Between Snow and Wolf

MAGNETIC PRESS™

Written by Agnès Domergue
Illustrated by Hélène Canac

Translation by Maria Vahrenhorst
Localization and Editing by Mike Kennedy
Lettering & Production Assistance by Chris Northrop

MAGNETIC™

ISBN: 978-1-951719-27-2
Library of Congress Control Number: 2021912648

Between Snow and Wolf by Agnès Domergue and Hélène Canac, Published 2021 by Magnetic Press, LLC.
Originally published as *"Entre Neige et Loup"* © 2019 Editions Jungle, All rights reserved. www.editions-jungle.com

Printed in China.

10 9 8 7 6 5 4 3 2 1

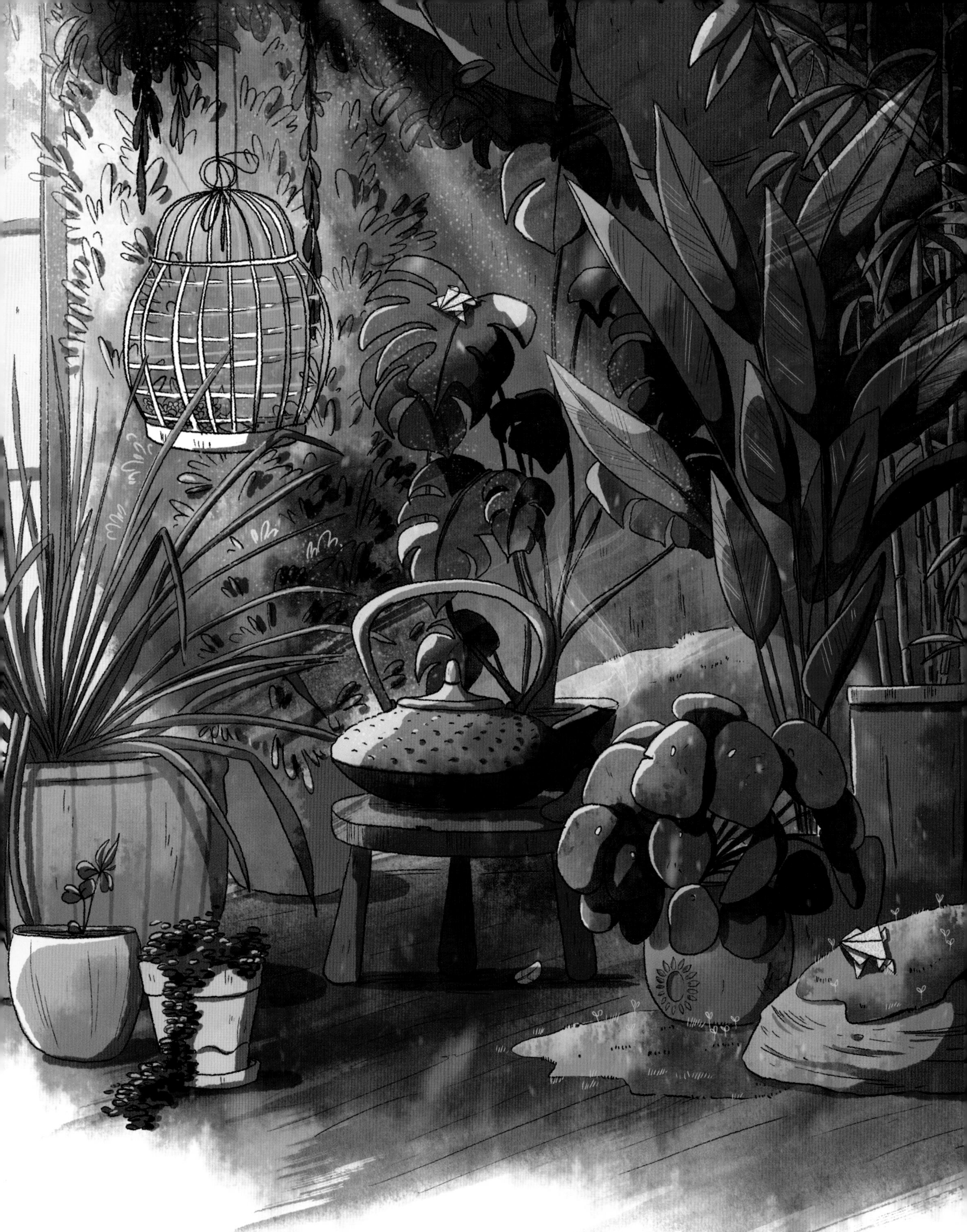

To the flower, the bird, the wind, and the moon.
And to Charlotte, my forever niece, born in the winter solstice.

— Agnès Domergue

To my mom.
A huge thank you to my Choupi for having given me time.
And to my favorite zombie for simply being there.

—Hélène Canac

"The only way to achieve the impossible is to believe that it is possible."
— Lewis Carroll

In the old pond
A frog jumps
A plop in the water!
(Haiku by Bashō)

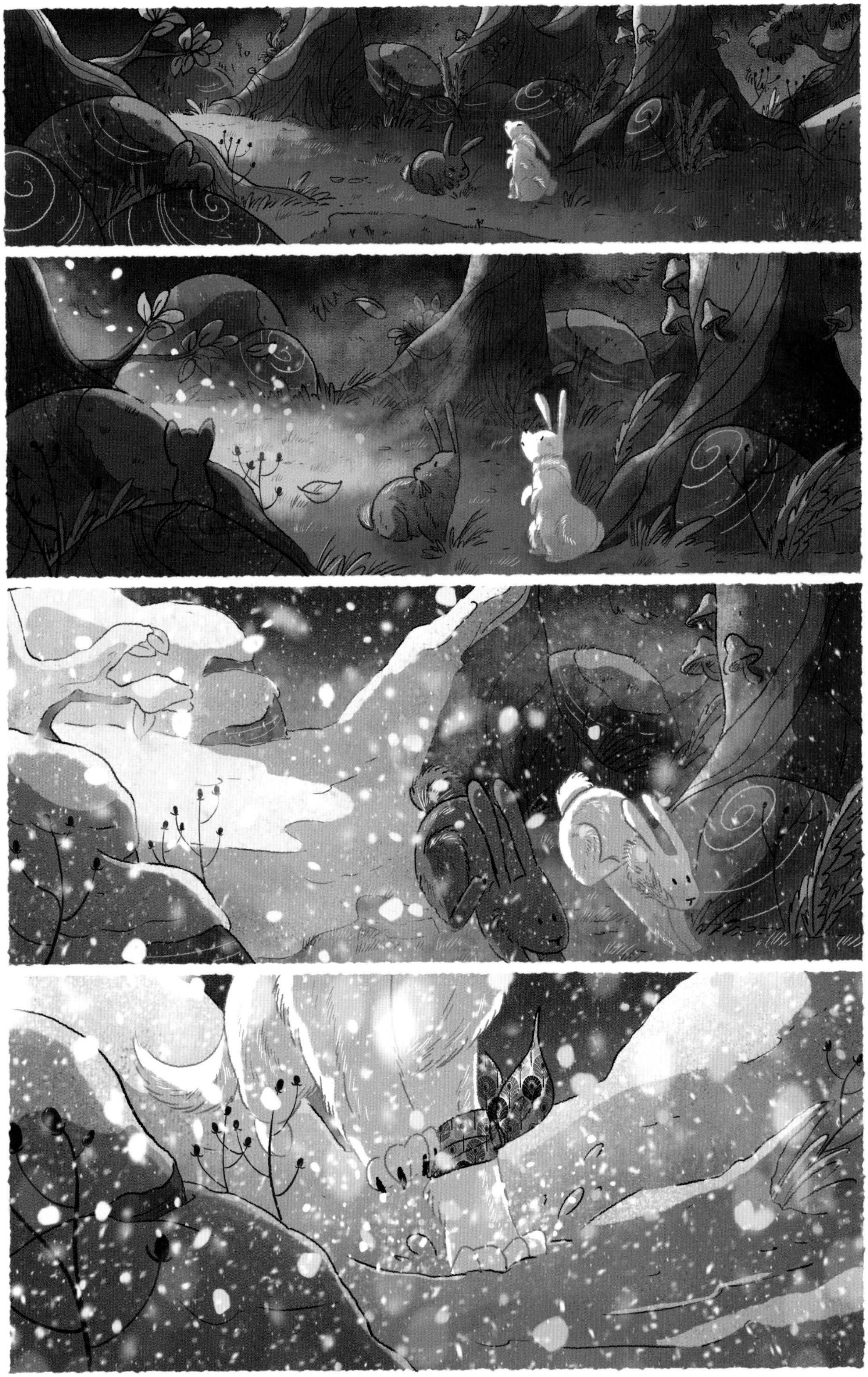

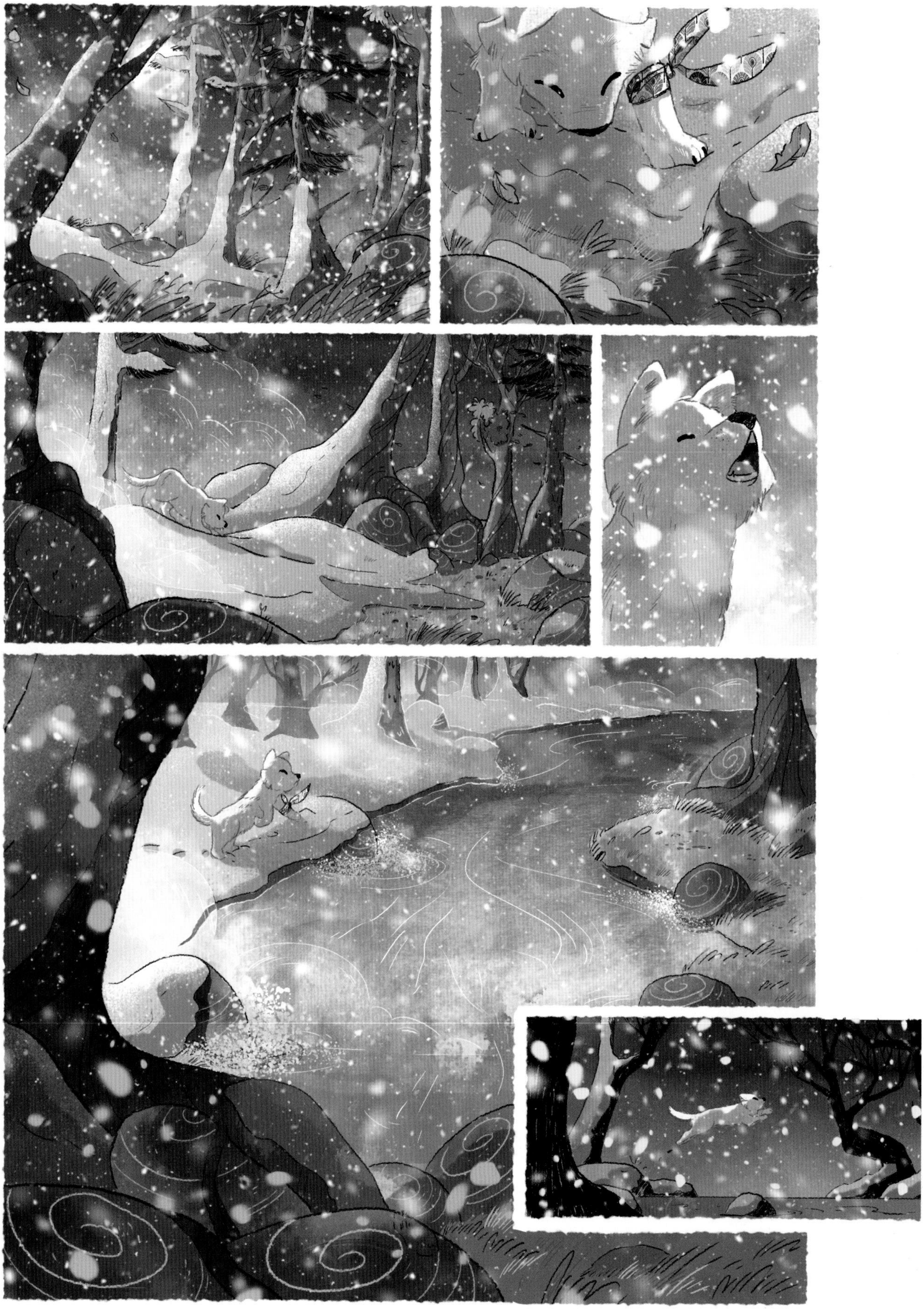

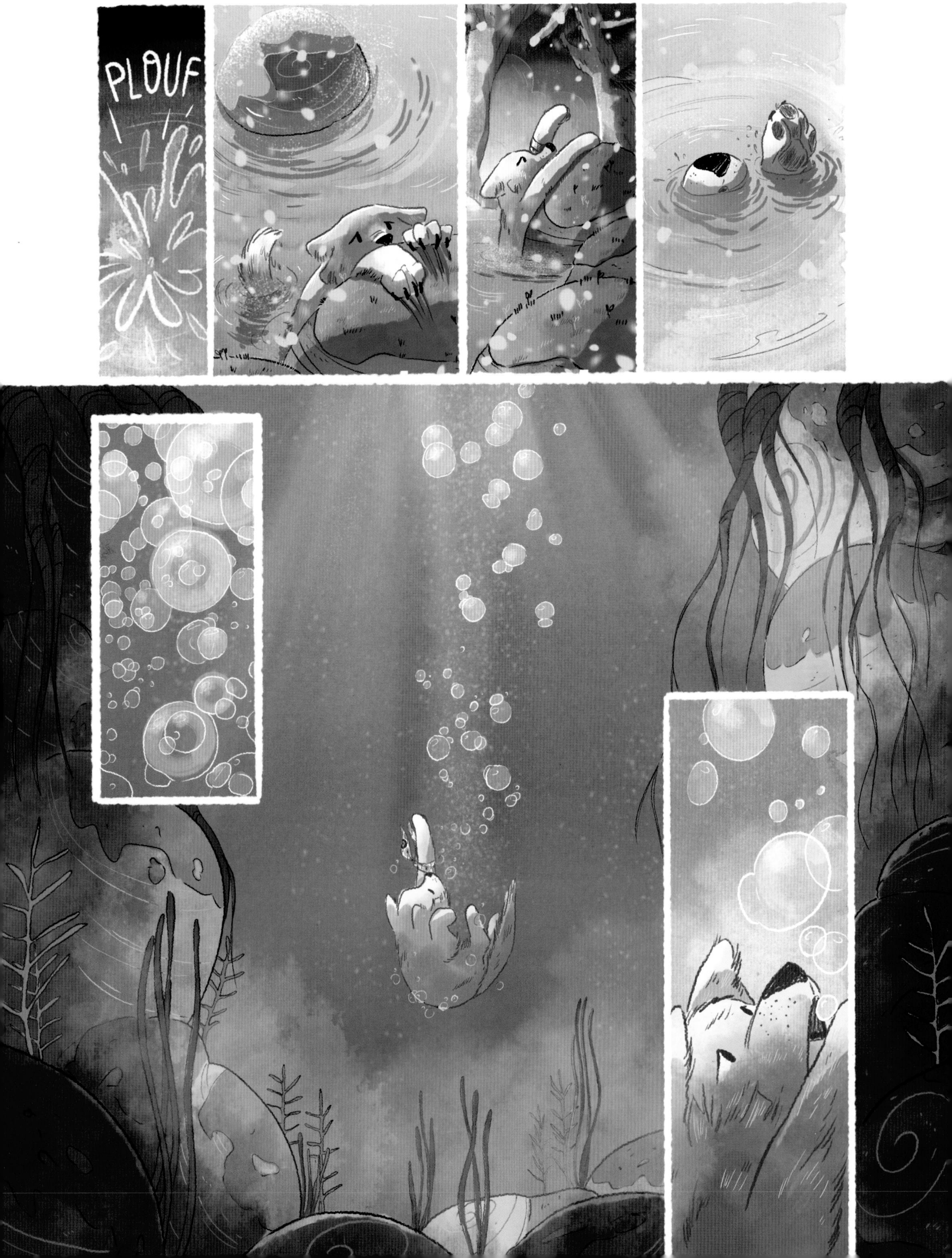
PLOUF

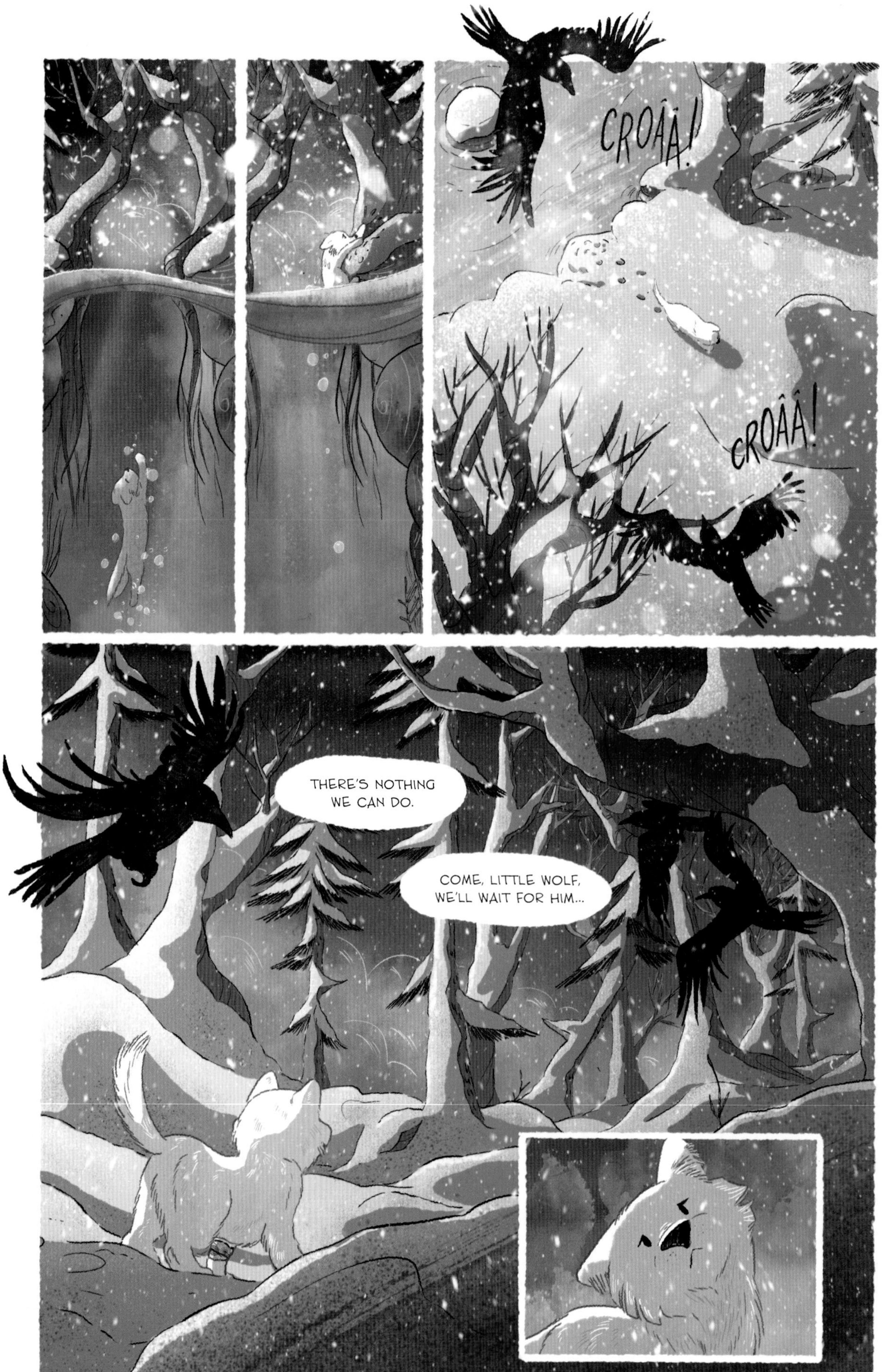

CROÂÂ!
CROÂÂ!
THERE'S NOTHING WE CAN DO.
COME, LITTLE WOLF, WE'LL WAIT FOR HIM...

The Japanese Garden

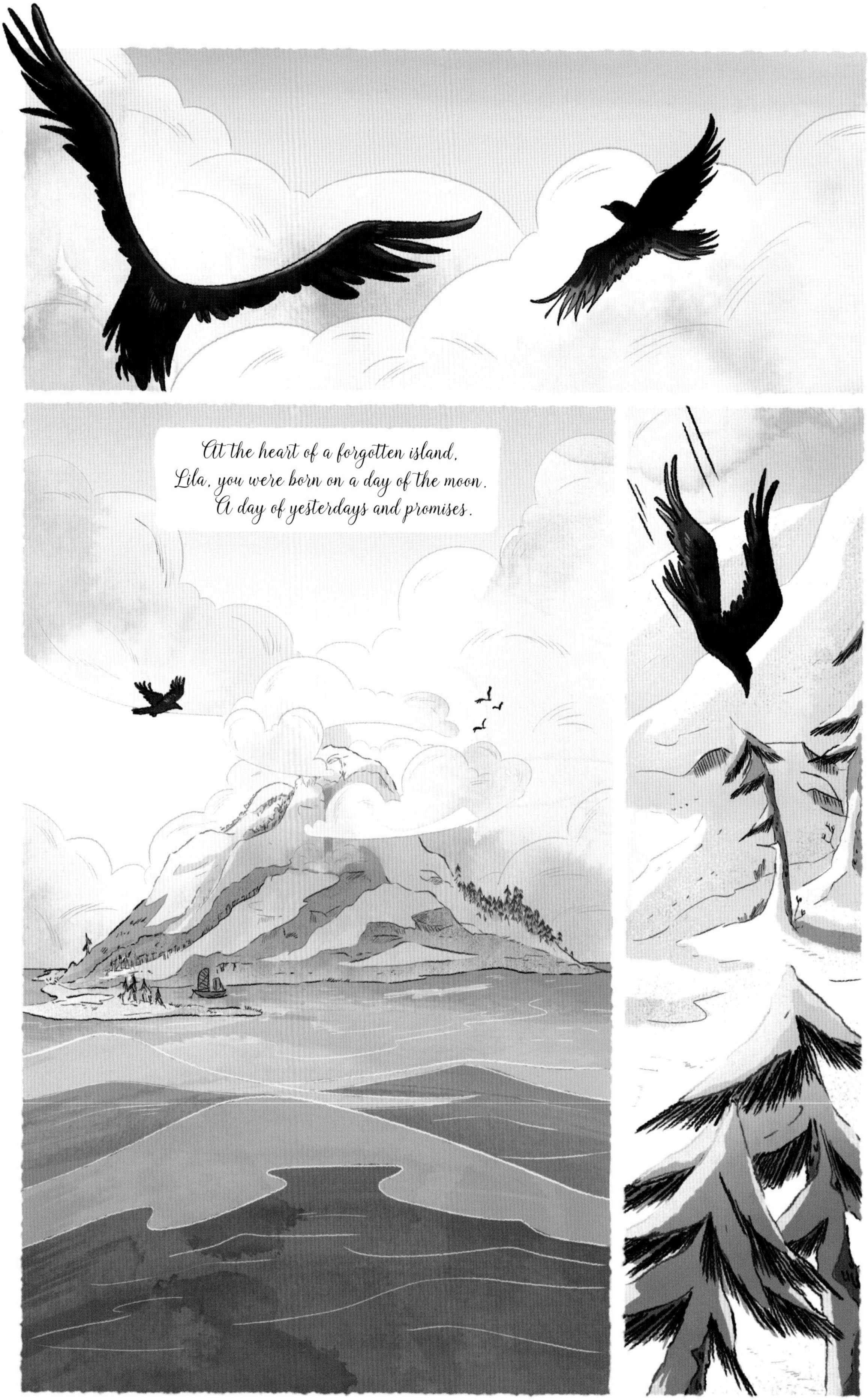
At the heart of a forgotten island,
Lila, you were born on a day of the moon.
A day of yesterdays and promises.

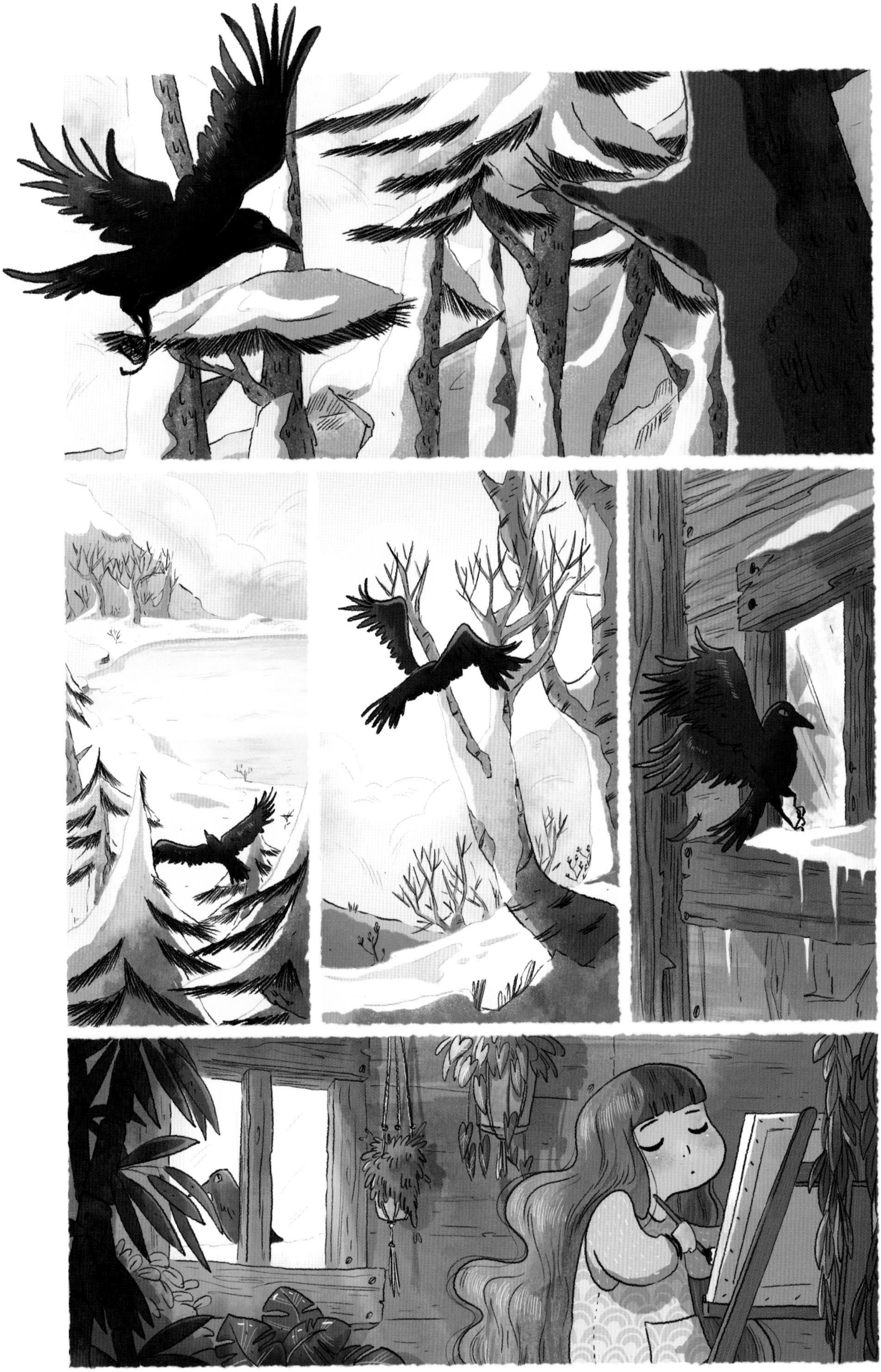

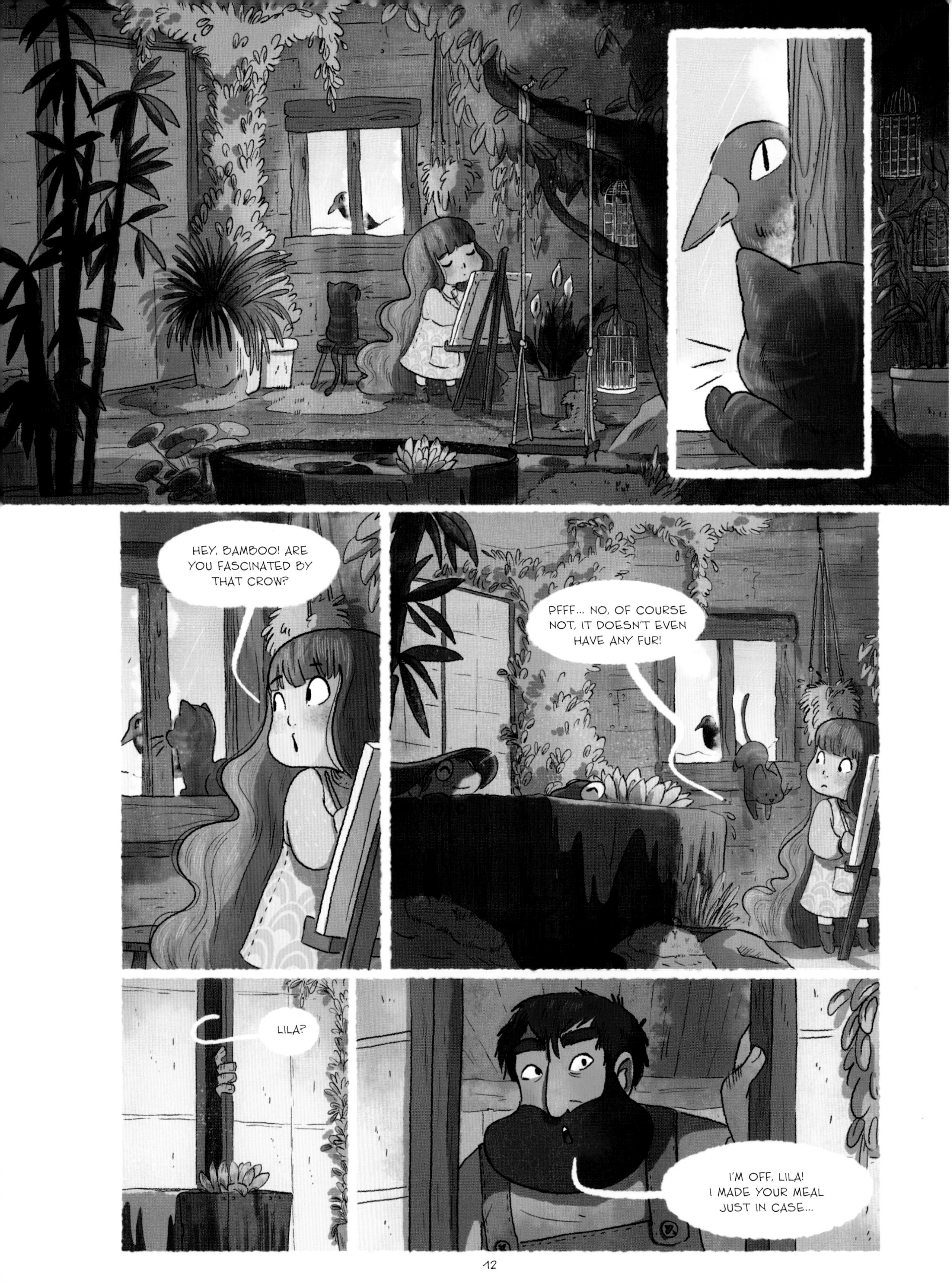
HEY, BAMBOO! ARE YOU FASCINATED BY THAT CROW?
PFFF... NO, OF COURSE NOT, IT DOESN'T EVEN HAVE ANY FUR!
LILA?
I'M OFF, LILA! I MADE YOUR MEAL JUST IN CASE...

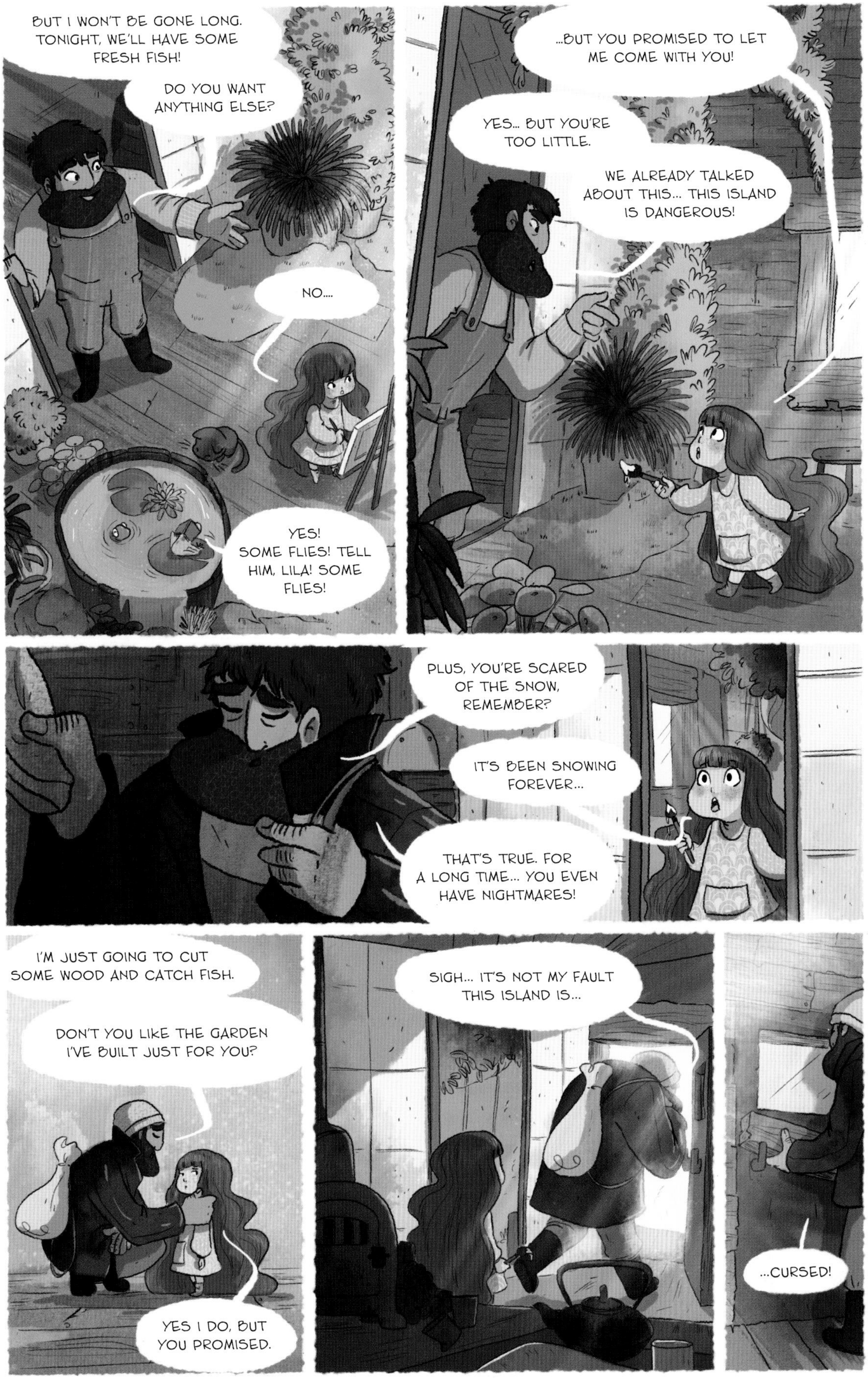
BUT I WON'T BE GONE LONG. TONIGHT, WE'LL HAVE SOME FRESH FISH!
DO YOU WANT ANYTHING ELSE?
NO....
YES! SOME FLIES! TELL HIM, LILA! SOME FLIES!
...BUT YOU PROMISED TO LET ME COME WITH YOU!
YES... BUT YOU'RE TOO LITTLE.
WE ALREADY TALKED ABOUT THIS... THIS ISLAND IS DANGEROUS!
PLUS, YOU'RE SCARED OF THE SNOW, REMEMBER?
IT'S BEEN SNOWING FOREVER...
THAT'S TRUE. FOR A LONG TIME... YOU EVEN HAVE NIGHTMARES!
I'M JUST GOING TO CUT SOME WOOD AND CATCH FISH.
DON'T YOU LIKE THE GARDEN I'VE BUILT JUST FOR YOU?
YES I DO, BUT YOU PROMISED.
SIGH... IT'S NOT MY FAULT THIS ISLAND IS...
...CURSED!

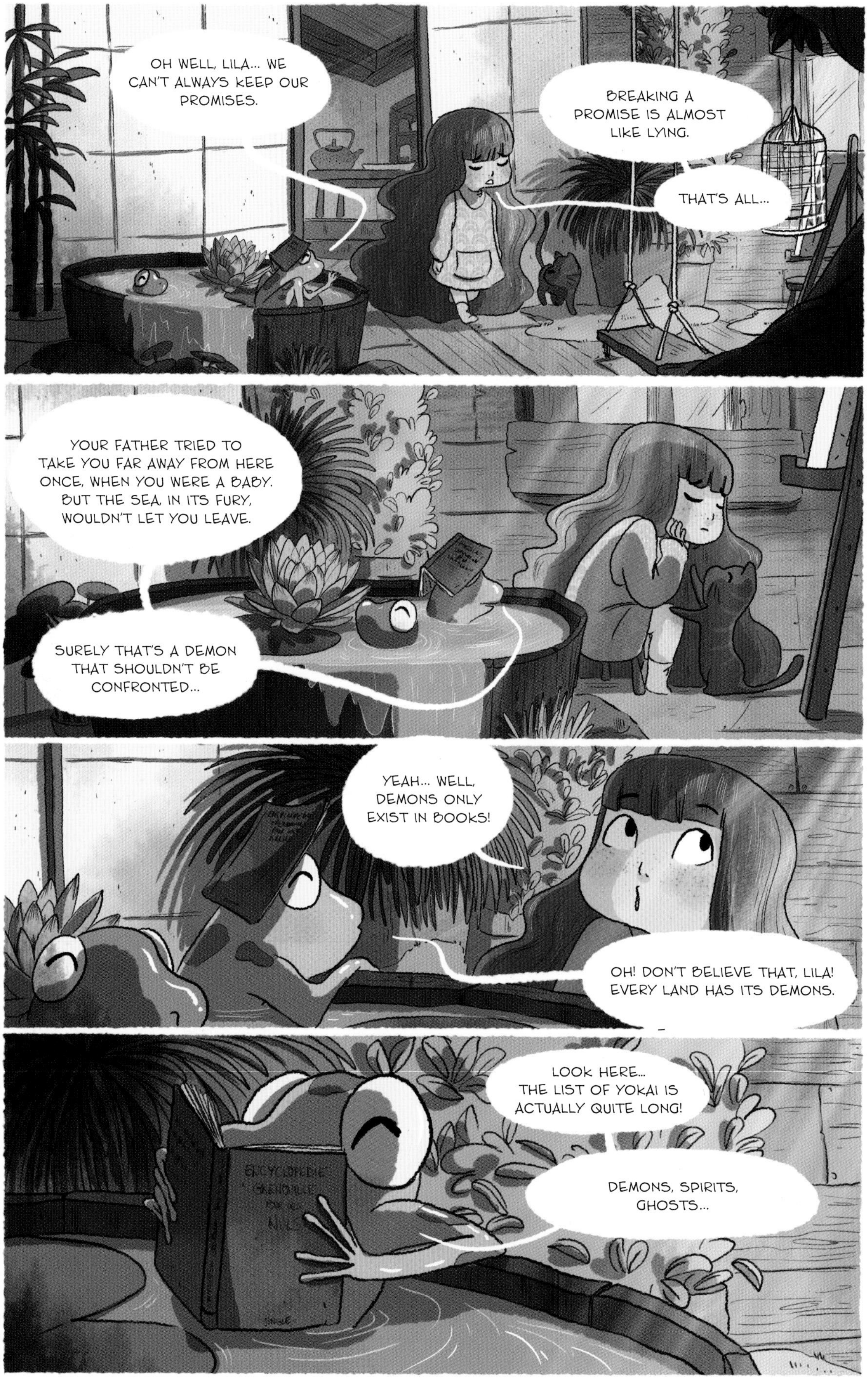
OH WELL, LILA... WE CAN'T ALWAYS KEEP OUR PROMISES.
BREAKING A PROMISE IS ALMOST LIKE LYING.
THAT'S ALL...
YOUR FATHER TRIED TO TAKE YOU FAR AWAY FROM HERE ONCE, WHEN YOU WERE A BABY. BUT THE SEA, IN ITS FURY, WOULDN'T LET YOU LEAVE.
SURELY THAT'S A DEMON THAT SHOULDN'T BE CONFRONTED...
YEAH... WELL, DEMONS ONLY EXIST IN BOOKS!
OH! DON'T BELIEVE THAT, LILA! EVERY LAND HAS ITS DEMONS.
LOOK HERE... THE LIST OF YOKAI IS ACTUALLY QUITE LONG!
ENCYCLOPEDIE GRENOUILLE POUR LES NULS
DEMONS, SPIRITS, GHOSTS...

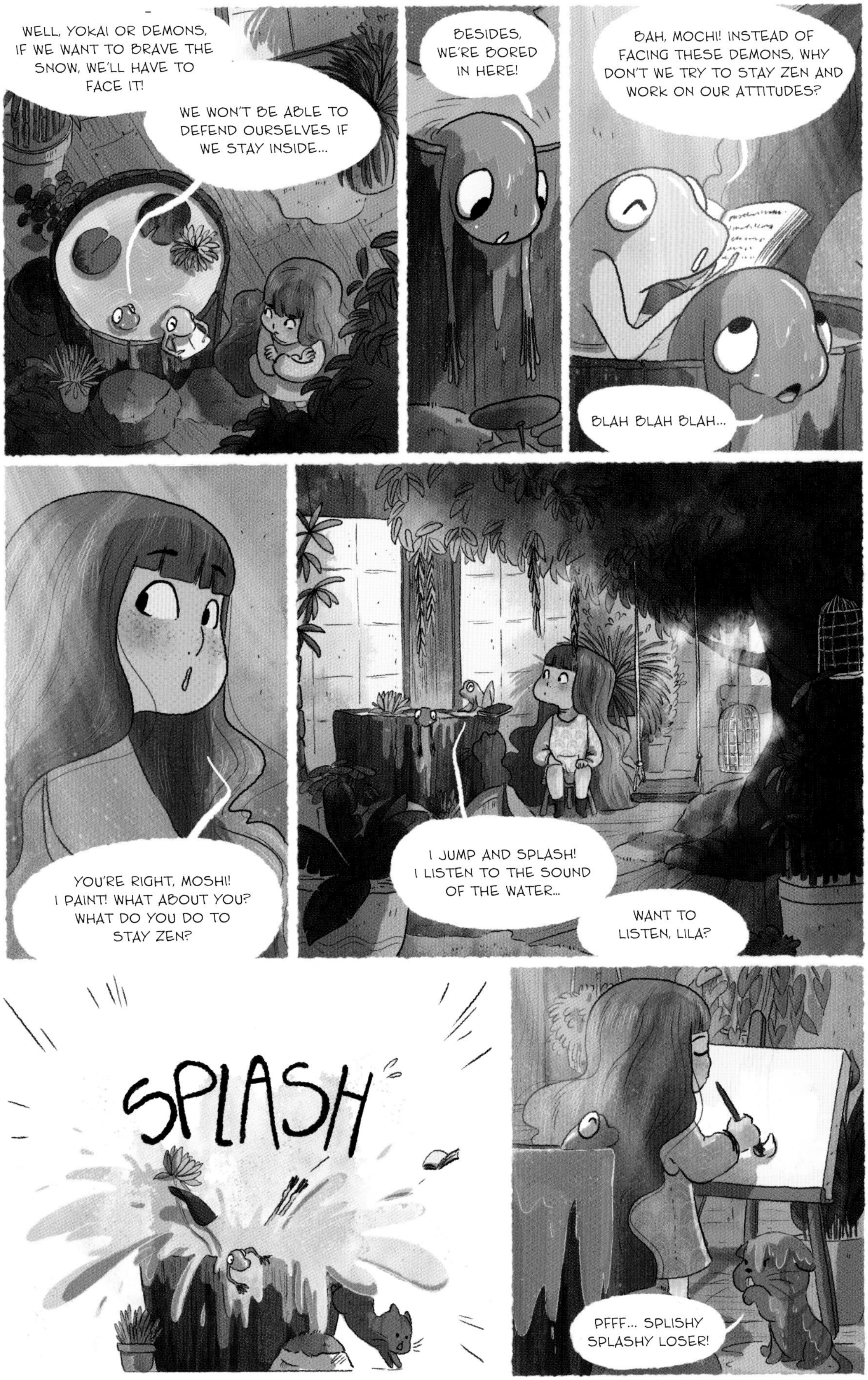
WELL, YOKAI OR DEMONS, IF WE WANT TO BRAVE THE SNOW, WE'LL HAVE TO FACE IT!
WE WON'T BE ABLE TO DEFEND OURSELVES IF WE STAY INSIDE...
BESIDES, WE'RE BORED IN HERE!
BAH, MOCHI! INSTEAD OF FACING THESE DEMONS, WHY DON'T WE TRY TO STAY ZEN AND WORK ON OUR ATTITUDES?
BLAH BLAH BLAH...
YOU'RE RIGHT, MOSHI! I PAINT! WHAT ABOUT YOU? WHAT DO YOU DO TO STAY ZEN?
I JUMP AND SPLASH! I LISTEN TO THE SOUND OF THE WATER...
WANT TO LISTEN, LILA?
SPLASH
PFFF... SPLISHY SPLASHY LOSER!

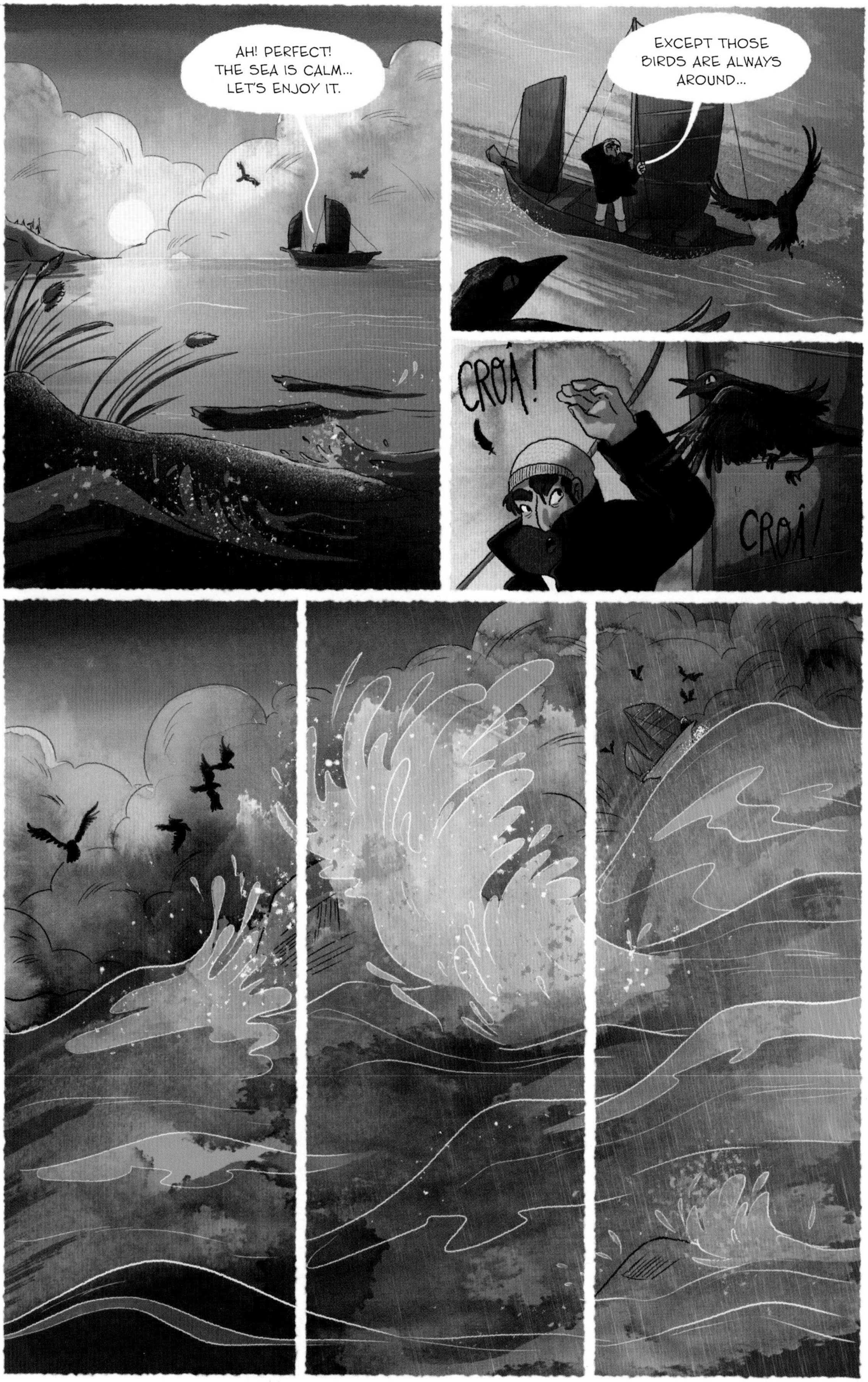
AH! PERFECT!
THE SEA IS CALM...
LET'S ENJOY IT.
EXCEPT THOSE
BIRDS ARE ALWAYS
AROUND...
CROÂ!
CROÂ!

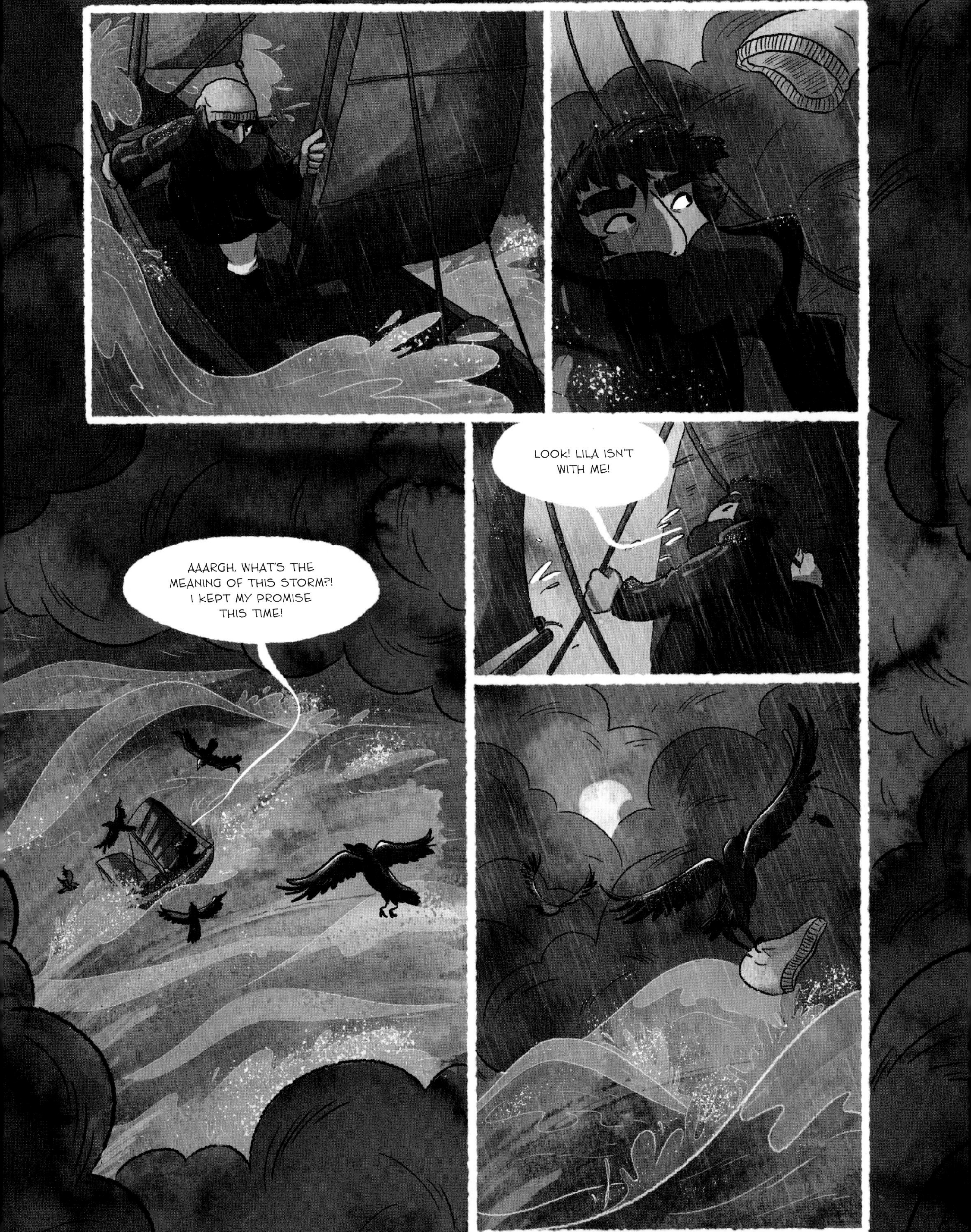
LOOK! LILA ISN'T WITH ME!
AAARGH, WHAT'S THE MEANING OF THIS STORM?! I KEPT MY PROMISE THIS TIME!

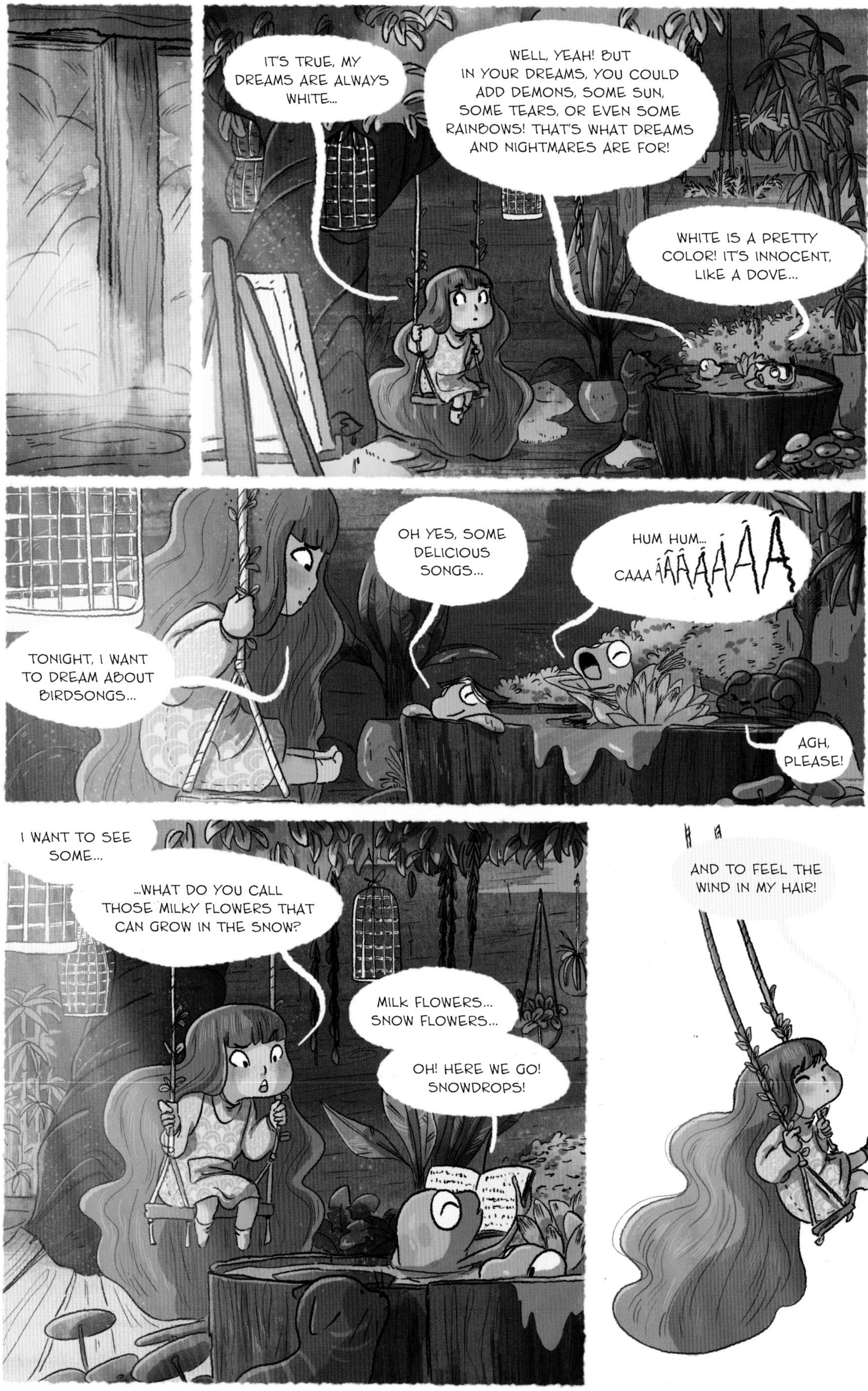
IT'S TRUE, MY DREAMS ARE ALWAYS WHITE...
WELL, YEAH! BUT IN YOUR DREAMS, YOU COULD ADD DEMONS, SOME SUN, SOME TEARS, OR EVEN SOME RAINBOWS! THAT'S WHAT DREAMS AND NIGHTMARES ARE FOR!
WHITE IS A PRETTY COLOR! IT'S INNOCENT, LIKE A DOVE...
TONIGHT, I WANT TO DREAM ABOUT BIRDSONGS...
OH YES, SOME DELICIOUS SONGS...
HUM HUM... CAAAÂÂÂÂÂÂÂÂ
AGH, PLEASE!
I WANT TO SEE SOME...
...WHAT DO YOU CALL THOSE MILKY FLOWERS THAT CAN GROW IN THE SNOW?
MILK FLOWERS... SNOW FLOWERS...
OH! HERE WE GO! SNOWDROPS!
AND TO FEEL THE WIND IN MY HAIR!

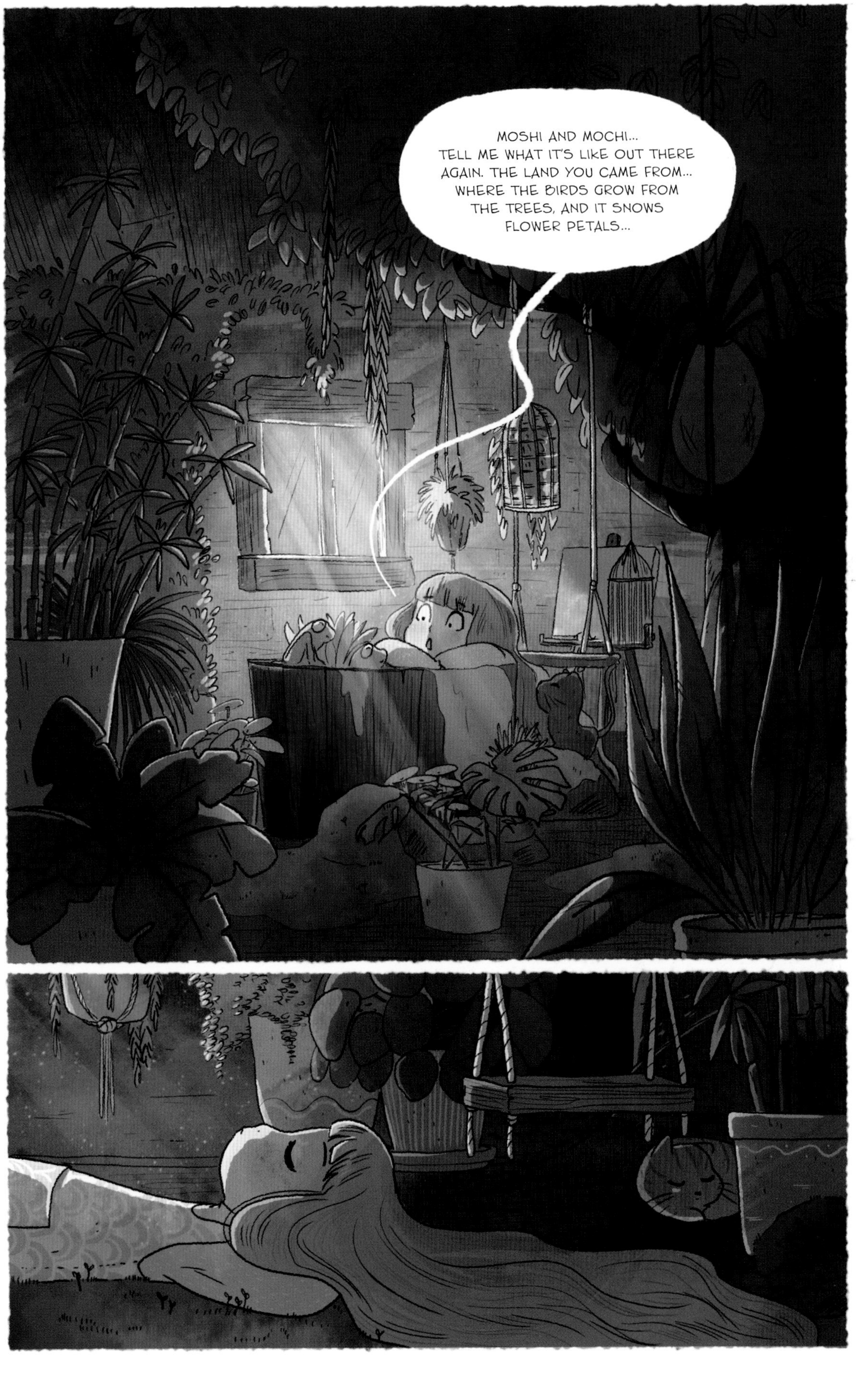
MOSHI AND MOCHI... TELL ME WHAT IT'S LIKE OUT THERE AGAIN. THE LAND YOU CAME FROM... WHERE THE BIRDS GROW FROM THE TREES, AND IT SNOWS FLOWER PETALS...

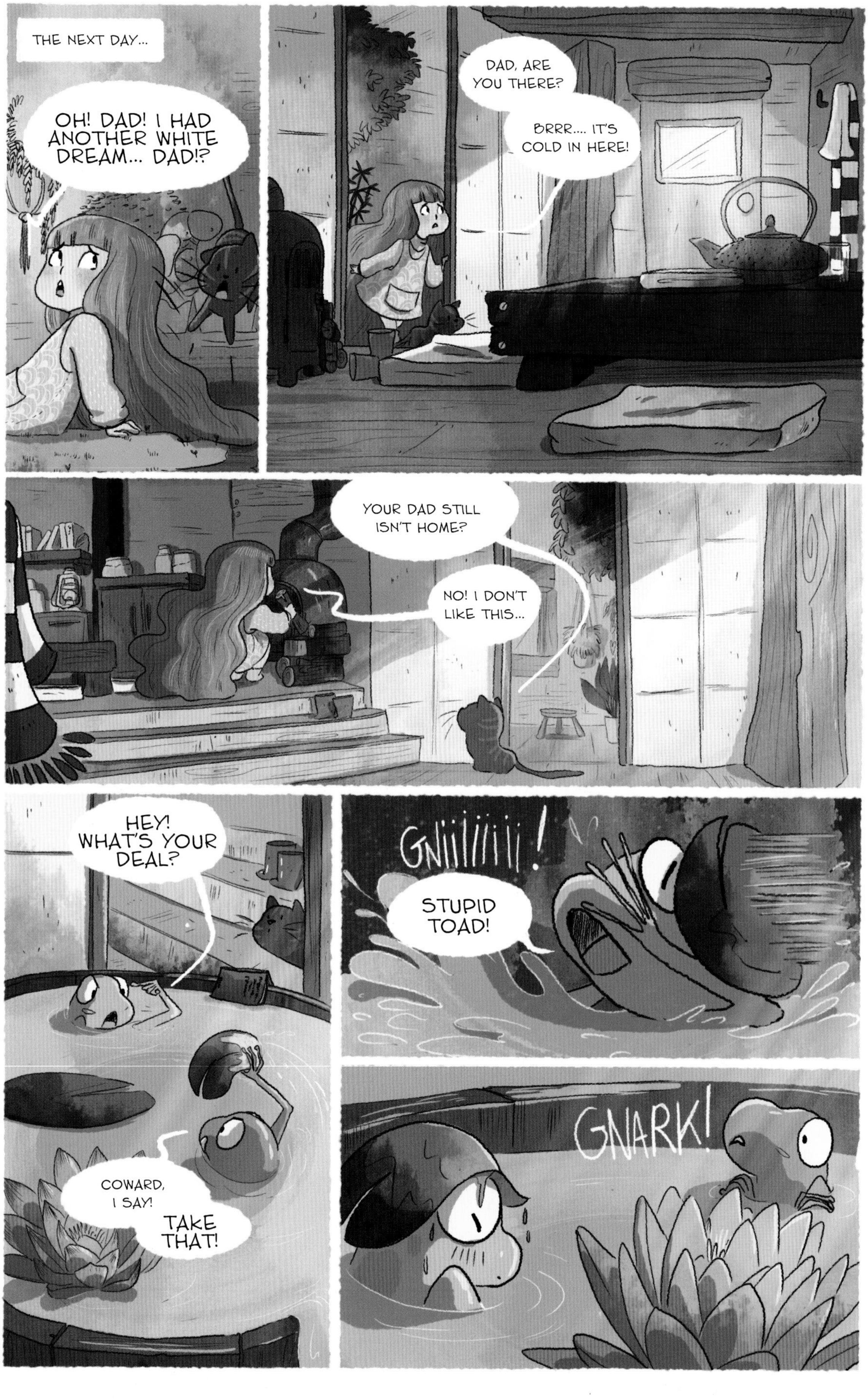
THE NEXT DAY...
OH! DAD! I HAD ANOTHER WHITE DREAM... DAD!?
DAD, ARE YOU THERE?
BRRR.... IT'S COLD IN HERE!
YOUR DAD STILL ISN'T HOME?
NO! I DON'T LIKE THIS...
HEY! WHAT'S YOUR DEAL?
GNIIIIIIII!
STUPID TOAD!
COWARD, I SAY!
TAKE THAT!
GNARK!

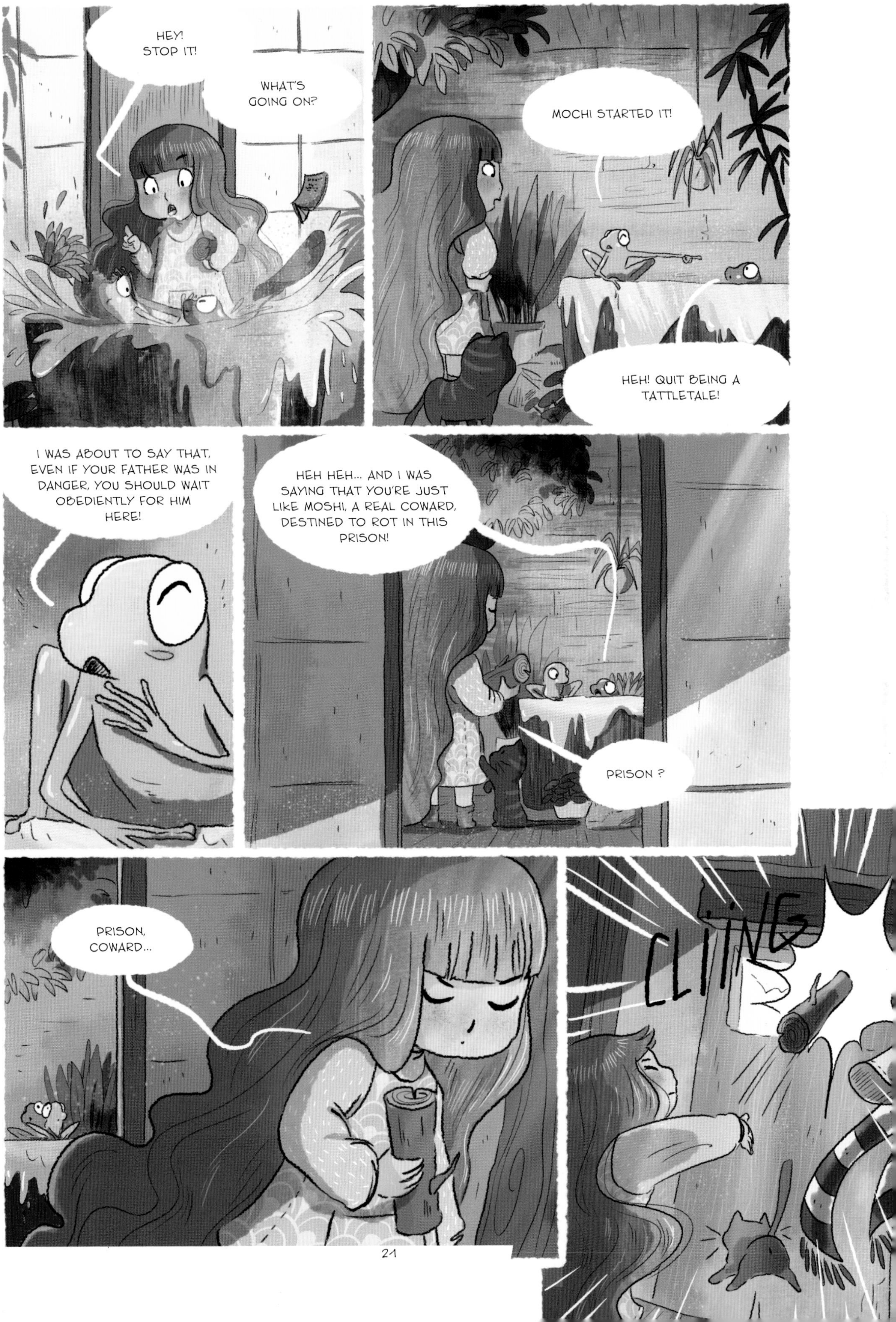
HEY!
STOP IT!
WHAT'S GOING ON?
MOCHI STARTED IT!
HEH! QUIT BEING A TATTLETALE!
I WAS ABOUT TO SAY THAT, EVEN IF YOUR FATHER WAS IN DANGER, YOU SHOULD WAIT OBEDIENTLY FOR HIM HERE!
HEH HEH... AND I WAS SAYING THAT YOU'RE JUST LIKE MOSHI, A REAL COWARD, DESTINED TO ROT IN THIS PRISON!
PRISON ?
PRISON, COWARD...
CLIING

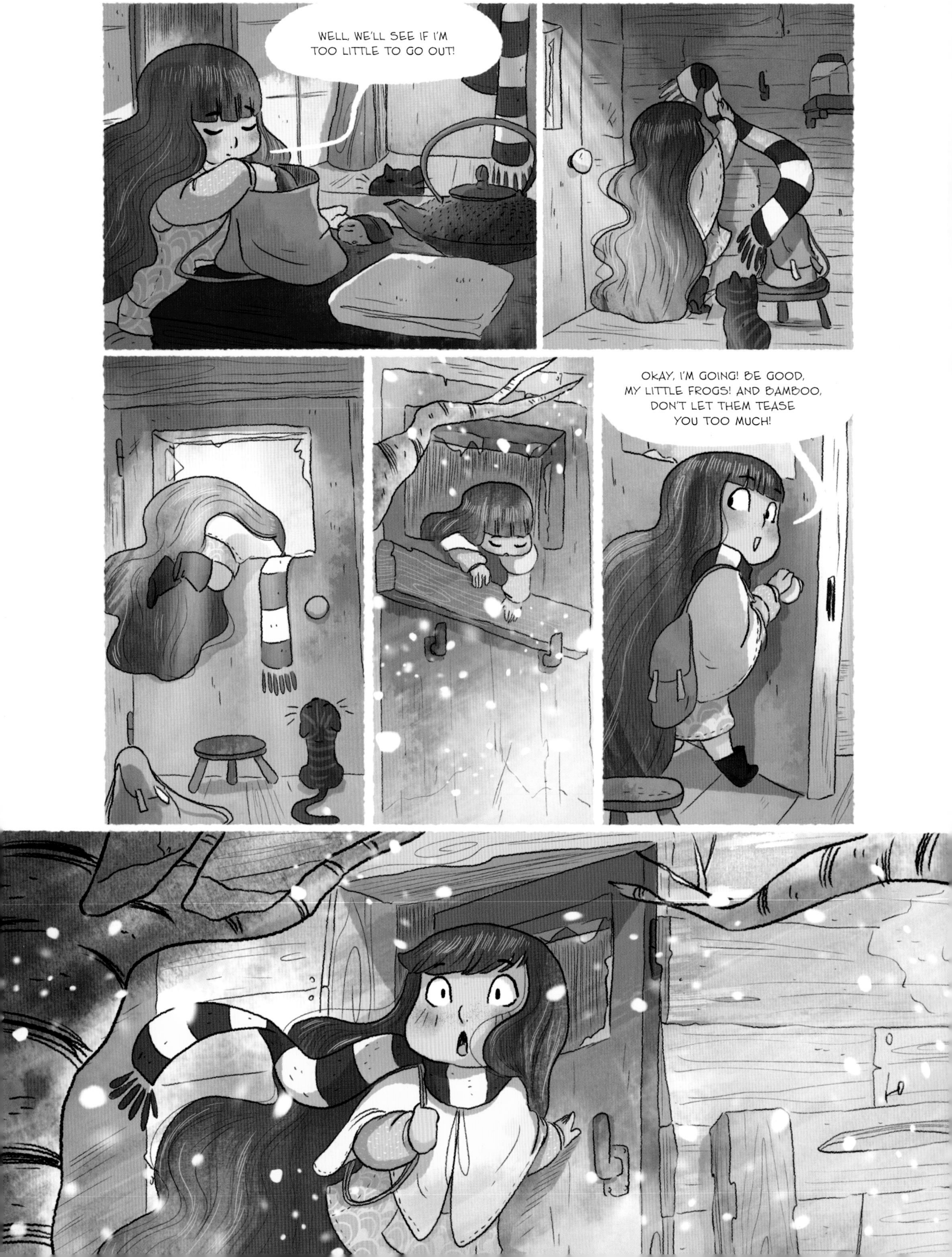
WELL, WE'LL SEE IF I'M TOO LITTLE TO GO OUT!
OKAY, I'M GOING! BE GOOD, MY LITTLE FROGS! AND BAMBOO, DON'T LET THEM TEASE YOU TOO MUCH!

The Jizo Forest

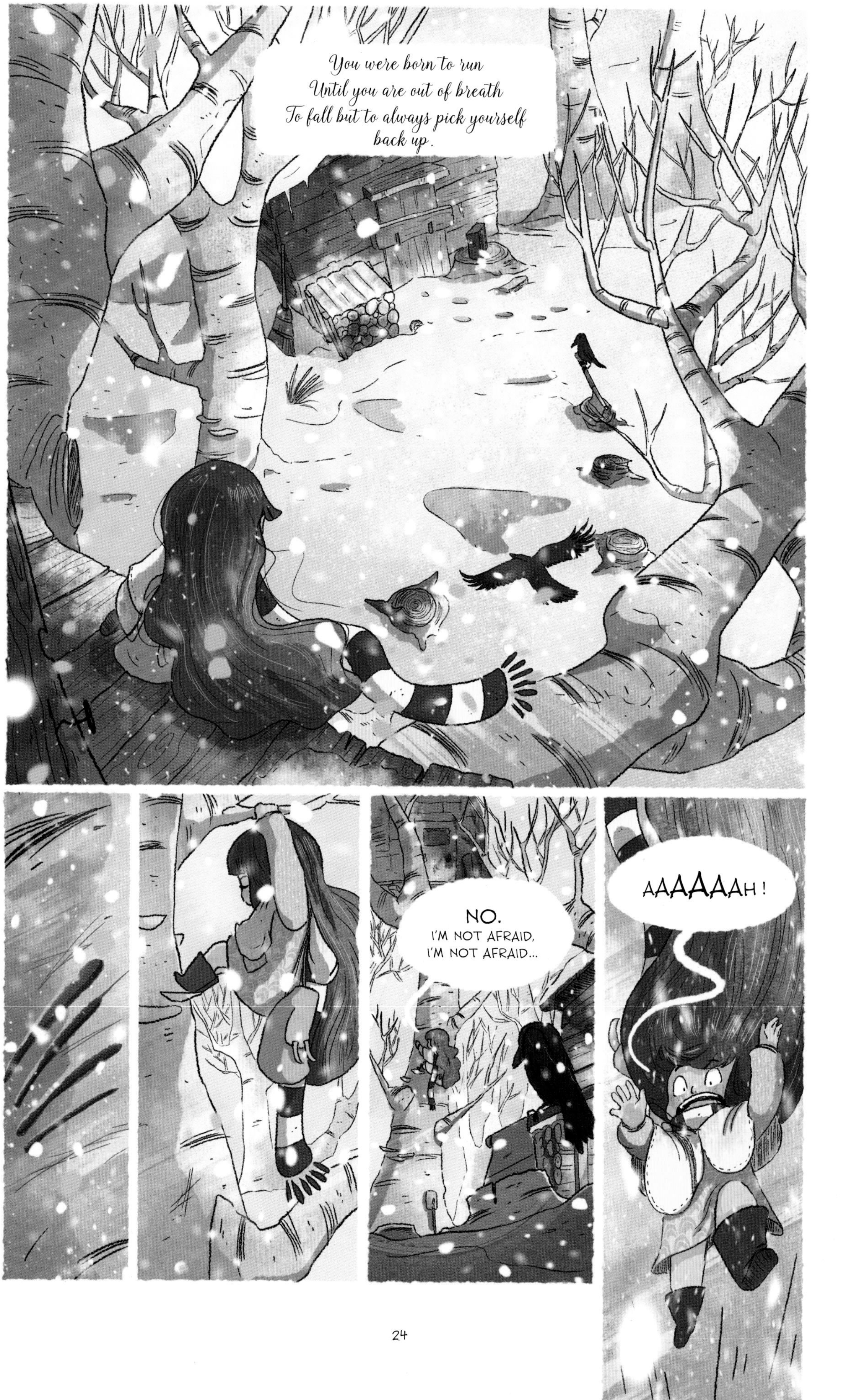
You were born to run
Until you are out of breath
To fall but to always pick yourself back up.
NO.
I'M NOT AFRAID,
I'M NOT AFRAID...
AAAAAAH!

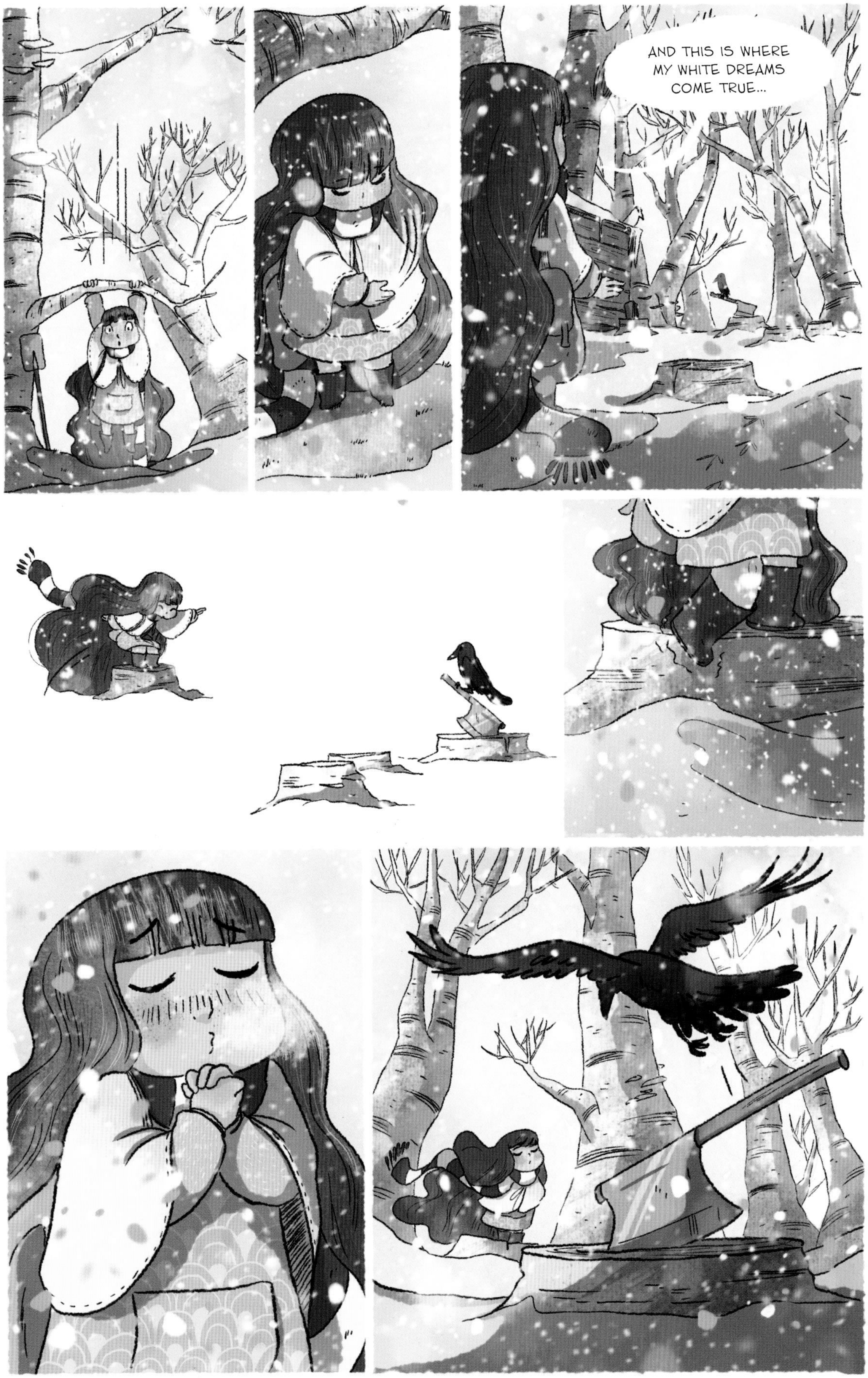
AND THIS IS WHERE MY WHITE DREAMS COME TRUE...

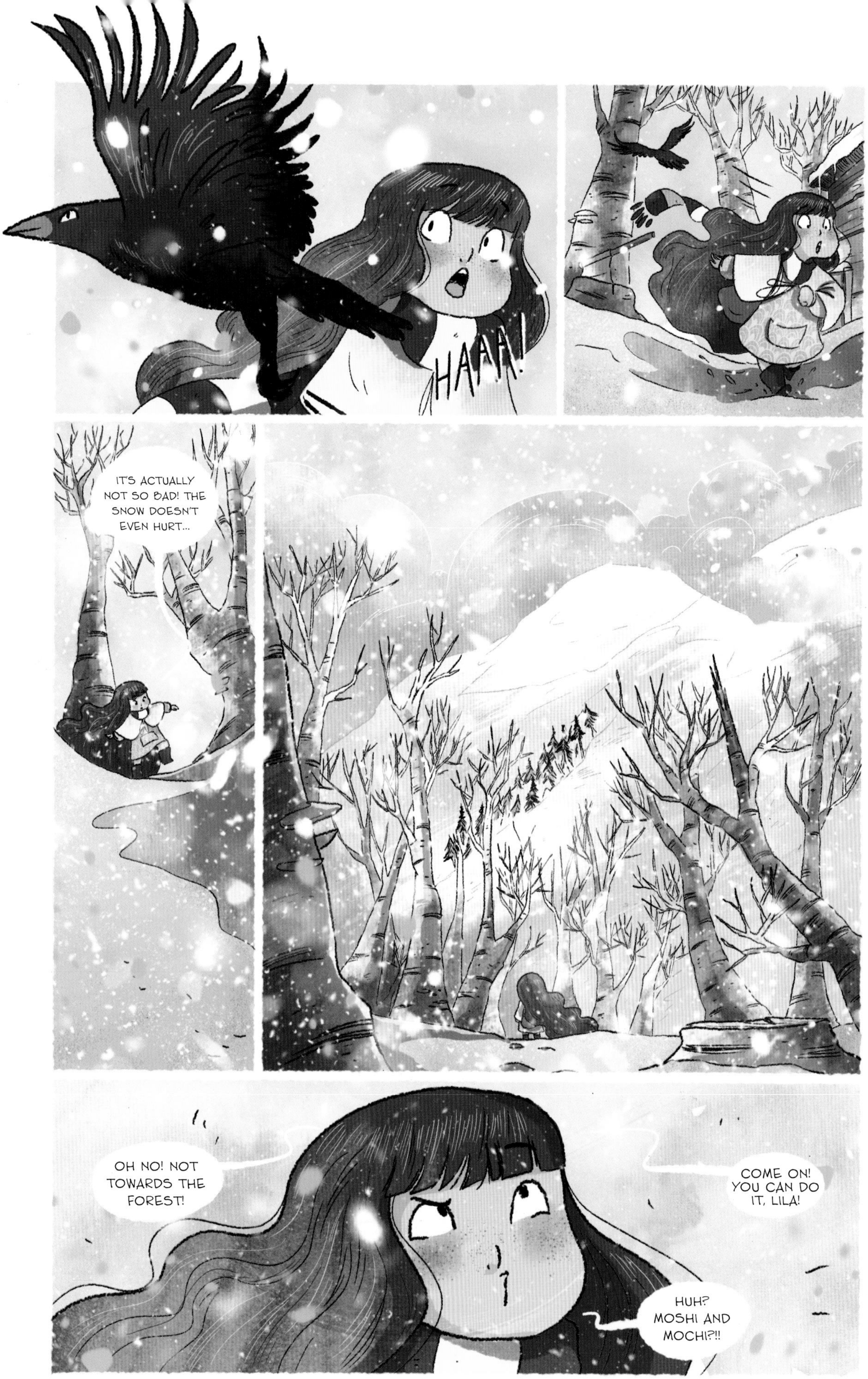
HAAA!
IT'S ACTUALLY NOT SO BAD! THE SNOW DOESN'T EVEN HURT...
OH NO! NOT TOWARDS THE FOREST!
COME ON! YOU CAN DO IT, LILA!
HUH? MOSHI AND MOCHI?!!

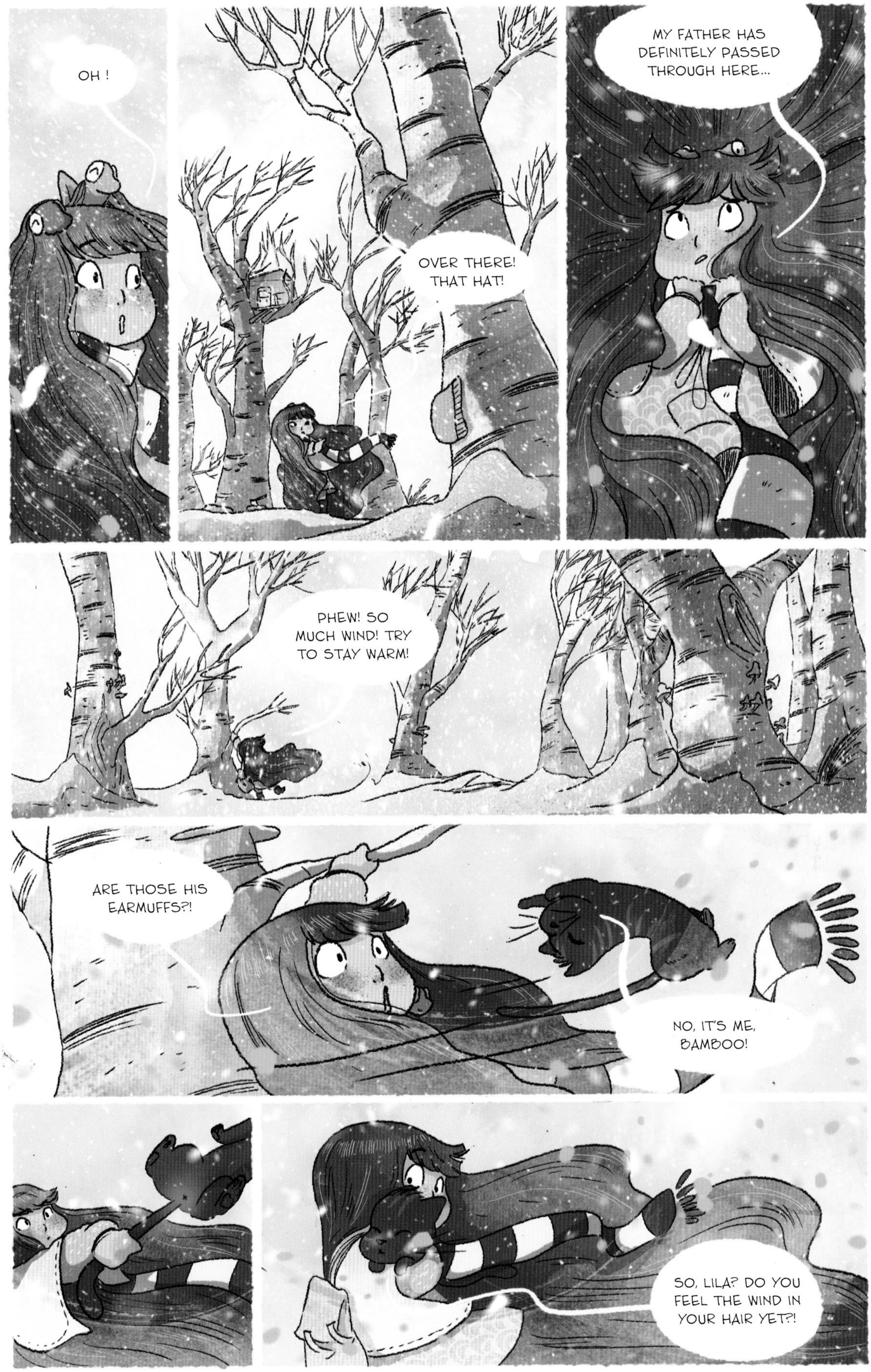
OH !
OVER THERE! THAT HAT!
MY FATHER HAS DEFINITELY PASSED THROUGH HERE...
PHEW! SO MUCH WIND! TRY TO STAY WARM!
ARE THOSE HIS EARMUFFS?!
NO, IT'S ME, BAMBOO!
SO, LILA? DO YOU FEEL THE WIND IN YOUR HAIR YET?!

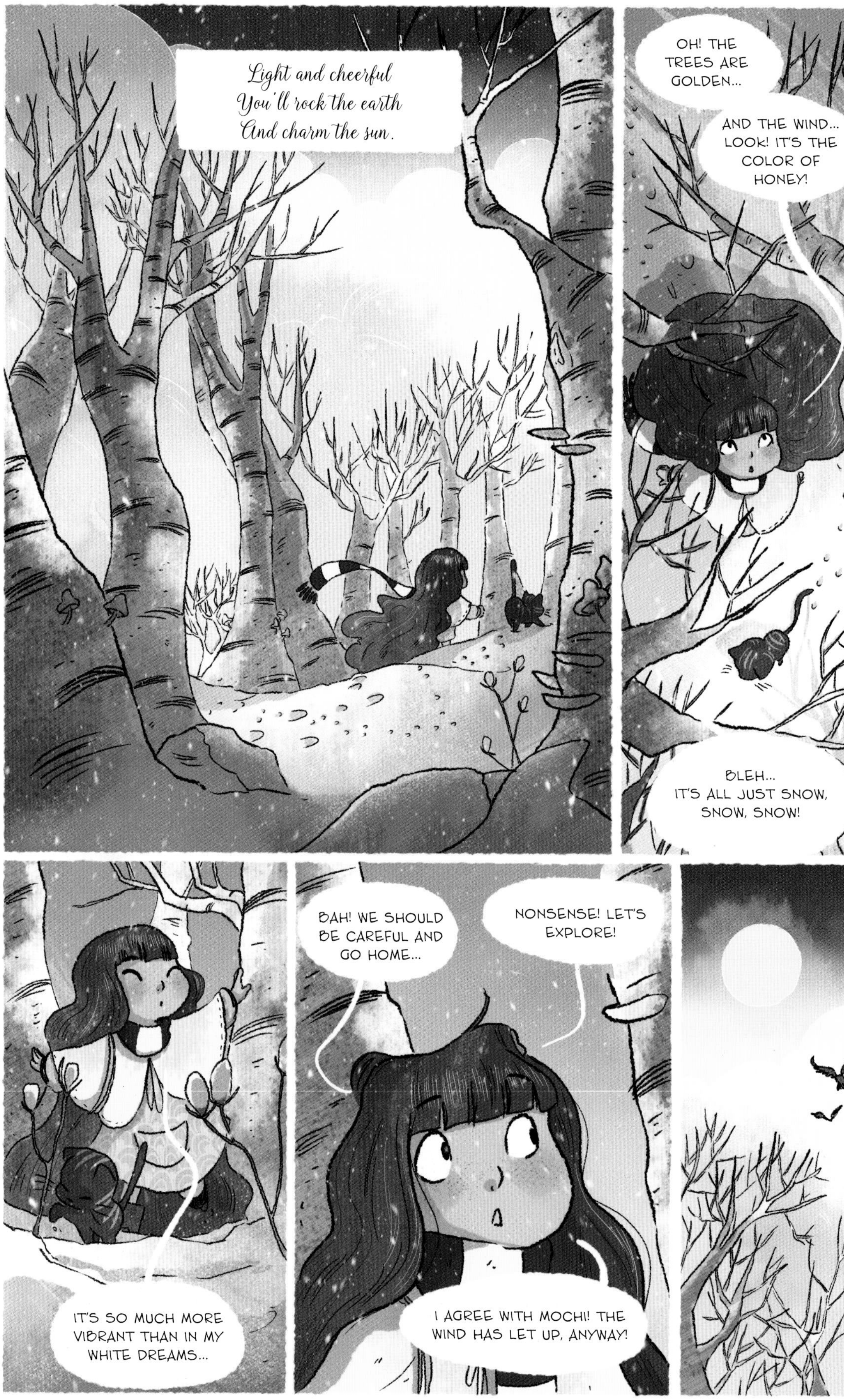
Light and cheerful
You'll rock the earth
And charm the sun.
OH! THE TREES ARE GOLDEN...
AND THE WIND... LOOK! IT'S THE COLOR OF HONEY!
BLEH... IT'S ALL JUST SNOW, SNOW, SNOW!
IT'S SO MUCH MORE VIBRANT THAN IN MY WHITE DREAMS...
BAH! WE SHOULD BE CAREFUL AND GO HOME...
NONSENSE! LET'S EXPLORE!
I AGREE WITH MOCHI! THE WIND HAS LET UP, ANYWAY!

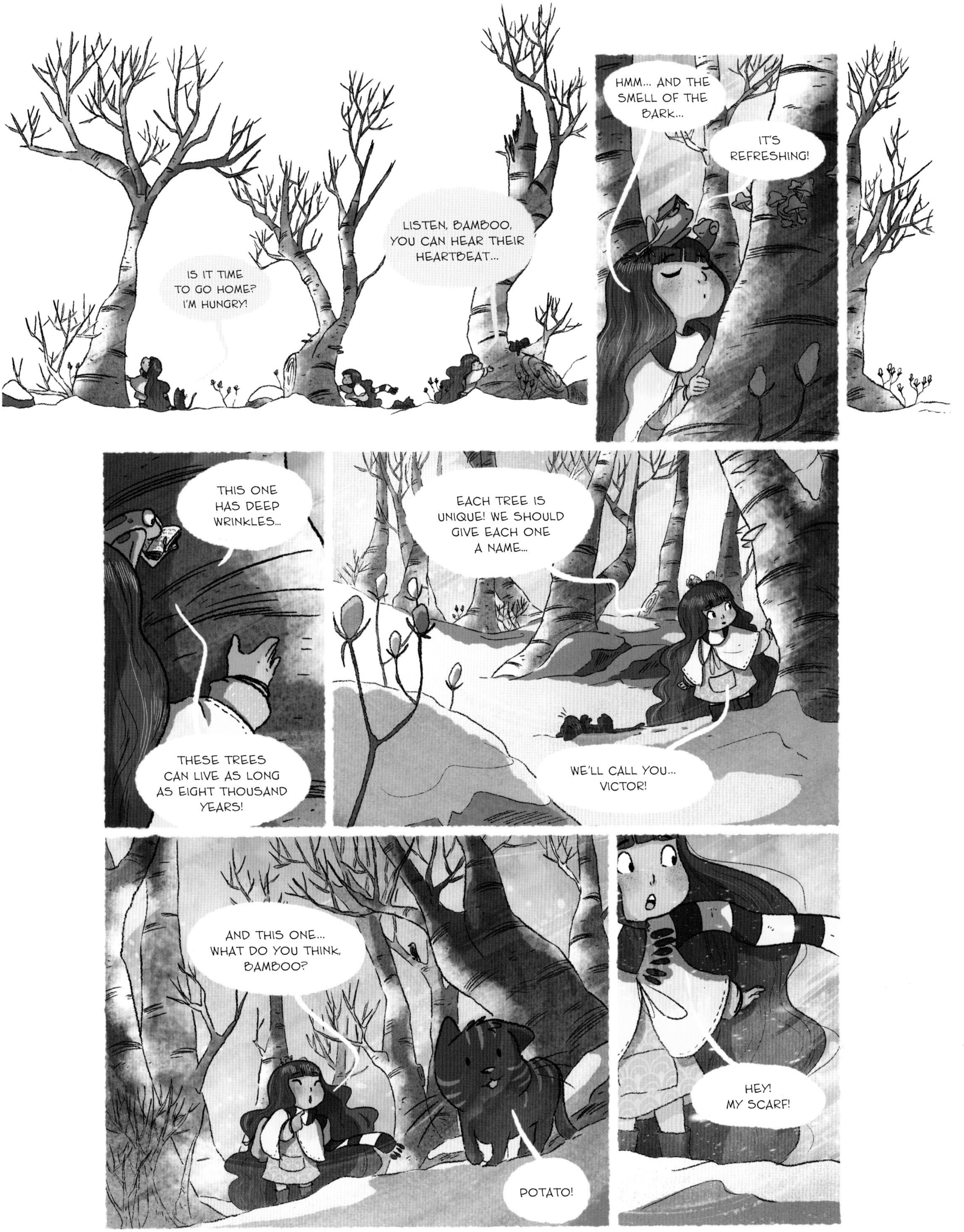
IS IT TIME TO GO HOME? I'M HUNGRY!
LISTEN, BAMBOO, YOU CAN HEAR THEIR HEARTBEAT...
HMM... AND THE SMELL OF THE BARK...
IT'S REFRESHING!
THIS ONE HAS DEEP WRINKLES...
THESE TREES CAN LIVE AS LONG AS EIGHT THOUSAND YEARS!
EACH TREE IS UNIQUE! WE SHOULD GIVE EACH ONE A NAME...
WE'LL CALL YOU... VICTOR!
AND THIS ONE... WHAT DO YOU THINK, BAMBOO?
POTATO!
HEY! MY SCARF!

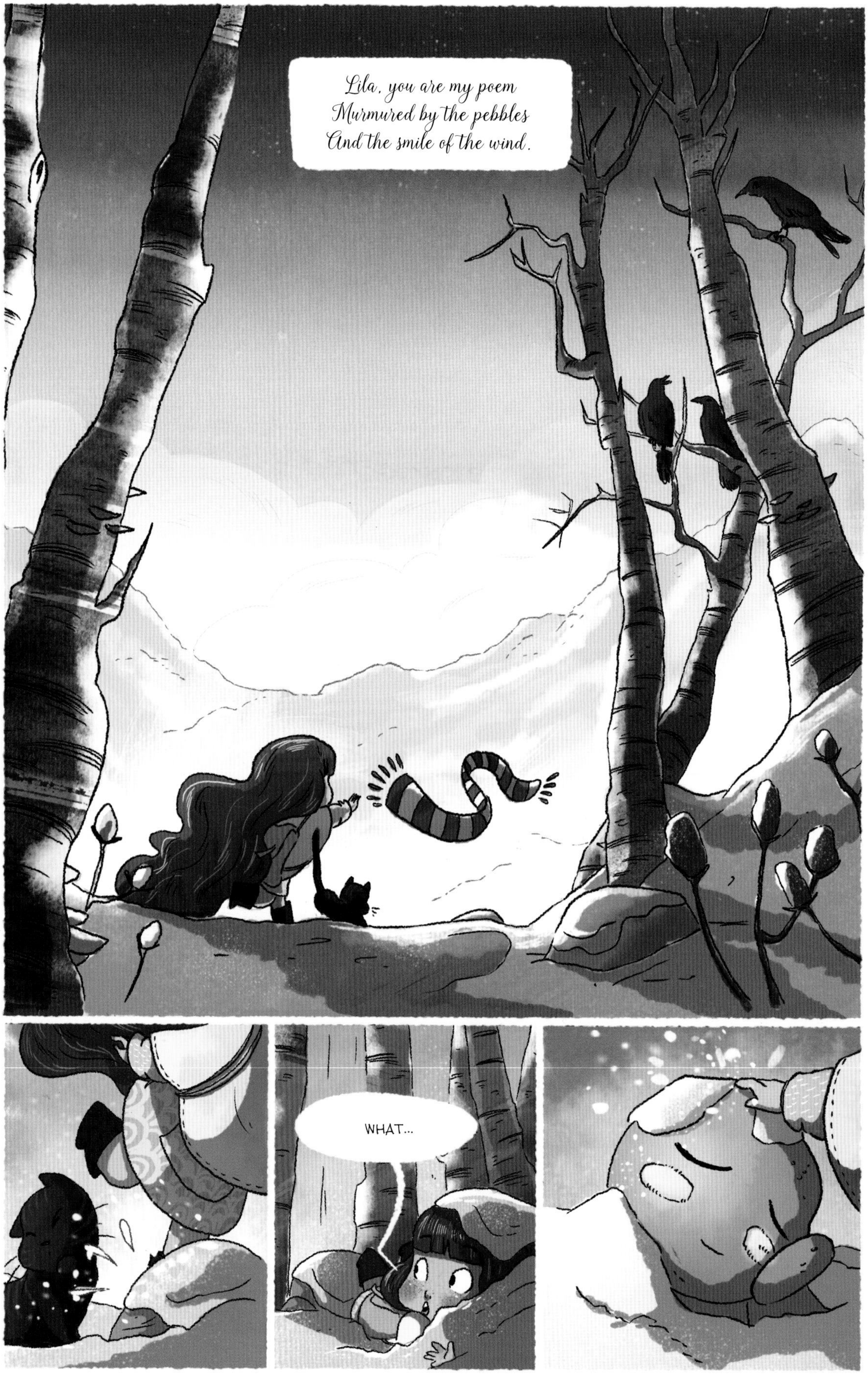
Lila, you are my poem
Murmured by the pebbles
And the smile of the wind.
WHAT...

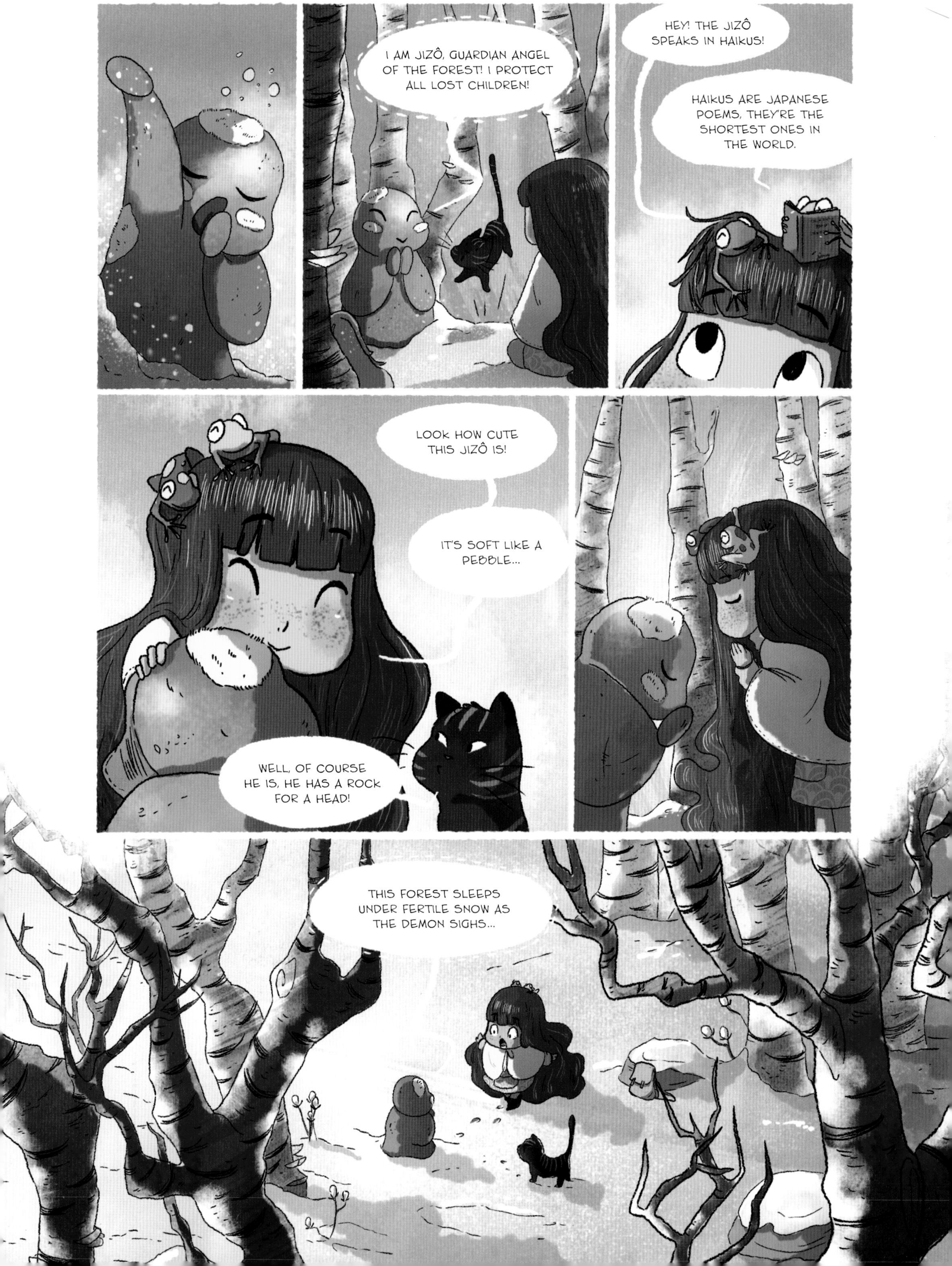
I AM JIZÔ, GUARDIAN ANGEL OF THE FOREST! I PROTECT ALL LOST CHILDREN!
HEY! THE JIZÔ SPEAKS IN HAIKUS!
HAIKUS ARE JAPANESE POEMS, THEY'RE THE SHORTEST ONES IN THE WORLD.
LOOK HOW CUTE THIS JIZÔ IS!
IT'S SOFT LIKE A PEBBLE...
WELL, OF COURSE HE IS, HE HAS A ROCK FOR A HEAD!
THIS FOREST SLEEPS UNDER FERTILE SNOW AS THE DEMON SIGHS...

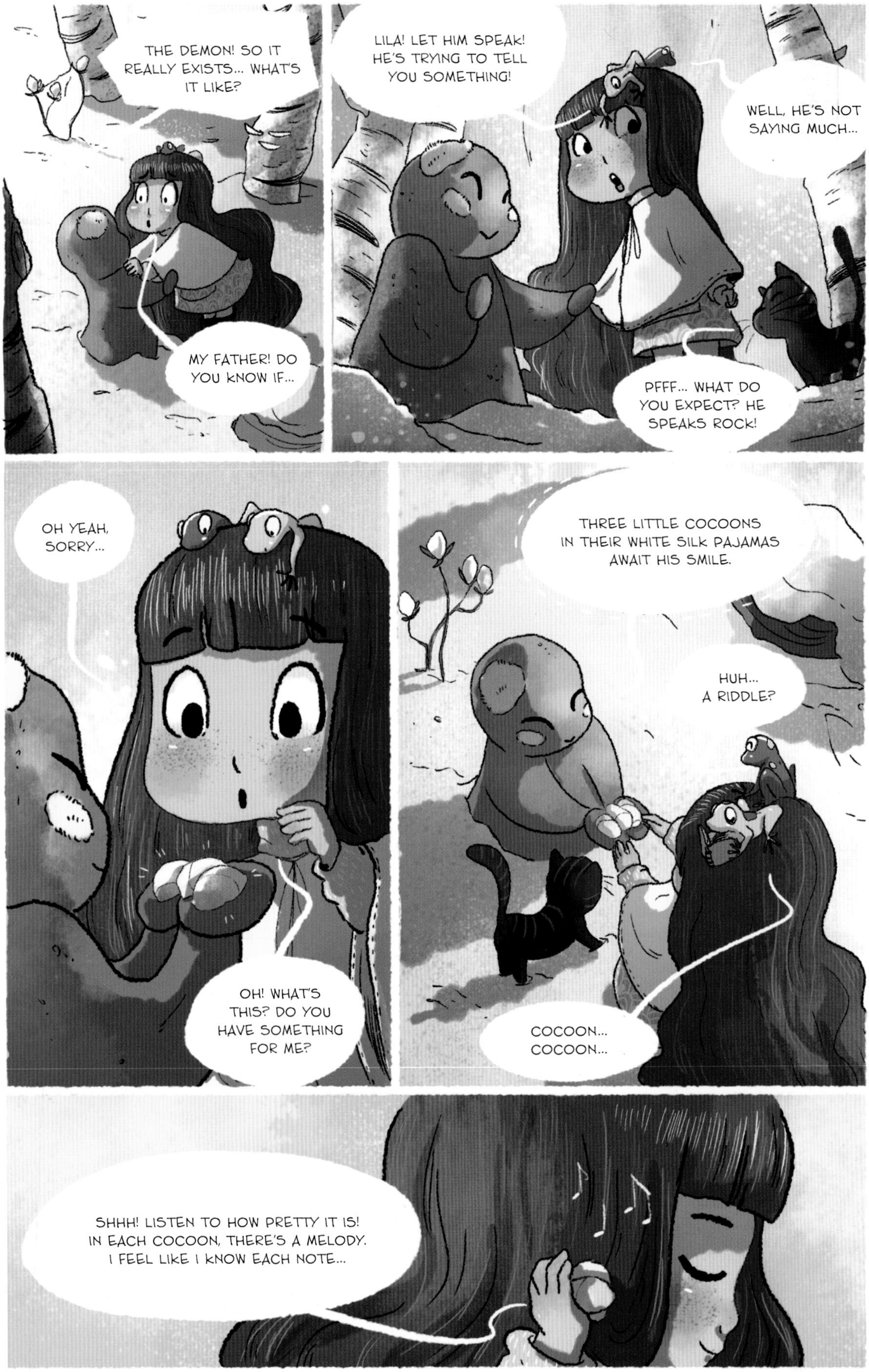
THE DEMON! SO IT REALLY EXISTS... WHAT'S IT LIKE?
MY FATHER! DO YOU KNOW IF...
LILA! LET HIM SPEAK! HE'S TRYING TO TELL YOU SOMETHING!
WELL, HE'S NOT SAYING MUCH...
PFFF... WHAT DO YOU EXPECT? HE SPEAKS ROCK!
OH YEAH, SORRY...
OH! WHAT'S THIS? DO YOU HAVE SOMETHING FOR ME?
THREE LITTLE COCOONS IN THEIR WHITE SILK PAJAMAS AWAIT HIS SMILE.
HUH... A RIDDLE?
COCOON... COCOON...
SHHH! LISTEN TO HOW PRETTY IT IS! IN EACH COCOON, THERE'S A MELODY. I FEEL LIKE I KNOW EACH NOTE...

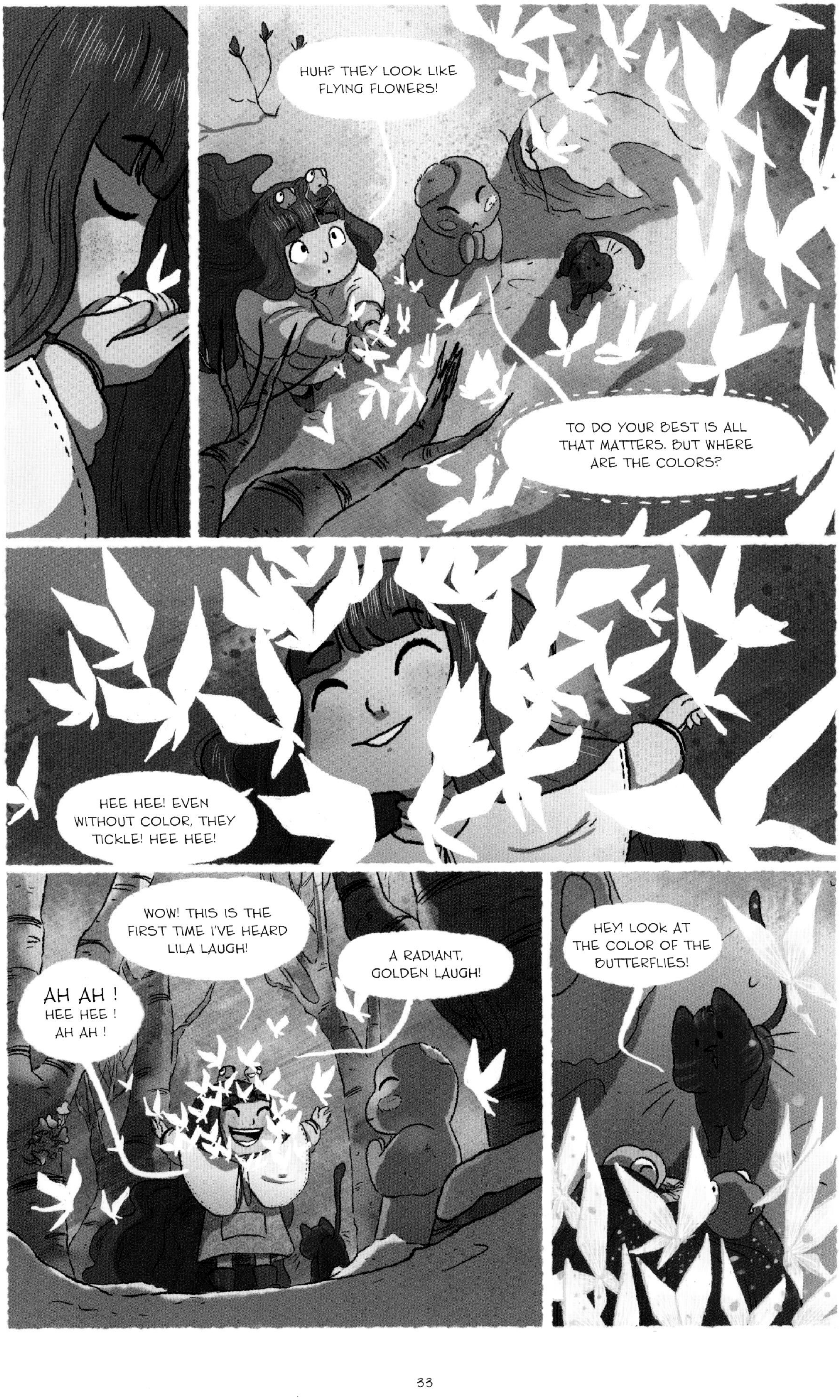
HUH? THEY LOOK LIKE FLYING FLOWERS!
TO DO YOUR BEST IS ALL THAT MATTERS. BUT WHERE ARE THE COLORS?
HEE HEE! EVEN WITHOUT COLOR, THEY TICKLE! HEE HEE!
AH AH ! HEE HEE ! AH AH !
WOW! THIS IS THE FIRST TIME I'VE HEARD LILA LAUGH!
A RADIANT, GOLDEN LAUGH!
HEY! LOOK AT THE COLOR OF THE BUTTERFLIES!

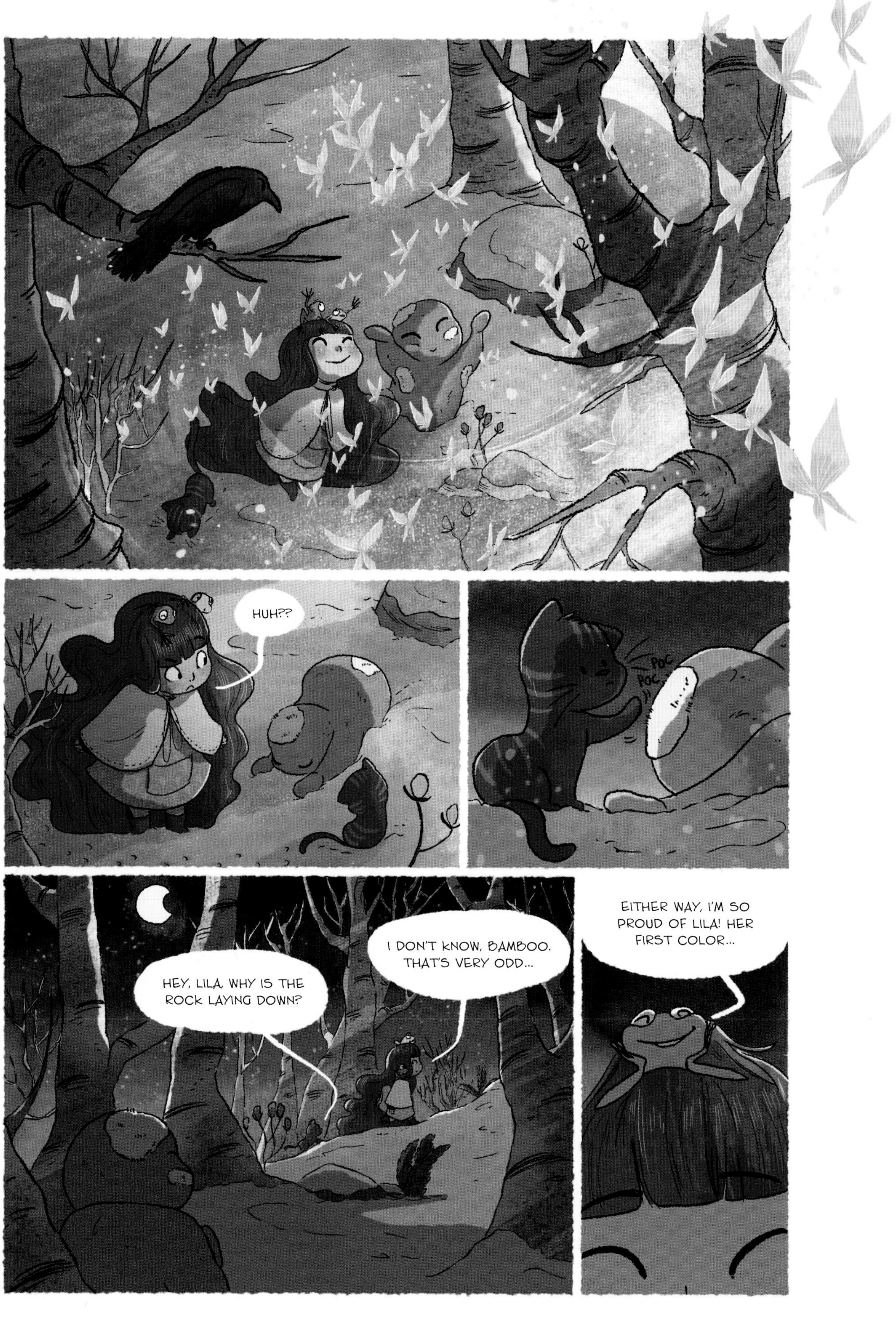
HUH??
POC
POC
HEY, LILA, WHY IS THE ROCK LAYING DOWN?
I DON'T KNOW, BAMBOO. THAT'S VERY ODD...
EITHER WAY, I'M SO PROUD OF LILA! HER FIRST COLOR...

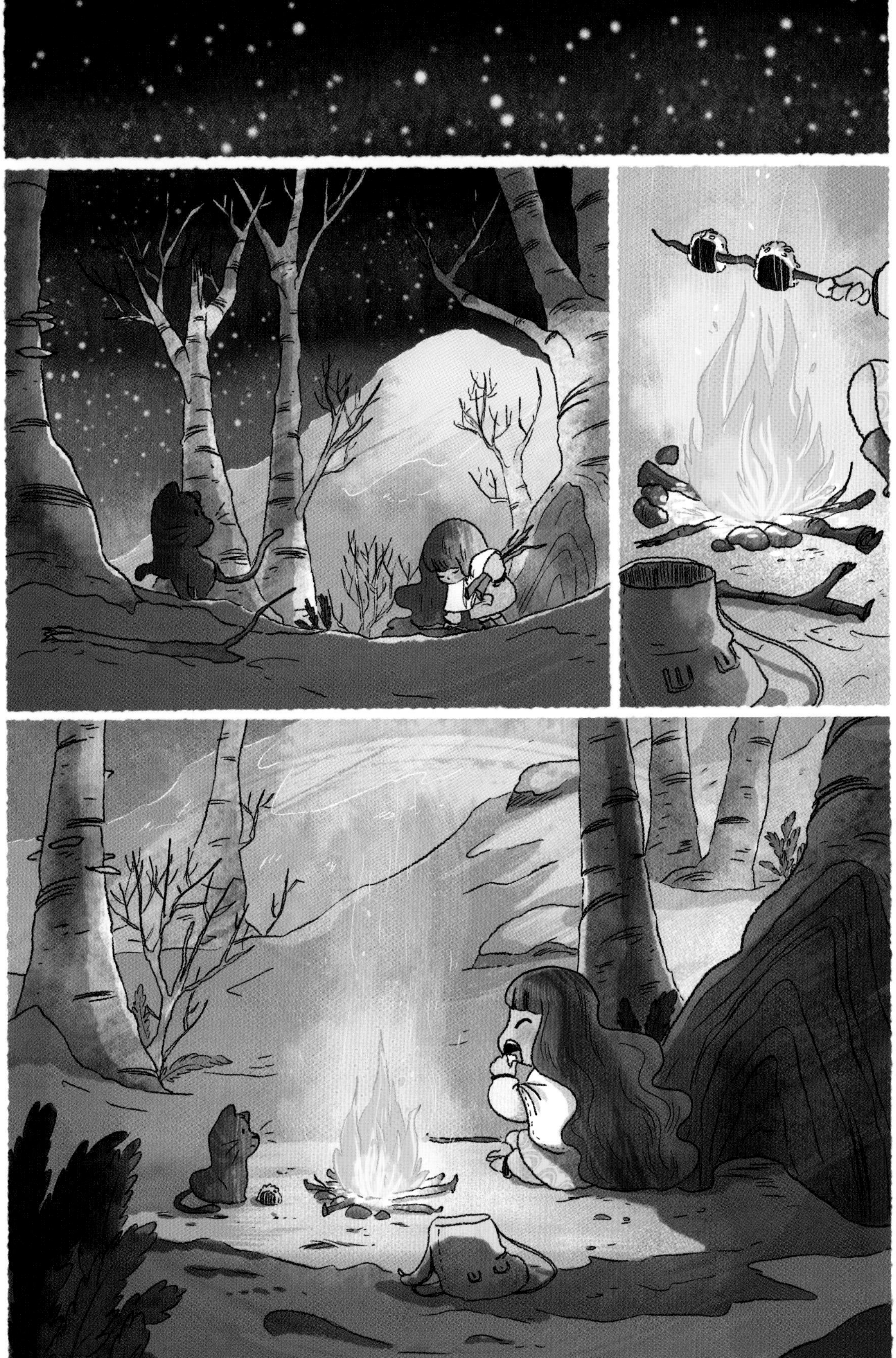

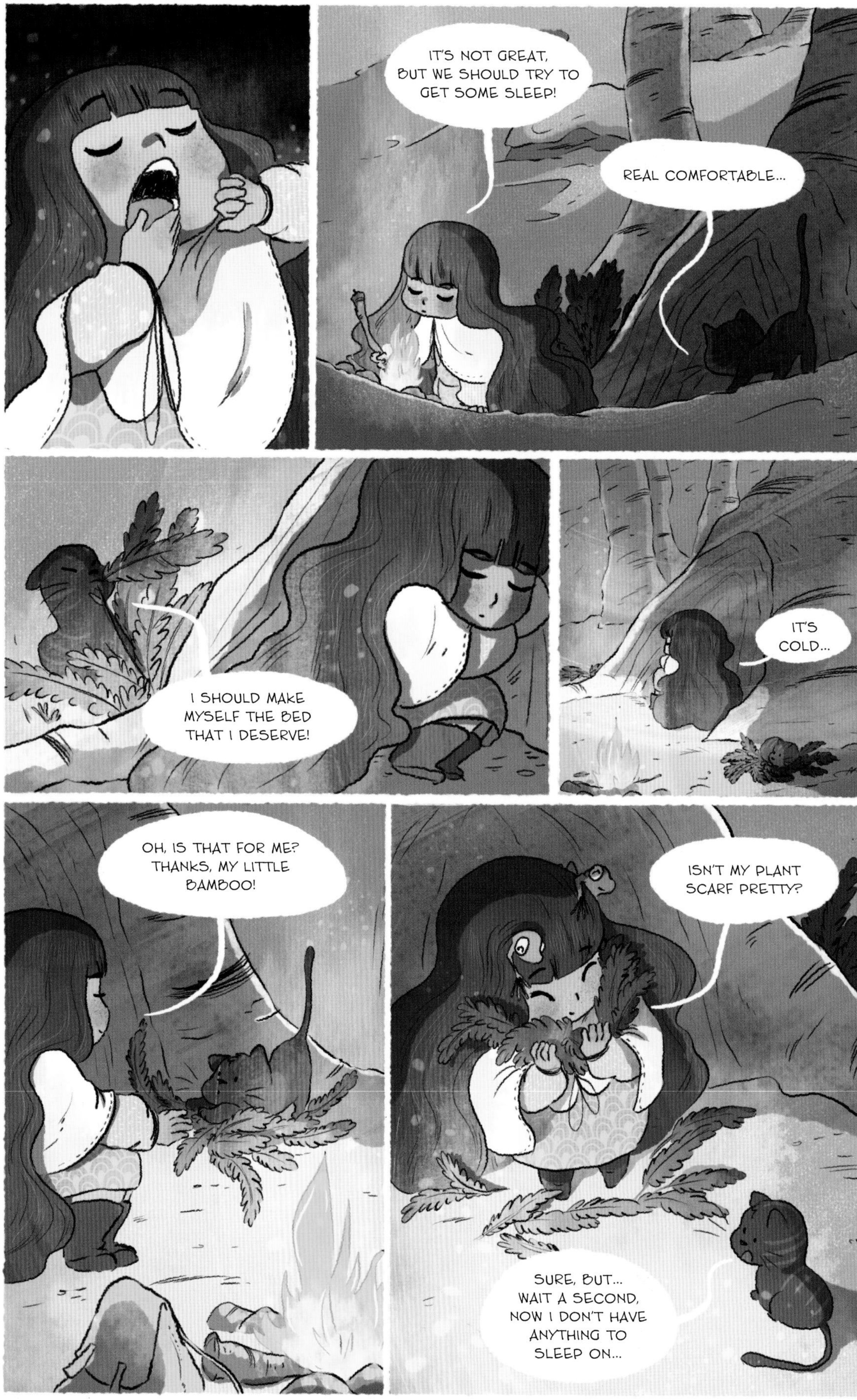
IT'S NOT GREAT, BUT WE SHOULD TRY TO GET SOME SLEEP!
REAL COMFORTABLE...
I SHOULD MAKE MYSELF THE BED THAT I DESERVE!
IT'S COLD...
OH, IS THAT FOR ME? THANKS, MY LITTLE BAMBOO!
ISN'T MY PLANT SCARF PRETTY?
SURE, BUT... WAIT A SECOND, NOW I DON'T HAVE ANYTHING TO SLEEP ON...

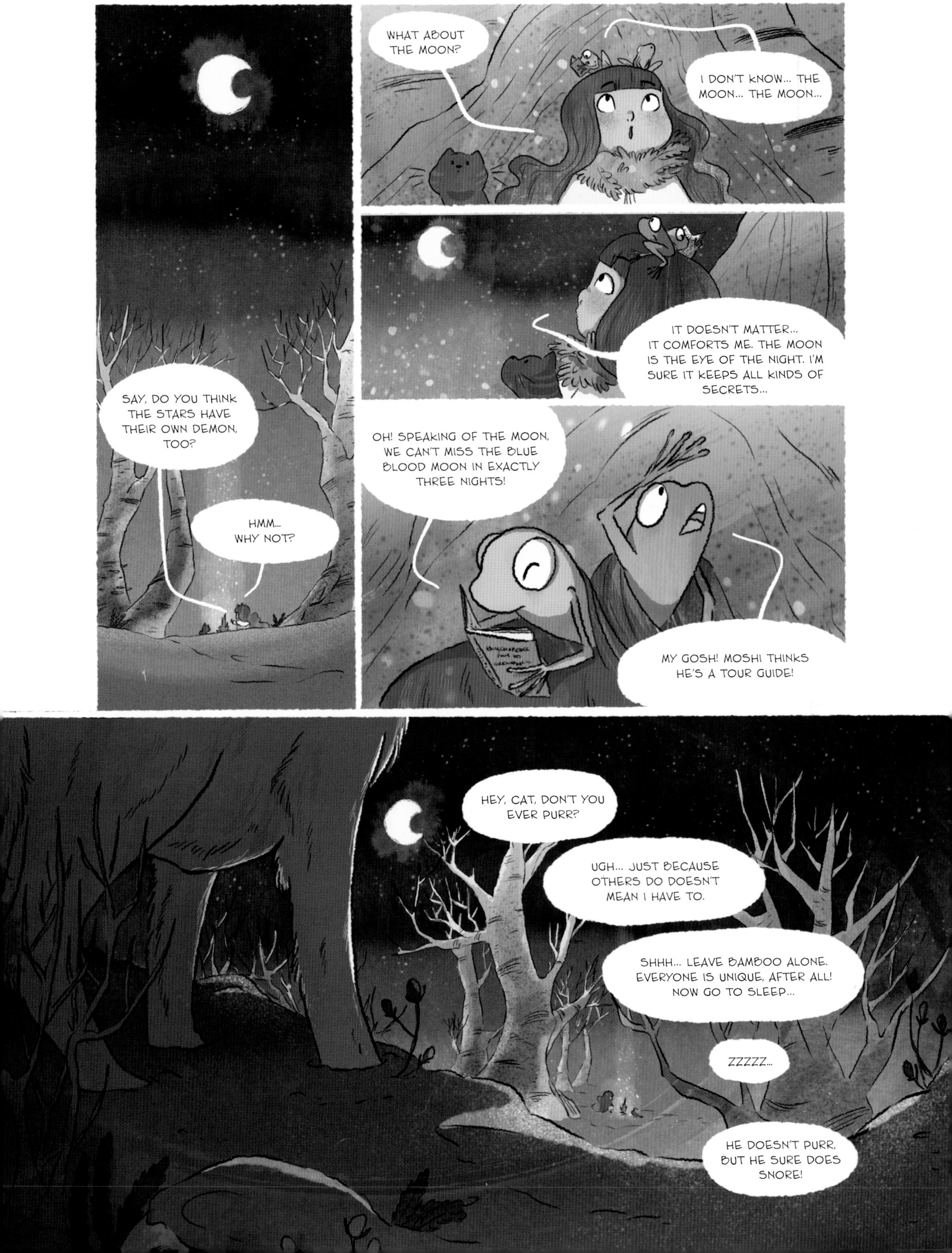
WHAT ABOUT THE MOON?
I DON'T KNOW... THE MOON... THE MOON...
IT DOESN'T MATTER... IT COMFORTS ME. THE MOON IS THE EYE OF THE NIGHT. I'M SURE IT KEEPS ALL KINDS OF SECRETS...
SAY, DO YOU THINK THE STARS HAVE THEIR OWN DEMON, TOO?
HMM... WHY NOT?
OH! SPEAKING OF THE MOON, WE CAN'T MISS THE BLUE BLOOD MOON IN EXACTLY THREE NIGHTS!
MY GOSH! MOSHI THINKS HE'S A TOUR GUIDE!
HEY, CAT, DON'T YOU EVER PURR?
UGH... JUST BECAUSE OTHERS DO DOESN'T MEAN I HAVE TO.
SHHH... LEAVE BAMBOO ALONE. EVERYONE IS UNIQUE, AFTER ALL! NOW GO TO SLEEP...
ZZZZZ...
HE DOESN'T PURR, BUT HE SURE DOES SNORE!

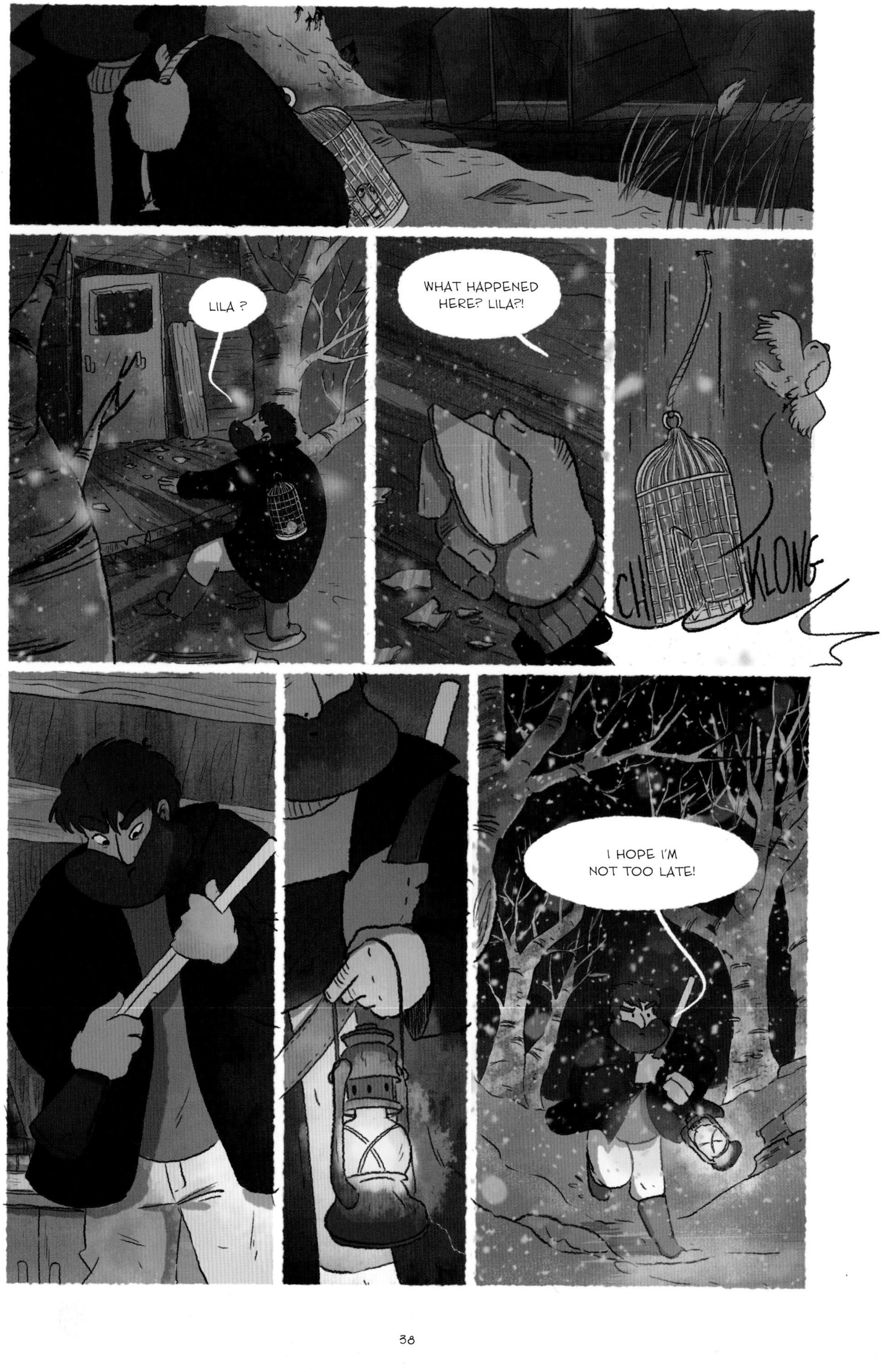
LILA ?
WHAT HAPPENED HERE? LILA?!
CHI KLONG
I HOPE I'M NOT TOO LATE!

The Pond of Memories

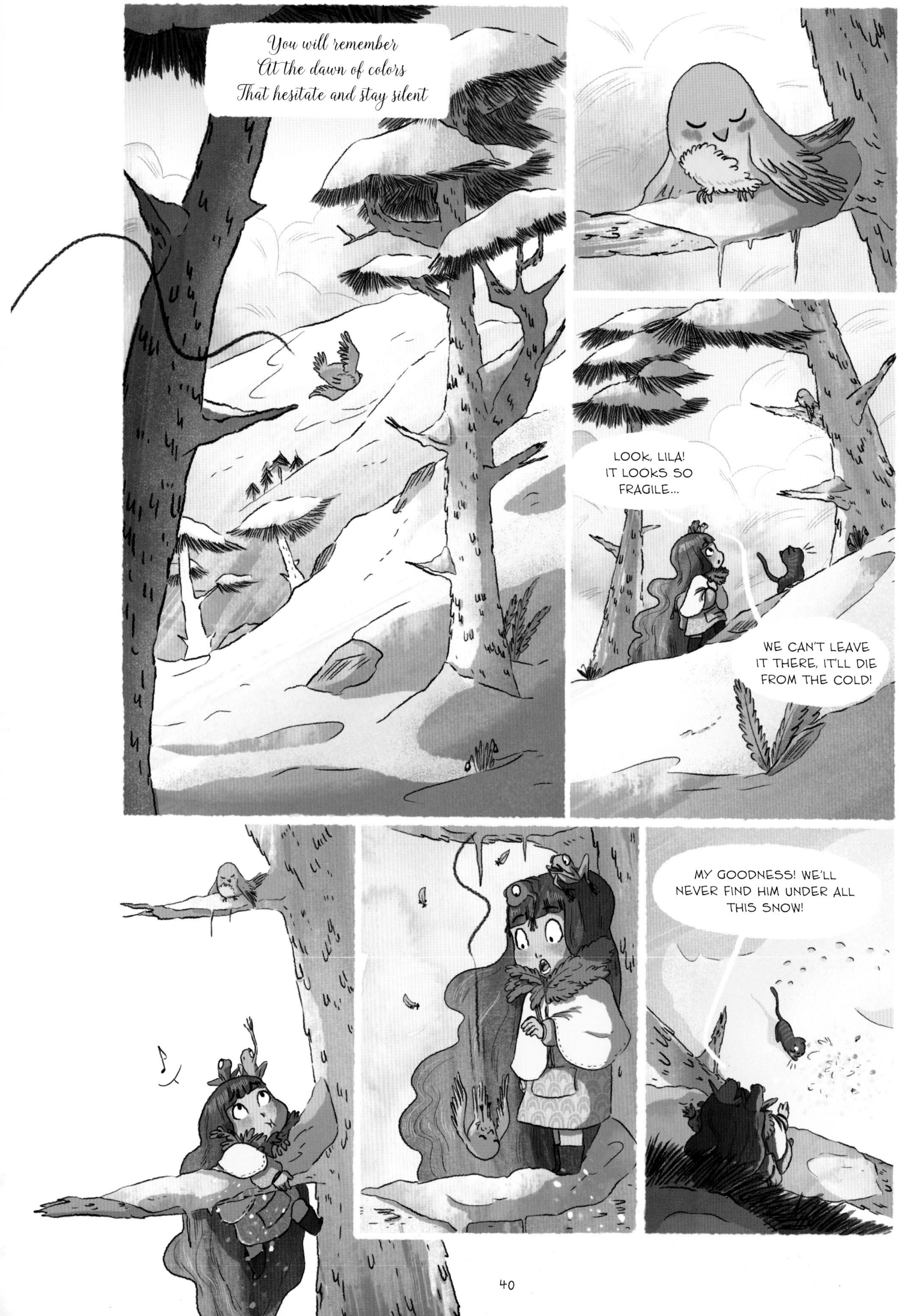
You will remember
At the dawn of colors
That hesitate and stay silent
LOOK, LILA! IT LOOKS SO FRAGILE...
WE CAN'T LEAVE IT THERE, IT'LL DIE FROM THE COLD!
MY GOODNESS! WE'LL NEVER FIND HIM UNDER ALL THIS SNOW!

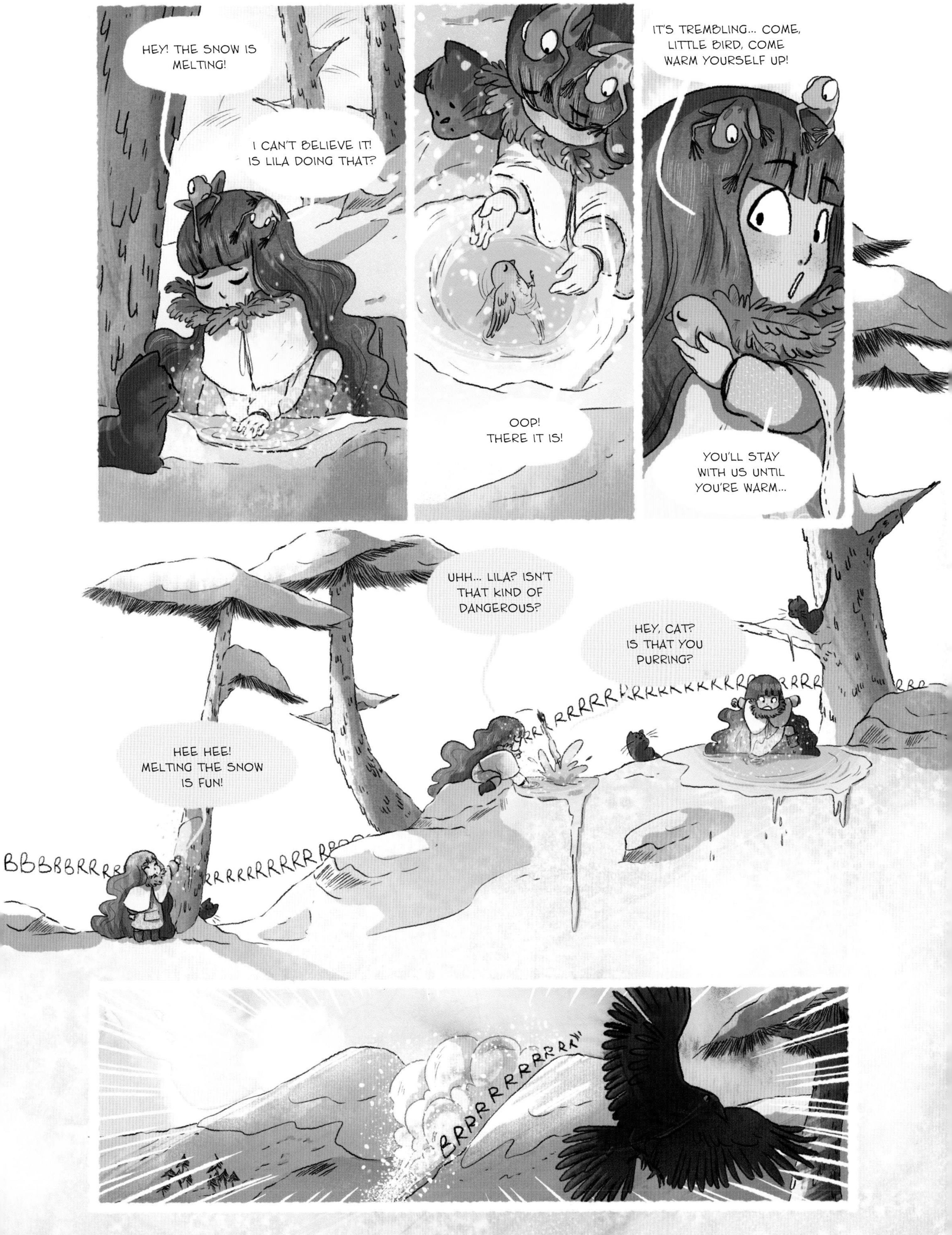
HEY! THE SNOW IS MELTING!
I CAN'T BELIEVE IT! IS LILA DOING THAT?
OOP! THERE IT IS!
IT'S TREMBLING... COME, LITTLE BIRD, COME WARM YOURSELF UP!
YOU'LL STAY WITH US UNTIL YOU'RE WARM...
UHH... LILA? ISN'T THAT KIND OF DANGEROUS?
HEY, CAT? IS THAT YOU PURRING?
RRRRRRRKKKKKKRRRRRRRR
HEE HEE! MELTING THE SNOW IS FUN!
BBBBBRRRRRRRRRRRRRRRR
BRRRRRRRRRRR

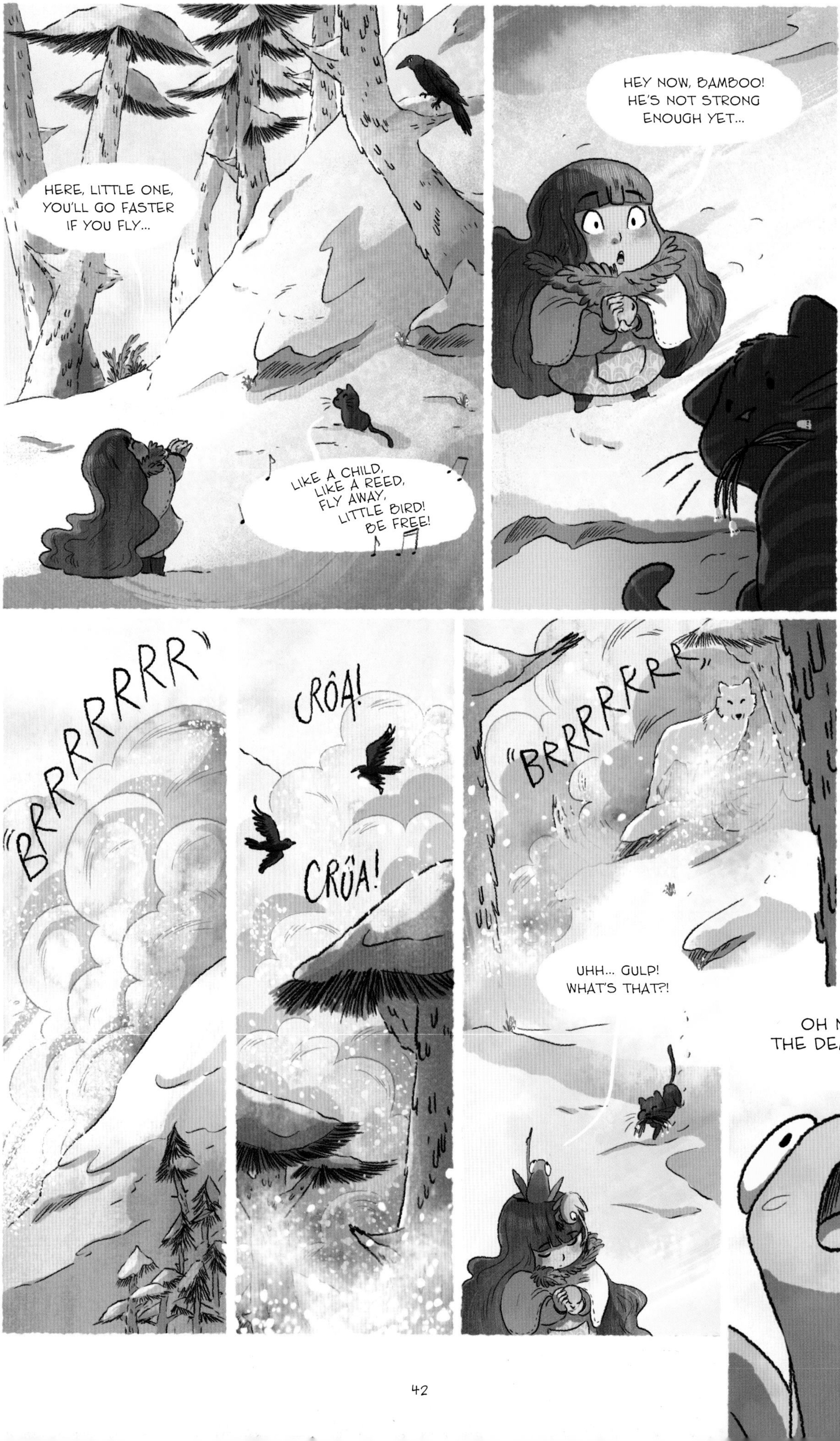
HERE, LITTLE ONE, YOU'LL GO FASTER IF YOU FLY...
LIKE A CHILD, LIKE A REED, FLY AWAY, LITTLE BIRD! BE FREE!
HEY NOW, BAMBOO! HE'S NOT STRONG ENOUGH YET...
"BRRRRRRR"
CRÔA!
CRÛA!
"BRRRRRRR"
UHH... GULP! WHAT'S THAT?!
OH NO! THE DEMONS!

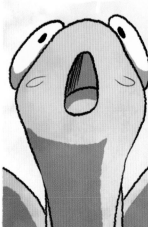

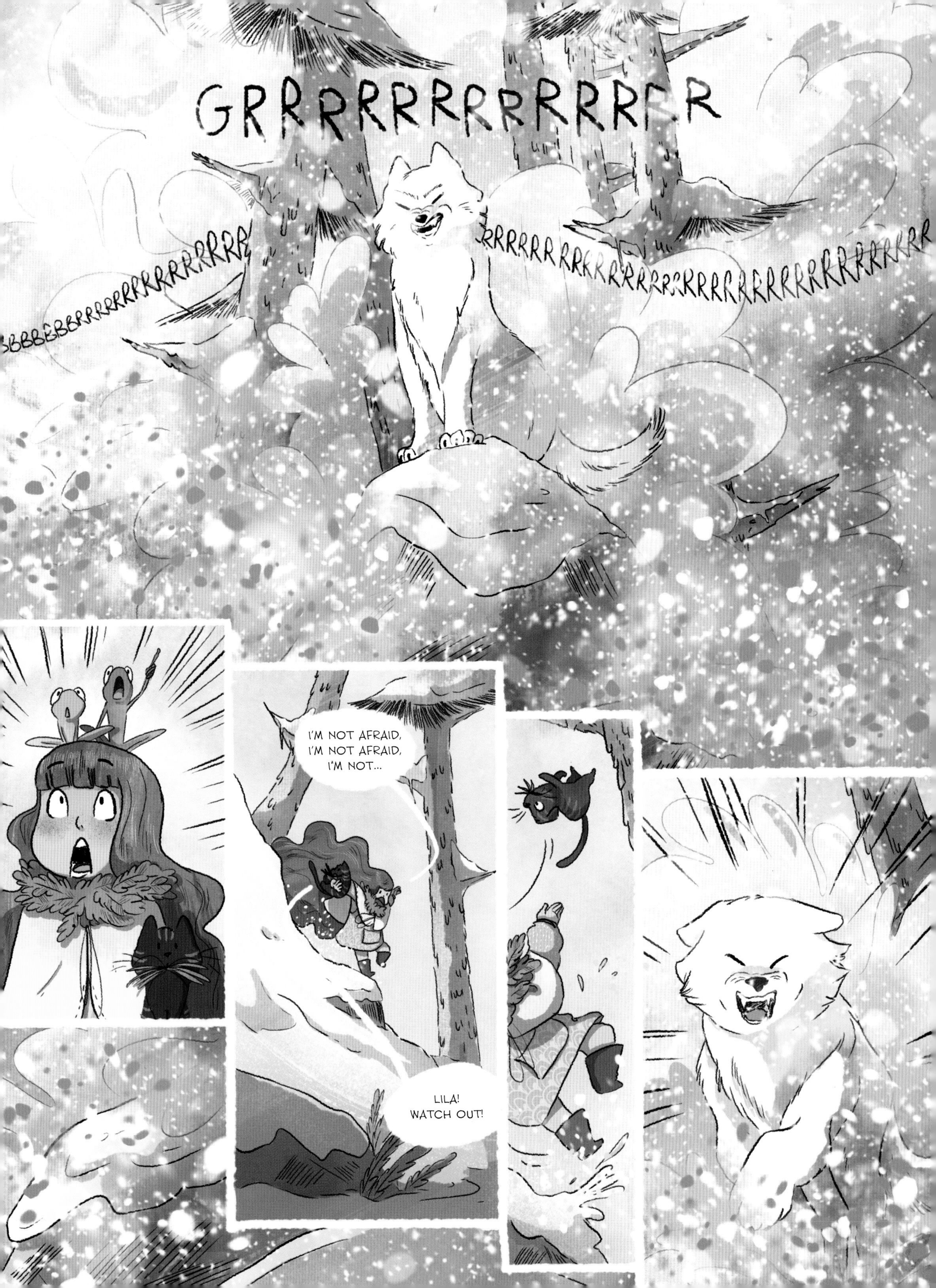
GRRRRRRRRRRRRR
I'M NOT AFRAID,
I'M NOT AFRAID,
I'M NOT...
LILA!
WATCH OUT!

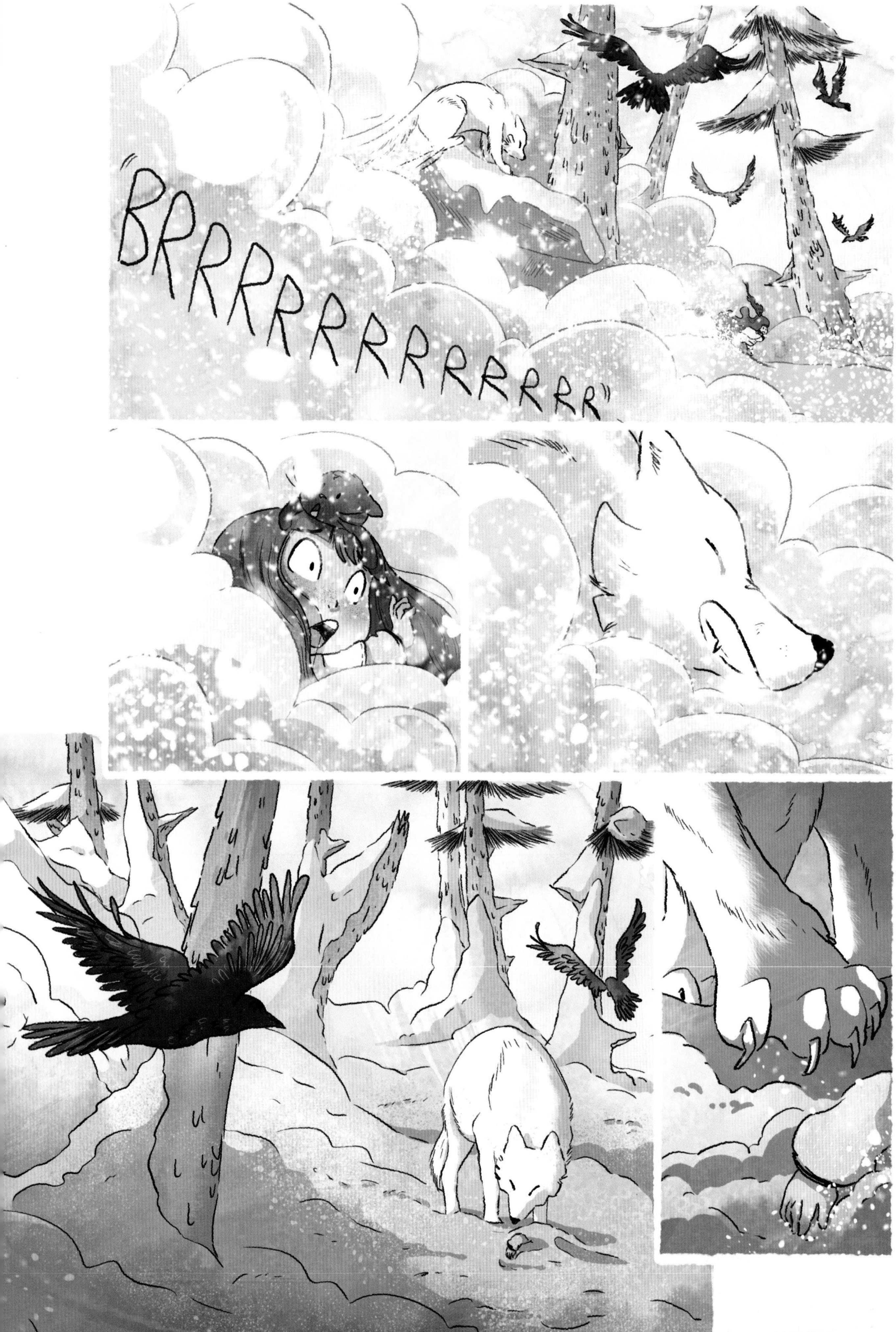
BRRRRRRRRRRRRR"

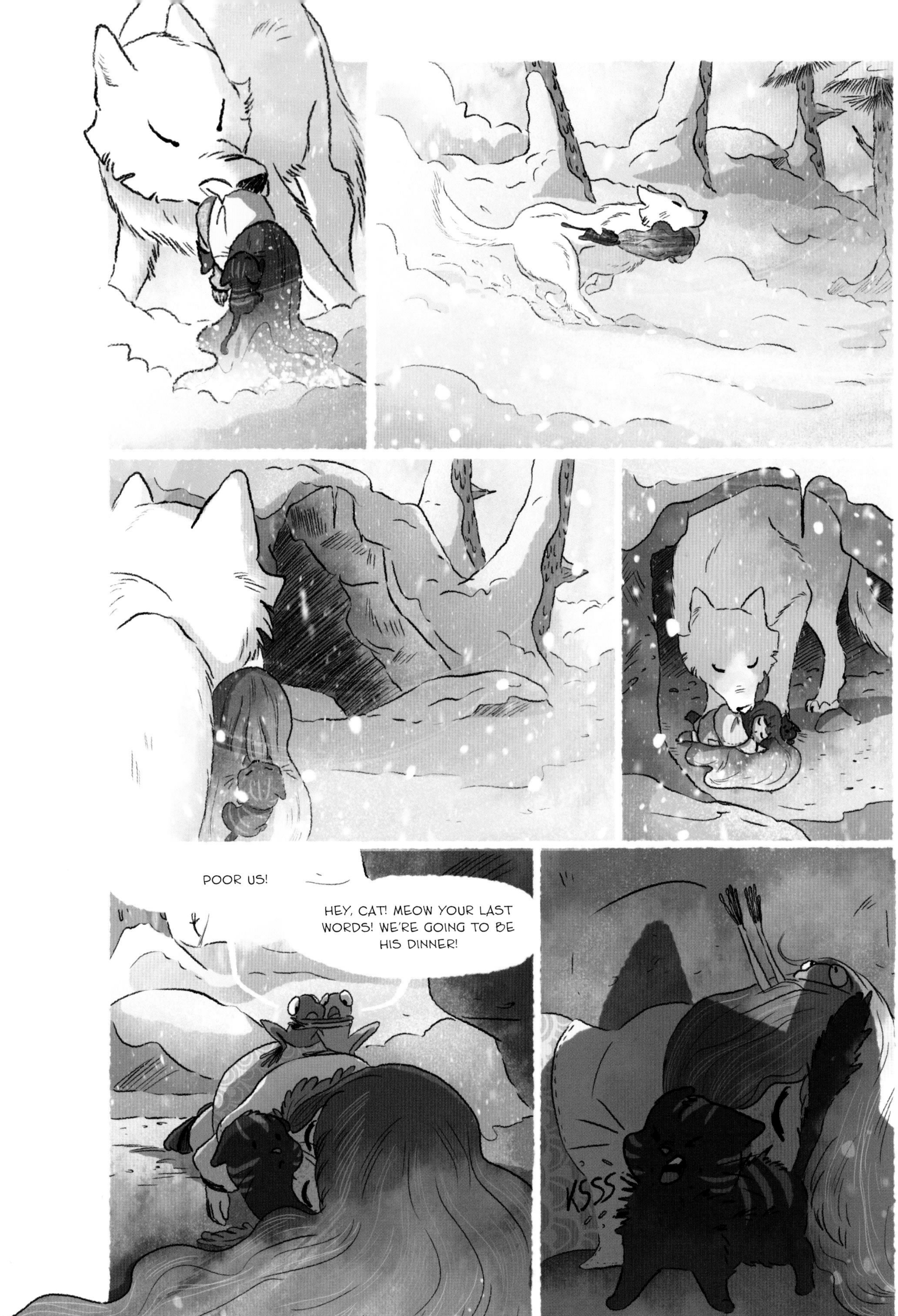
POOR US!
HEY, CAT! MEOW YOUR LAST WORDS! WE'RE GOING TO BE HIS DINNER!
KSSS

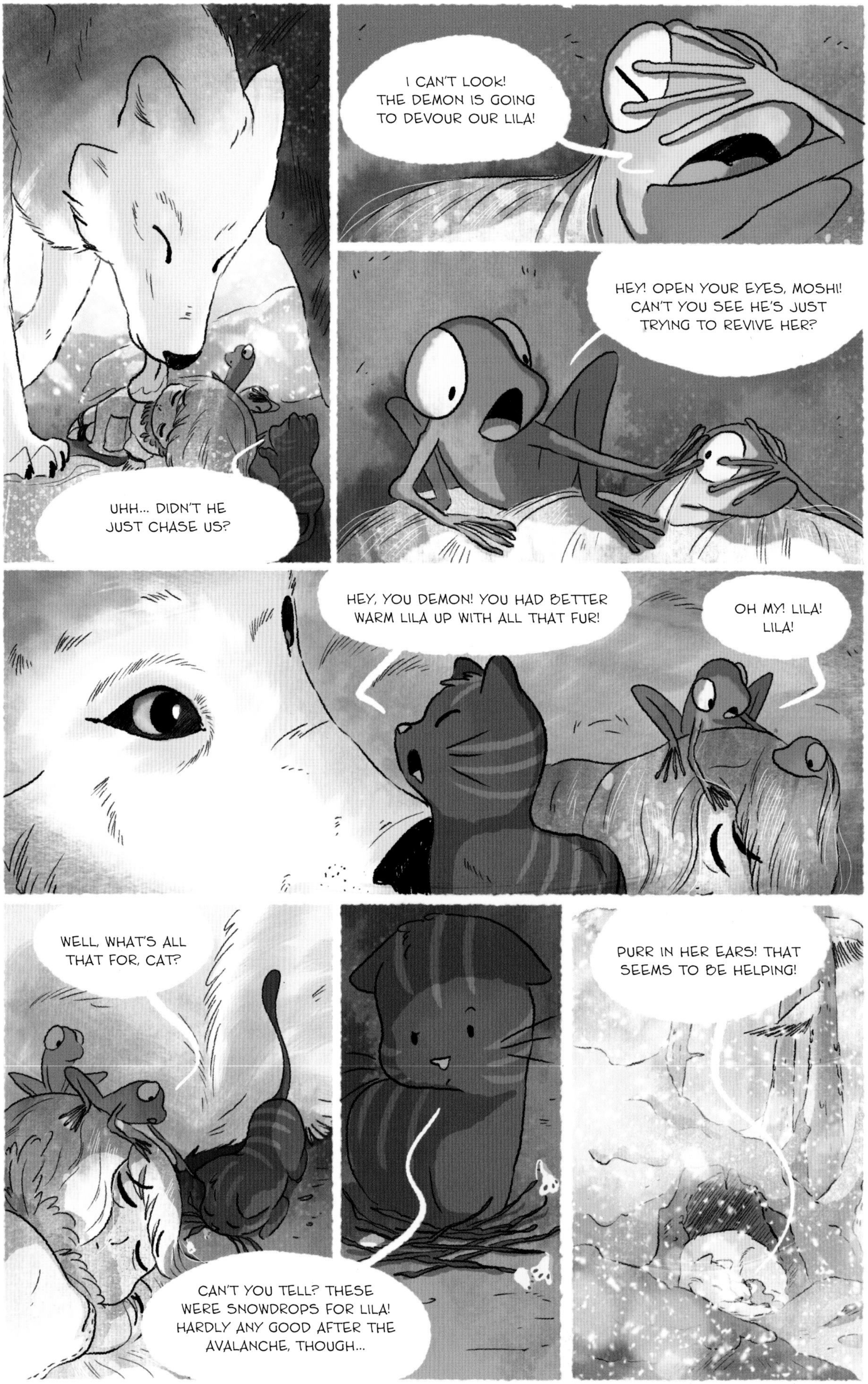
I CAN'T LOOK! THE DEMON IS GOING TO DEVOUR OUR LILA!
UHH... DIDN'T HE JUST CHASE US?
HEY! OPEN YOUR EYES, MOSHI! CAN'T YOU SEE HE'S JUST TRYING TO REVIVE HER?
HEY, YOU DEMON! YOU HAD BETTER WARM LILA UP WITH ALL THAT FUR!
OH MY! LILA! LILA!
WELL, WHAT'S ALL THAT FOR, CAT?
CAN'T YOU TELL? THESE WERE SNOWDROPS FOR LILA! HARDLY ANY GOOD AFTER THE AVALANCHE, THOUGH...
PURR IN HER EARS! THAT SEEMS TO BE HELPING!

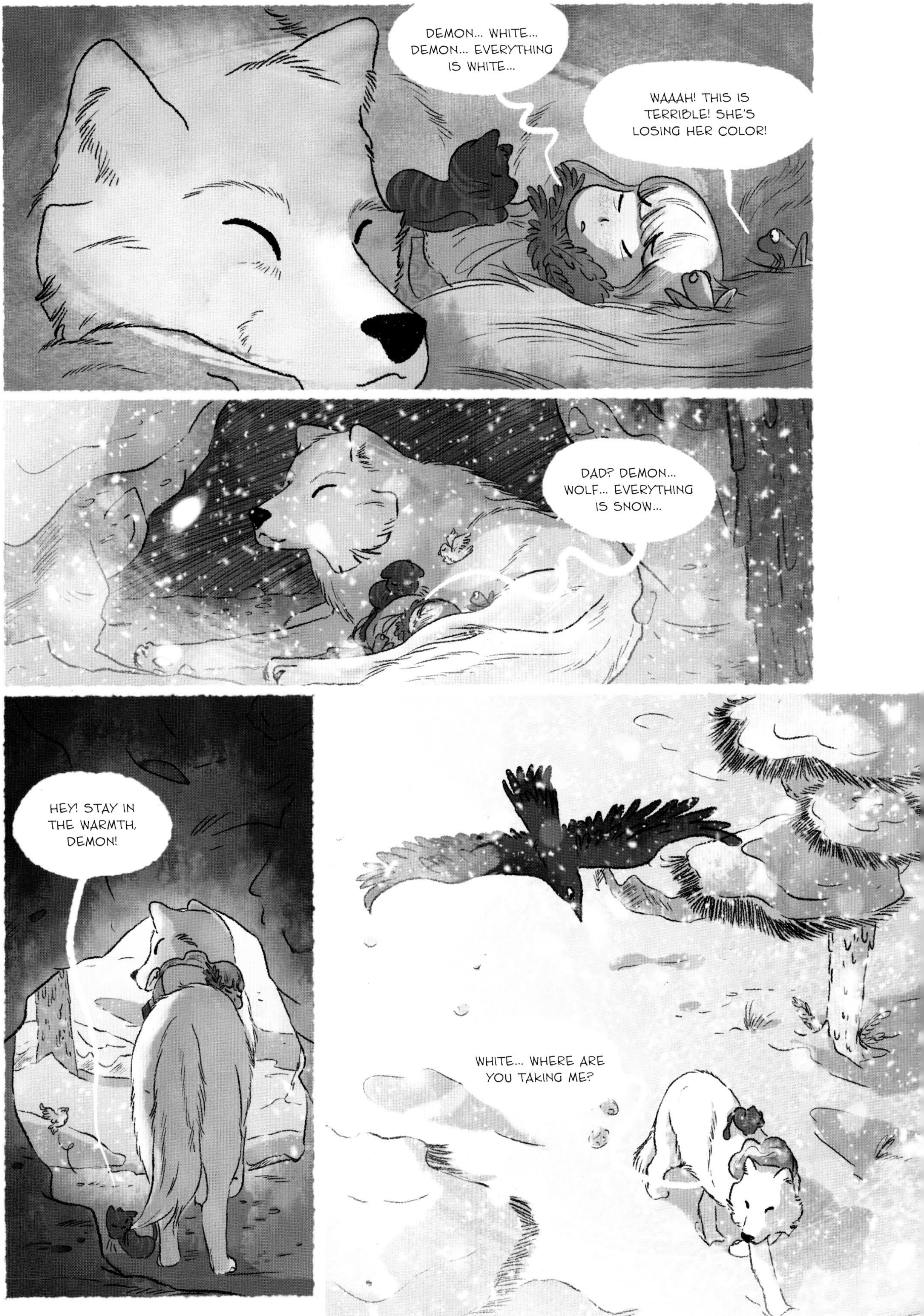
DEMON... WHITE... DEMON... EVERYTHING IS WHITE...
WAAAH! THIS IS TERRIBLE! SHE'S LOSING HER COLOR!
DAD? DEMON... WOLF... EVERYTHING IS SNOW...
HEY! STAY IN THE WARMTH, DEMON!
WHITE... WHERE ARE YOU TAKING ME?

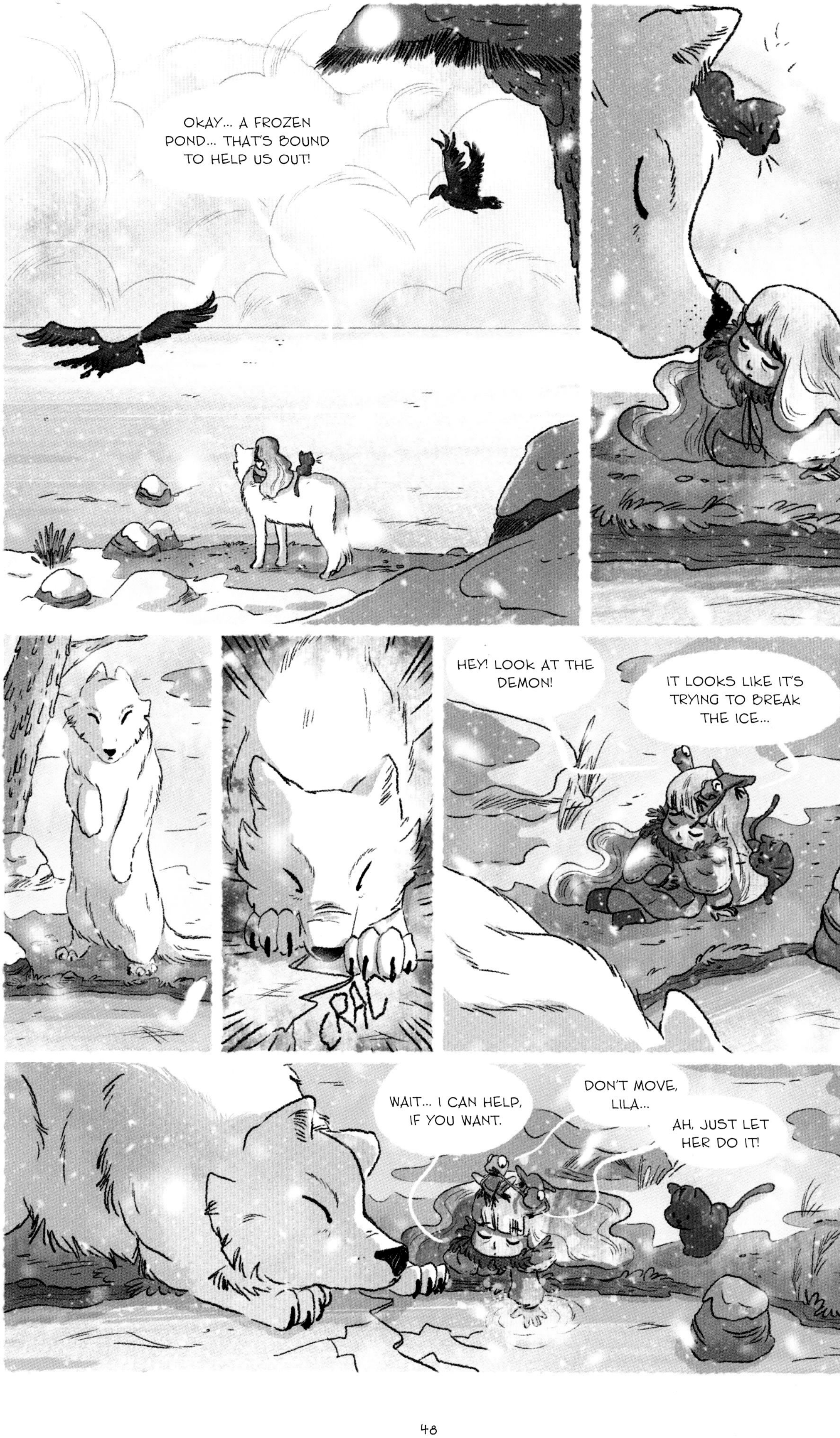
OKAY... A FROZEN POND... THAT'S BOUND TO HELP US OUT!
HEY! LOOK AT THE DEMON!
IT LOOKS LIKE IT'S TRYING TO BREAK THE ICE...
CRAC
WAIT... I CAN HELP, IF YOU WANT.
DON'T MOVE, LILA...
AH, JUST LET HER DO IT!

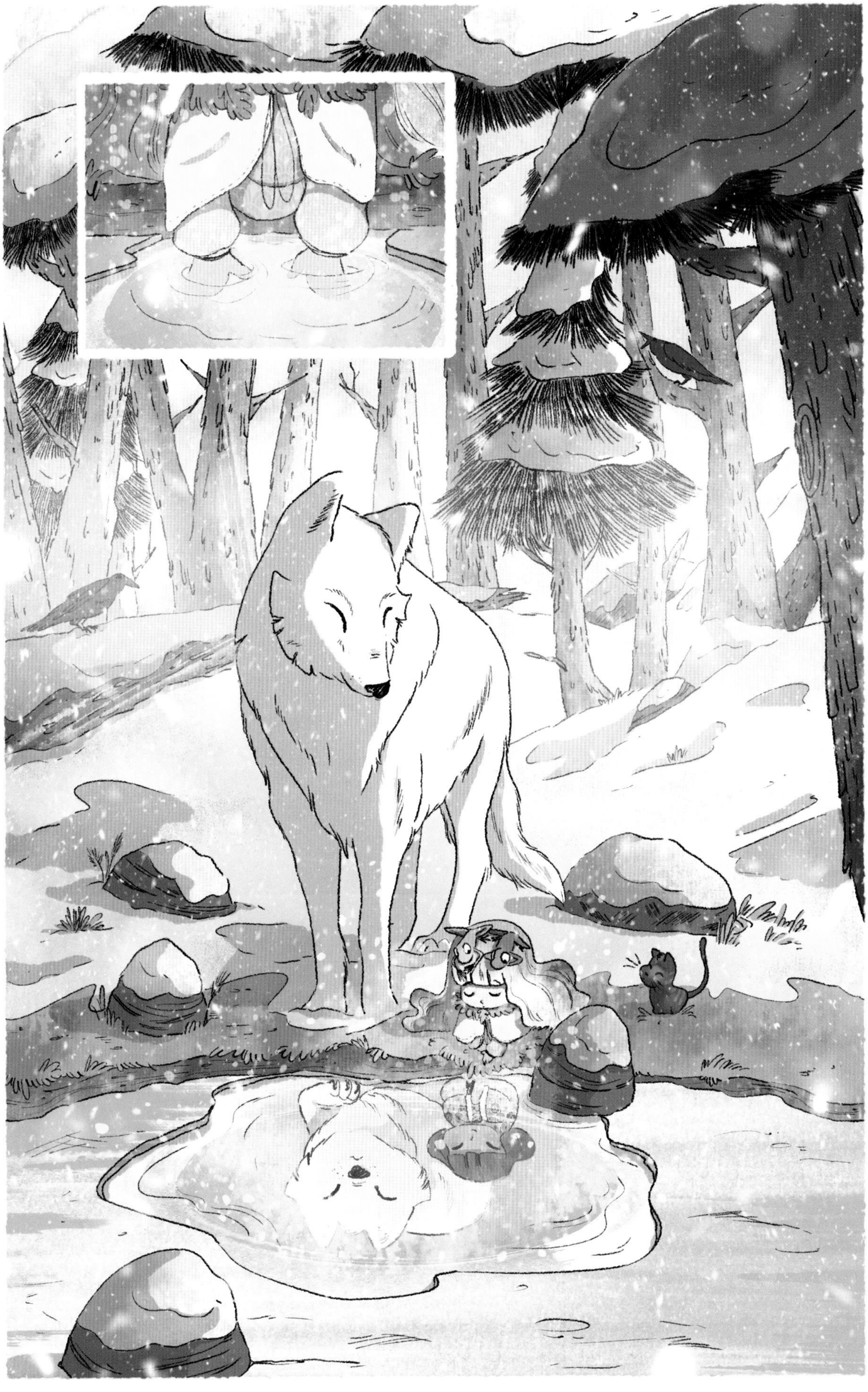

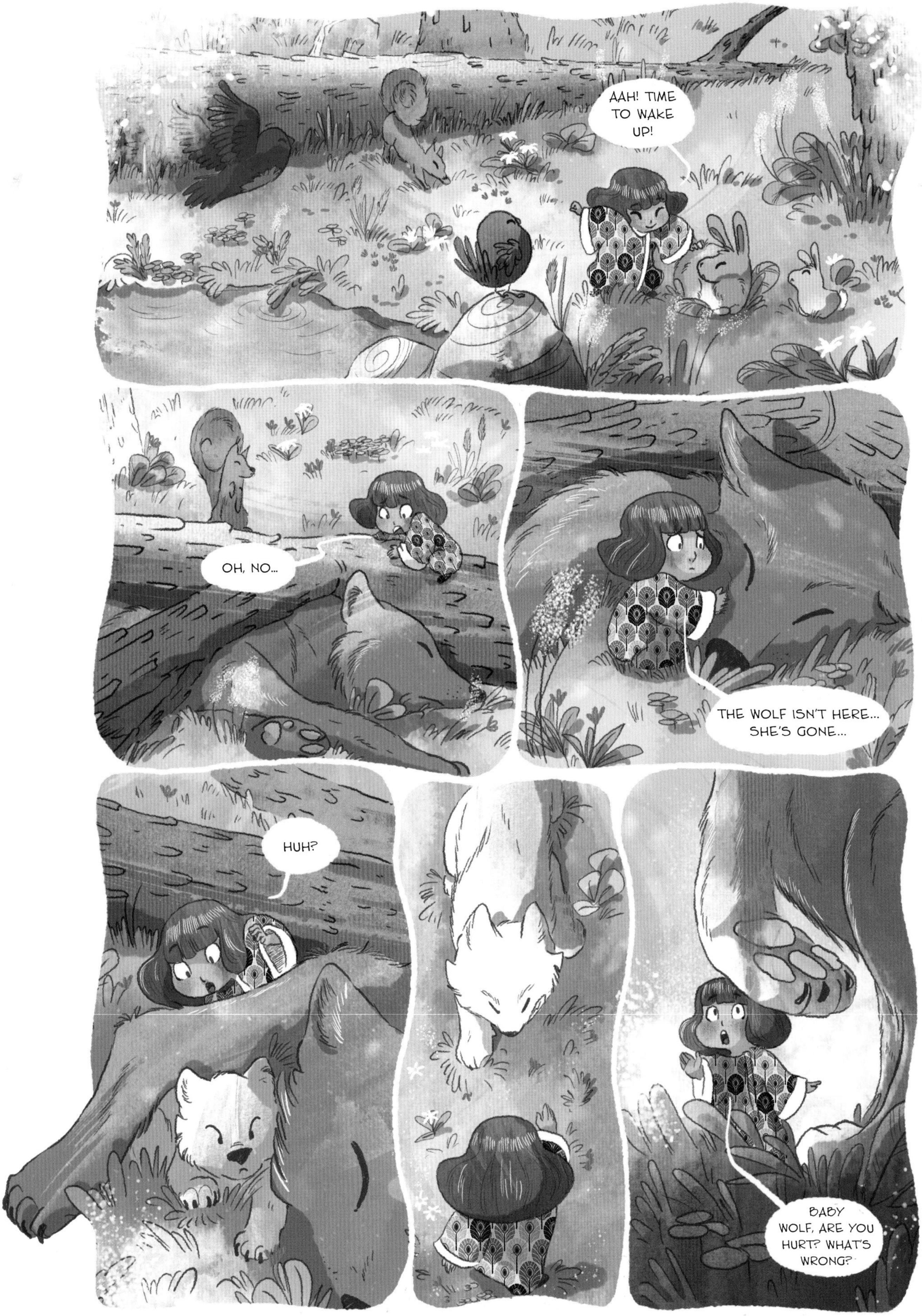
AAH! TIME TO WAKE UP!
OH, NO...
THE WOLF ISN'T HERE... SHE'S GONE...
HUH?
BABY WOLF, ARE YOU HURT? WHAT'S WRONG?

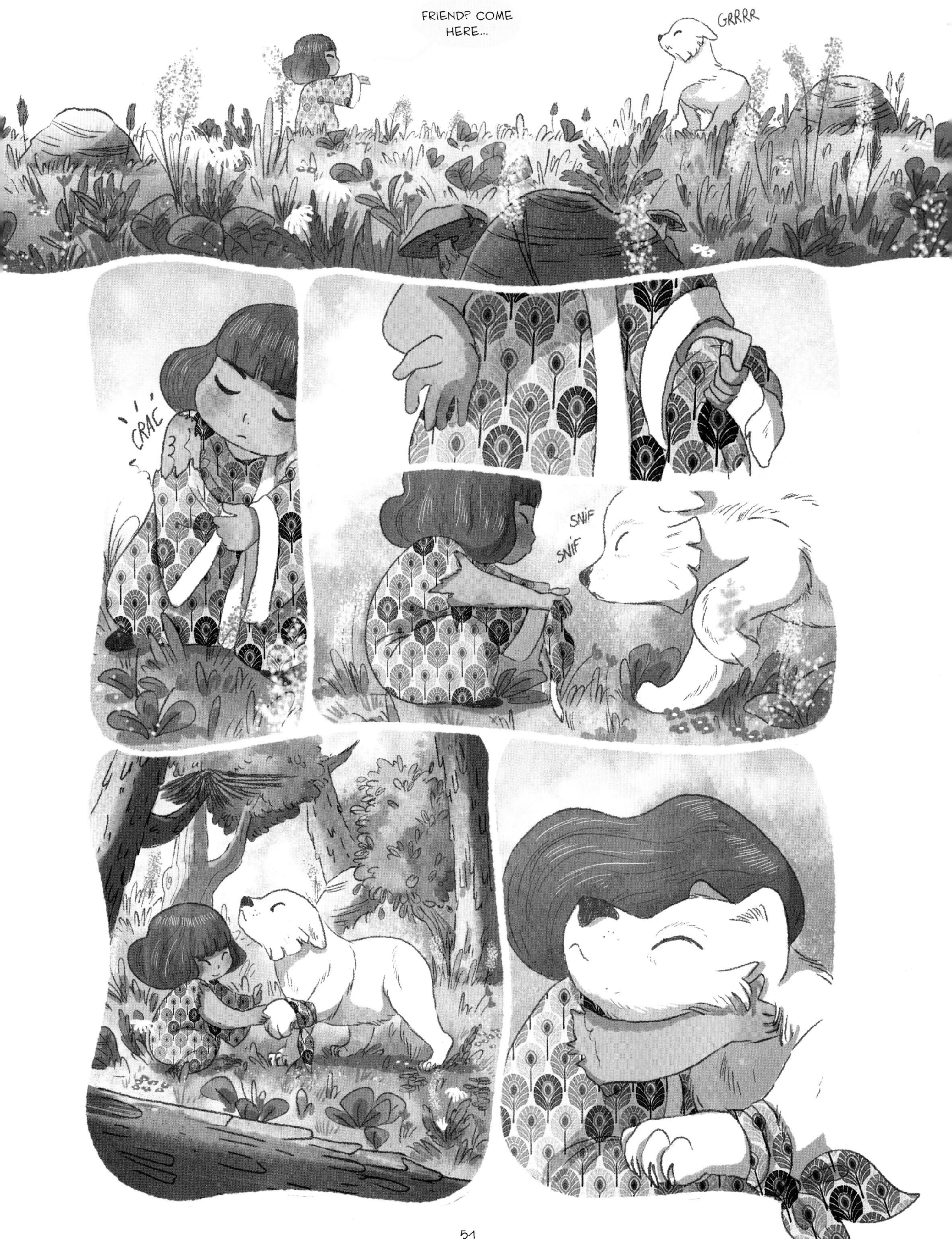
FRIEND? COME HERE...
GRRRR
CRAC
SNIF
SNIF

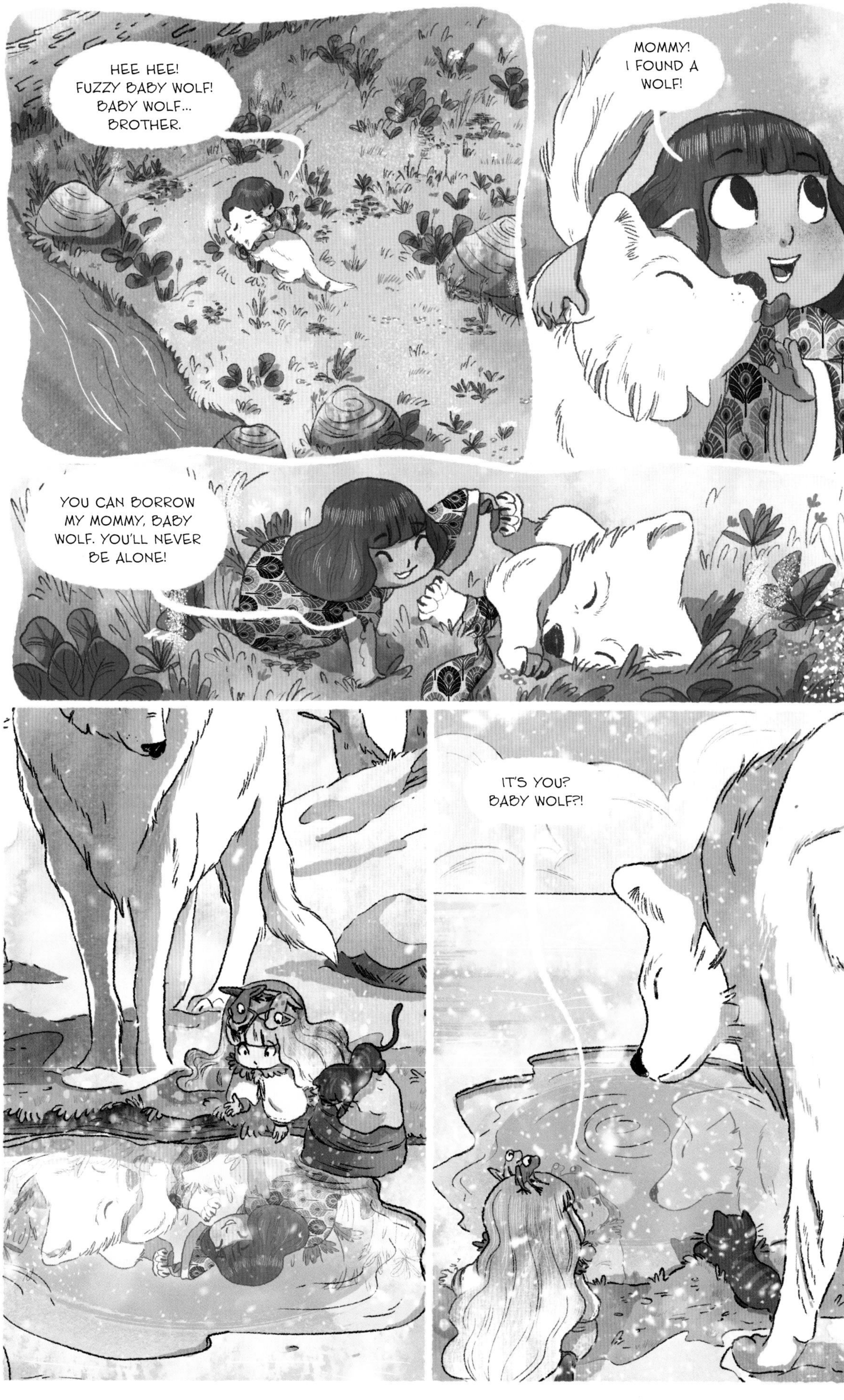
HEE HEE!
FUZZY BABY WOLF!
BABY WOLF...
BROTHER.
MOMMY!
I FOUND A
WOLF!
YOU CAN BORROW
MY MOMMY, BABY
WOLF. YOU'LL NEVER
BE ALONE!
IT'S YOU?
BABY WOLF?!

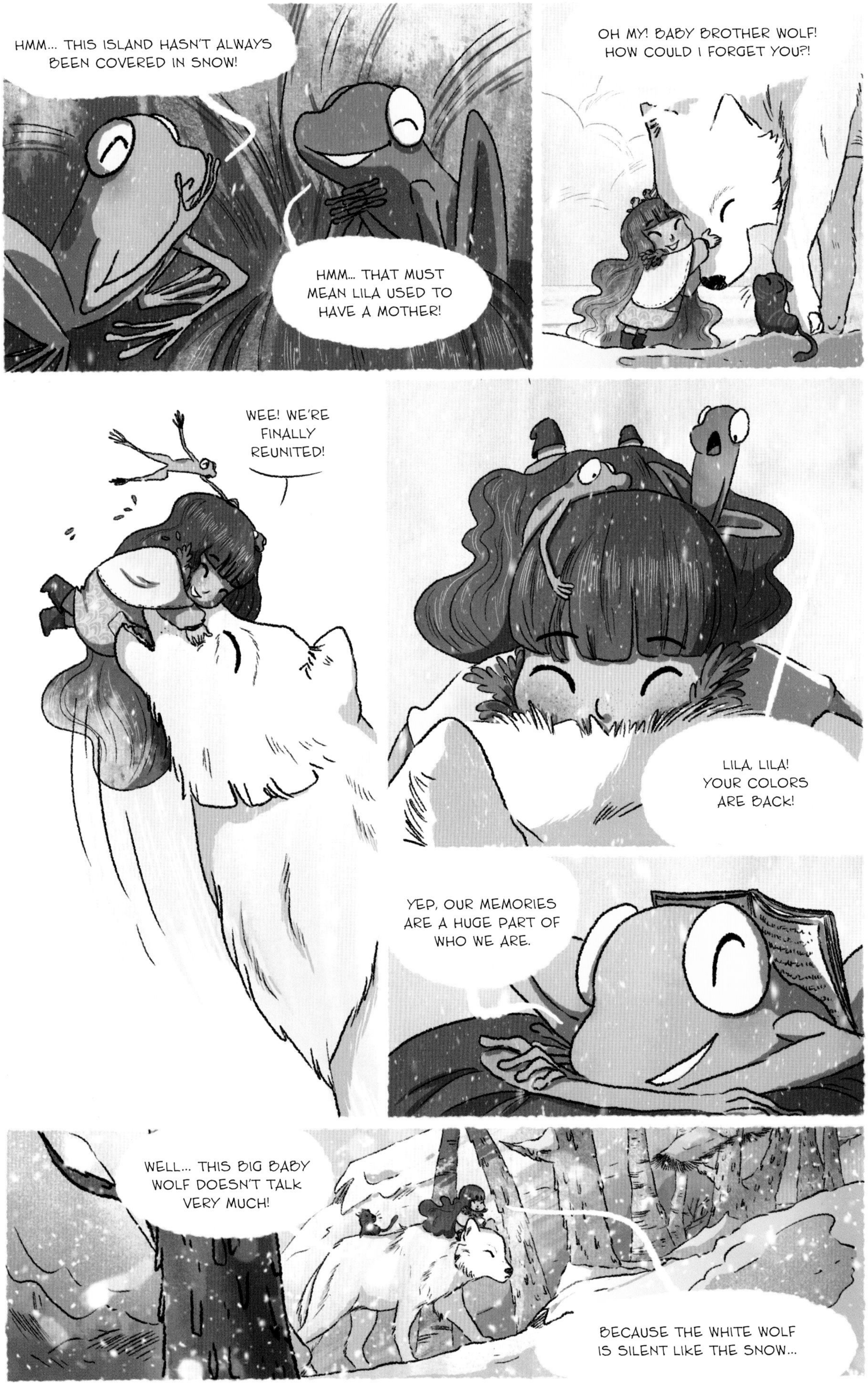
HMM... THIS ISLAND HASN'T ALWAYS BEEN COVERED IN SNOW!
HMM... THAT MUST MEAN LILA USED TO HAVE A MOTHER!
OH MY! BABY BROTHER WOLF! HOW COULD I FORGET YOU?!
WEE! WE'RE FINALLY REUNITED!
LILA, LILA! YOUR COLORS ARE BACK!
YEP, OUR MEMORIES ARE A HUGE PART OF WHO WE ARE.
WELL... THIS BIG BABY WOLF DOESN'T TALK VERY MUCH!
BECAUSE THE WHITE WOLF IS SILENT LIKE THE SNOW...

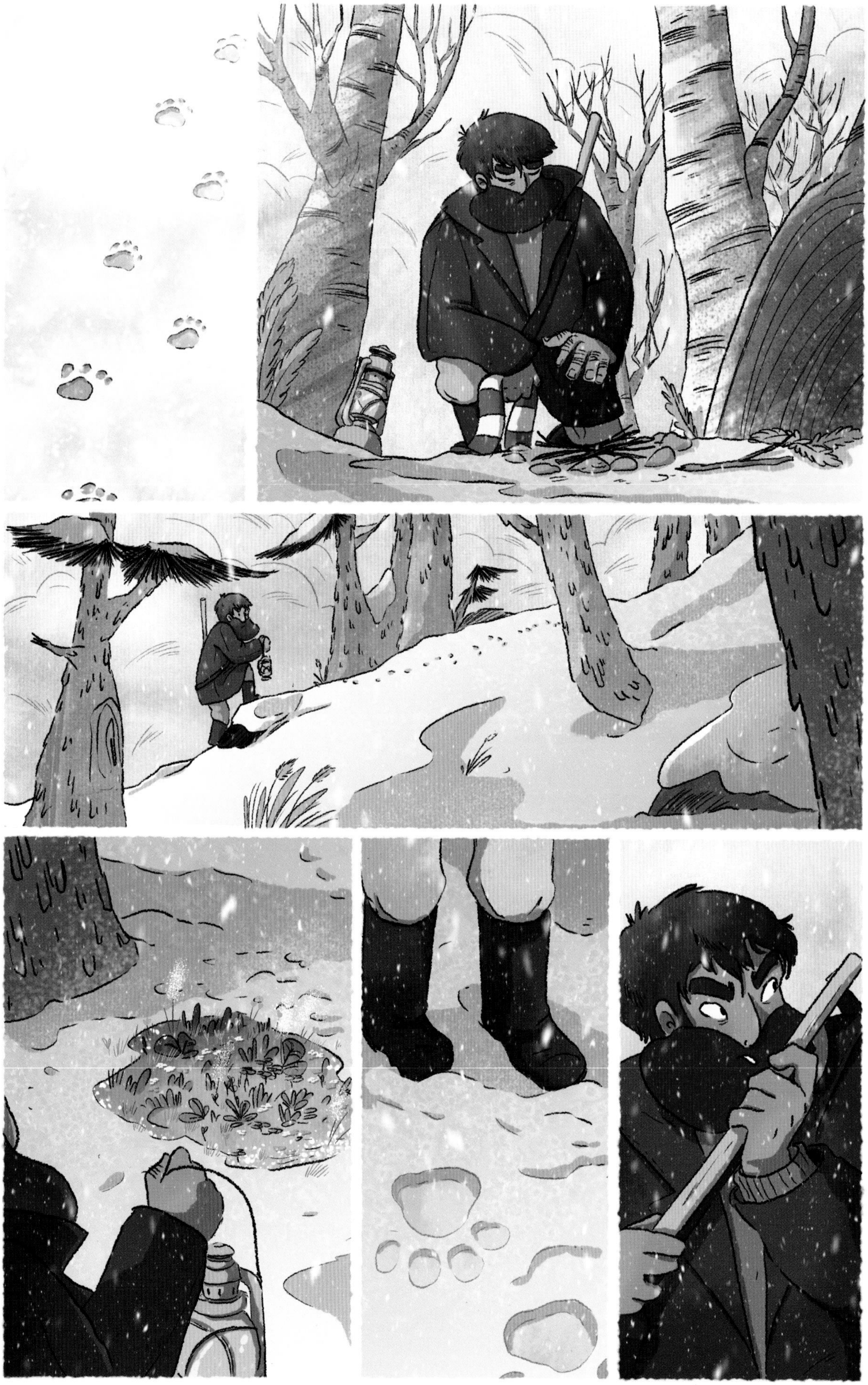

The River of the Moon Stone

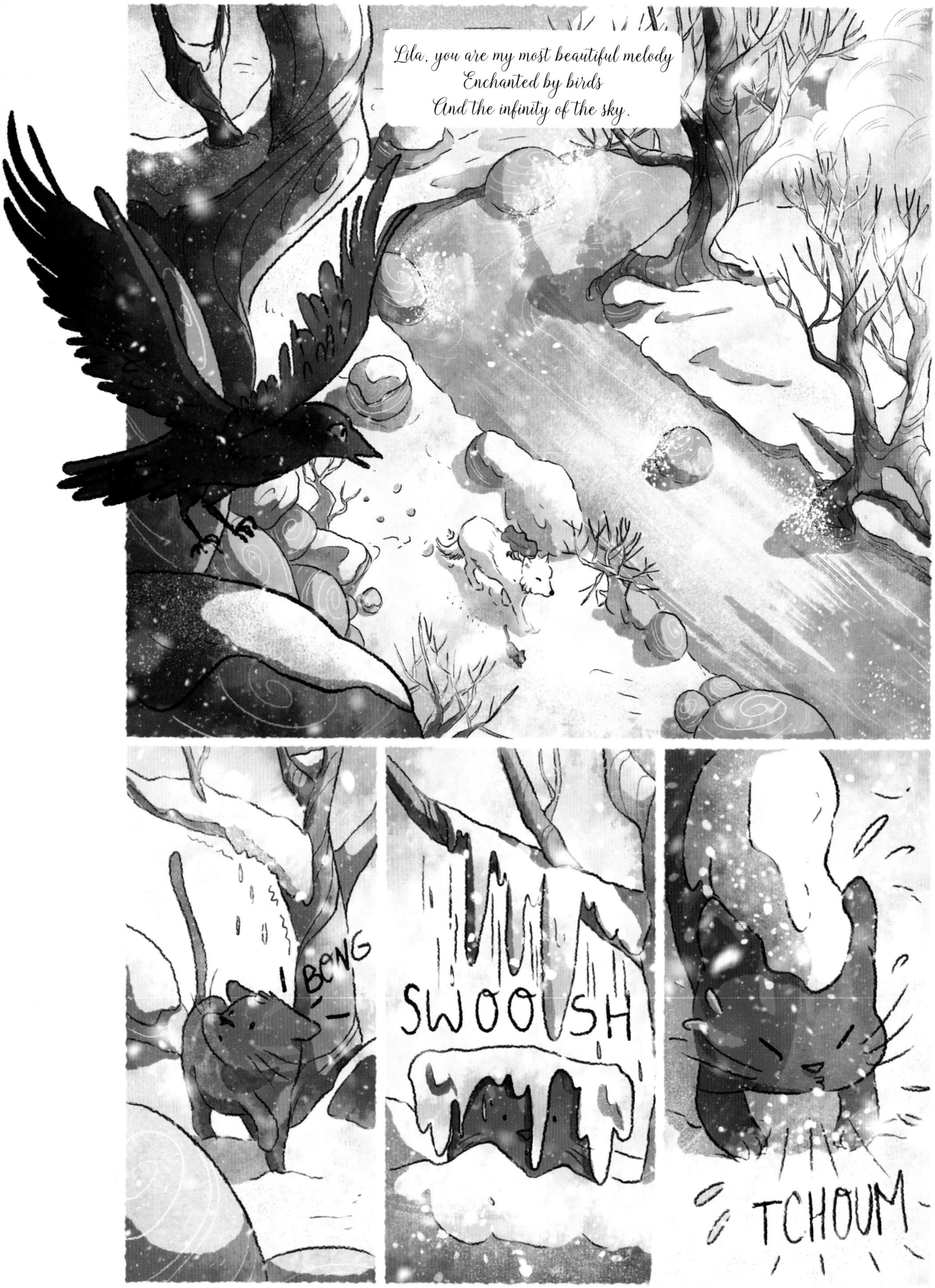
Lila, you are my most beautiful melody
Enchanted by birds
And the infinity of the sky.
BONG
SWOOOSH
TCHOUM

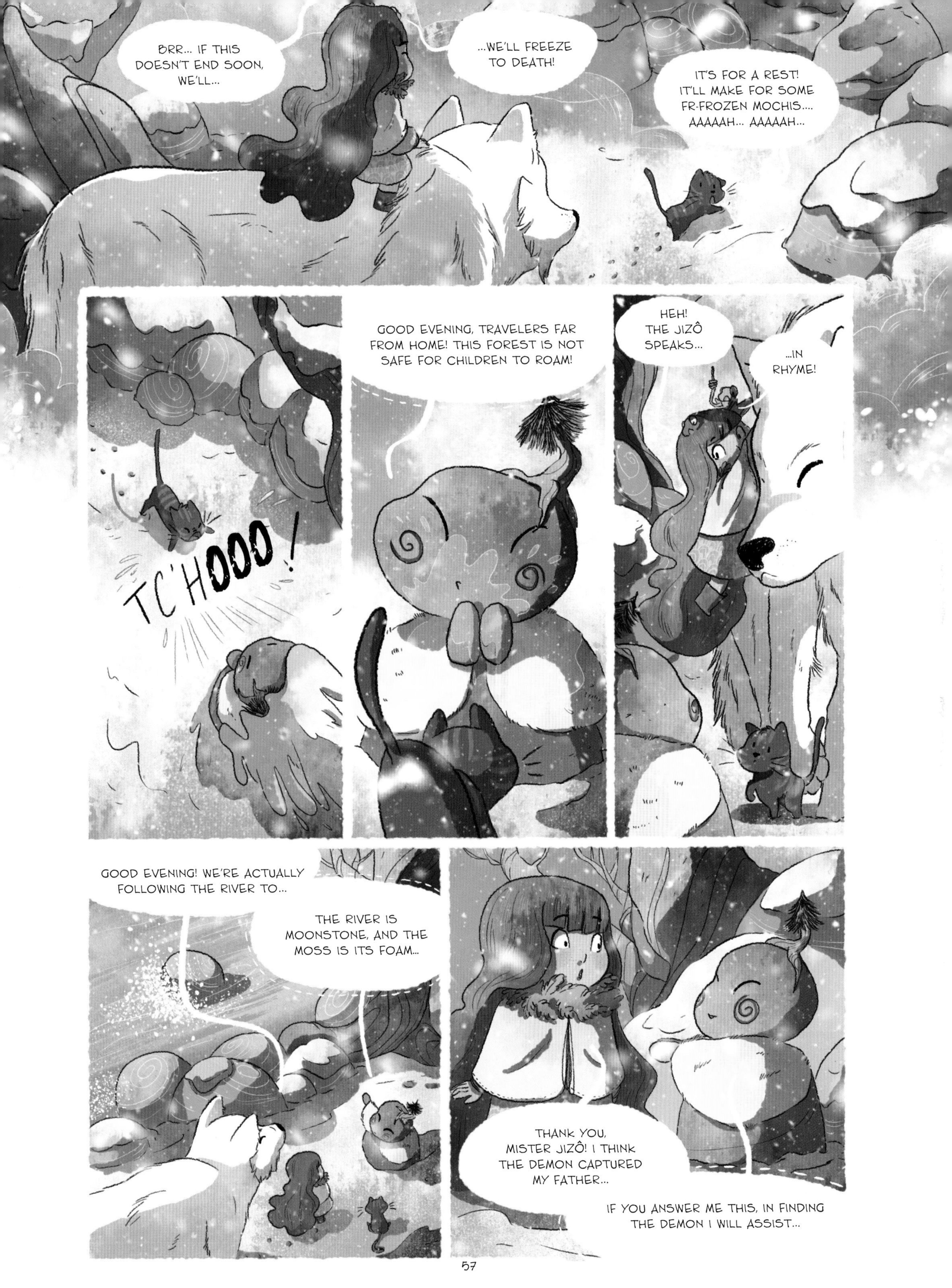

BRR... IF THIS DOESN'T END SOON, WE'LL...
...WE'LL FREEZE TO DEATH!
IT'S FOR A REST! IT'LL MAKE FOR SOME FR-FROZEN MOCHIS.... AAAAAH... AAAAAH...
TC'HOOO!
GOOD EVENING, TRAVELERS FAR FROM HOME! THIS FOREST IS NOT SAFE FOR CHILDREN TO ROAM!
HEH! THE JIZÔ SPEAKS...
...IN RHYME!
GOOD EVENING! WE'RE ACTUALLY FOLLOWING THE RIVER TO...
THE RIVER IS MOONSTONE, AND THE MOSS IS ITS FOAM...
THANK YOU, MISTER JIZÔ! I THINK THE DEMON CAPTURED MY FATHER...
IF YOU ANSWER ME THIS, IN FINDING THE DEMON I WILL ASSIST...

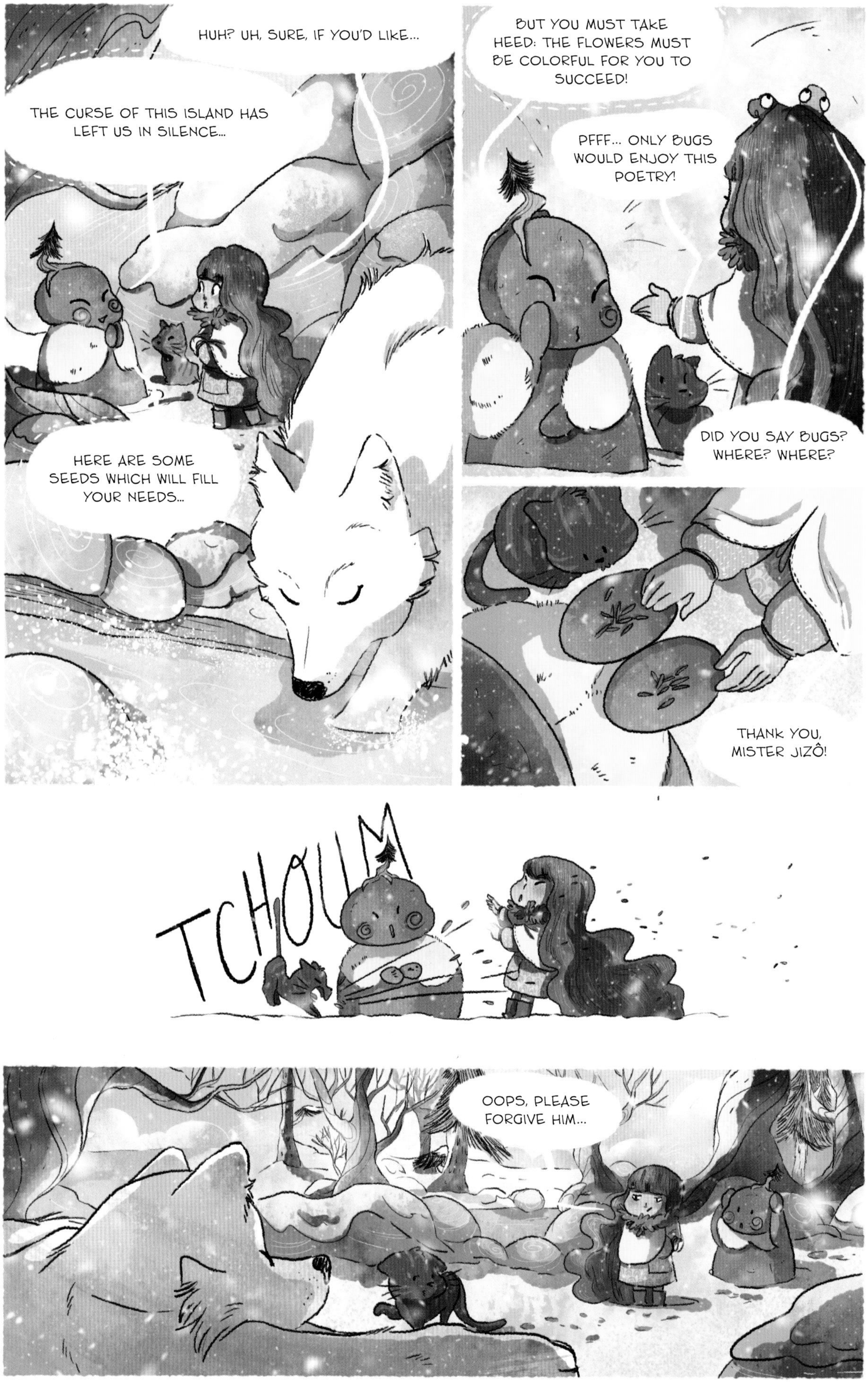

HUH? UH, SURE, IF YOU'D LIKE...
THE CURSE OF THIS ISLAND HAS LEFT US IN SILENCE...
HERE ARE SOME SEEDS WHICH WILL FILL YOUR NEEDS...
BUT YOU MUST TAKE HEED: THE FLOWERS MUST BE COLORFUL FOR YOU TO SUCCEED!
PFFF... ONLY BUGS WOULD ENJOY THIS POETRY!
DID YOU SAY BUGS? WHERE? WHERE?
THANK YOU, MISTER JIZÔ!
TCHOUM
OOPS, PLEASE FORGIVE HIM...

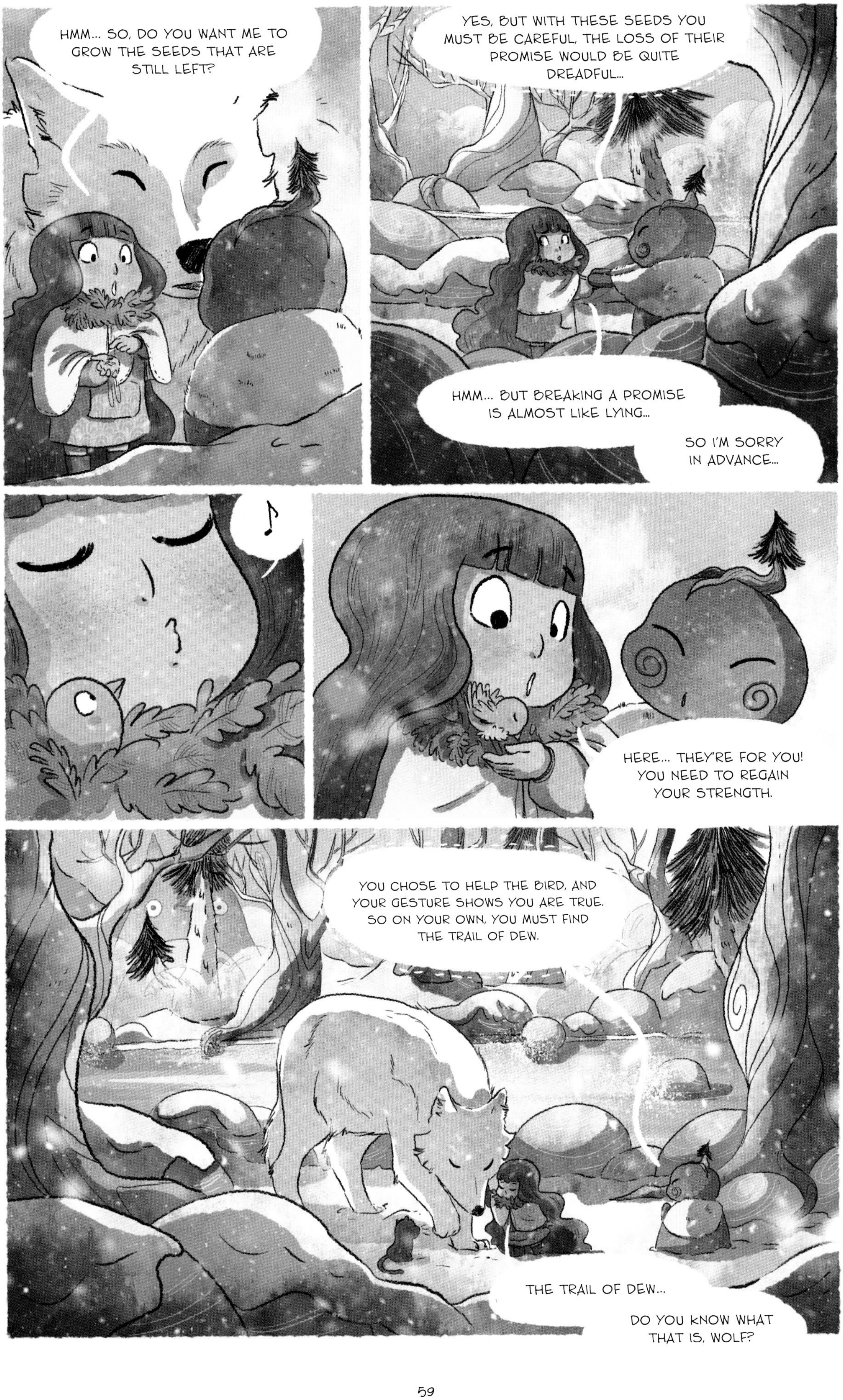
HMM... SO, DO YOU WANT ME TO GROW THE SEEDS THAT ARE STILL LEFT?
YES, BUT WITH THESE SEEDS YOU MUST BE CAREFUL, THE LOSS OF THEIR PROMISE WOULD BE QUITE DREADFUL...
HMM... BUT BREAKING A PROMISE IS ALMOST LIKE LYING...
SO I'M SORRY IN ADVANCE...
♪
HERE... THEY'RE FOR YOU! YOU NEED TO REGAIN YOUR STRENGTH.
YOU CHOSE TO HELP THE BIRD, AND YOUR GESTURE SHOWS YOU ARE TRUE. SO ON YOUR OWN, YOU MUST FIND THE TRAIL OF DEW.
THE TRAIL OF DEW...
DO YOU KNOW WHAT THAT IS, WOLF?

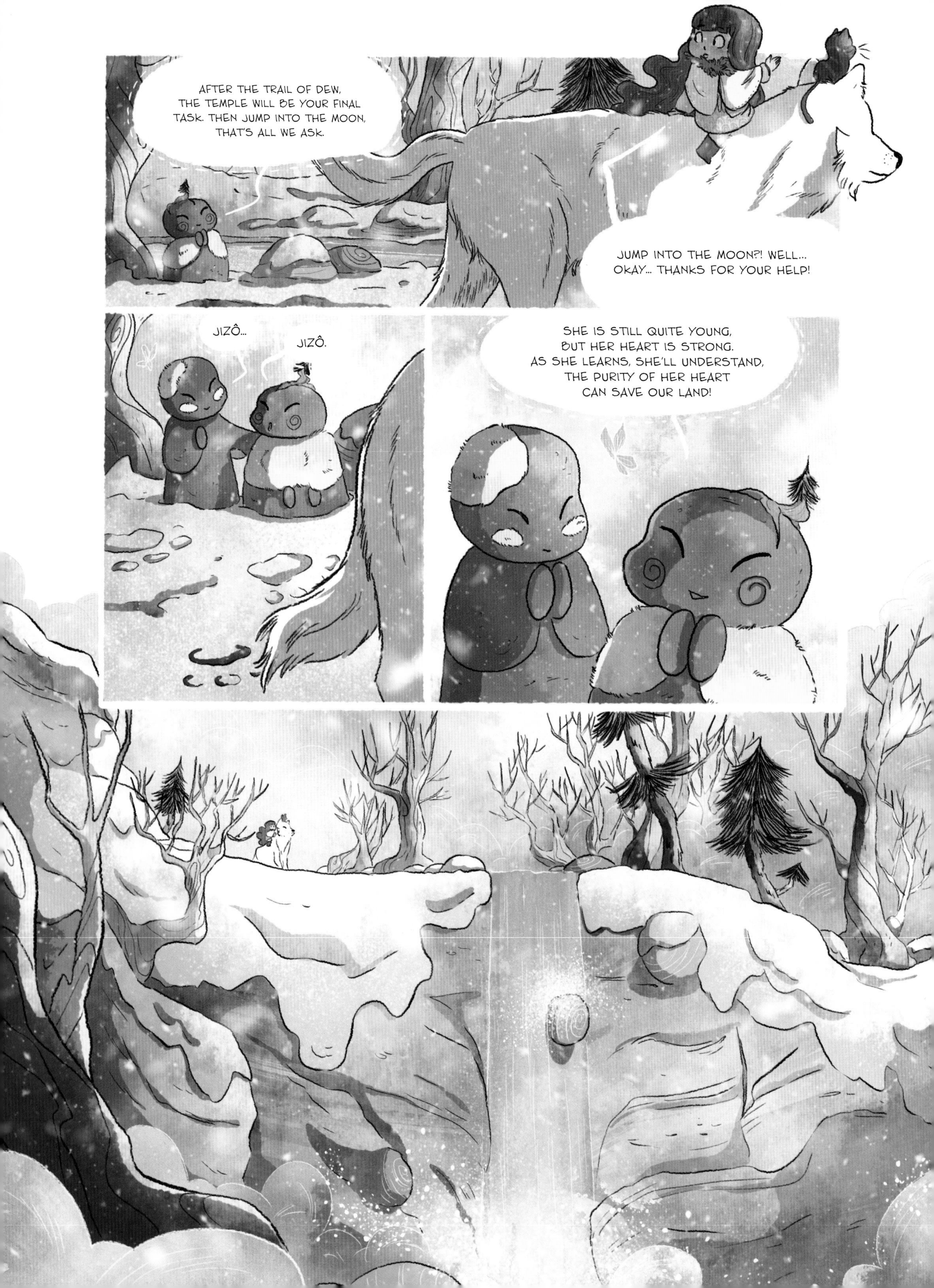
AFTER THE TRAIL OF DEW, THE TEMPLE WILL BE YOUR FINAL TASK. THEN JUMP INTO THE MOON, THAT'S ALL WE ASK.
JUMP INTO THE MOON?! WELL... OKAY... THANKS FOR YOUR HELP!
JIZÔ...
JIZÔ.
SHE IS STILL QUITE YOUNG, BUT HER HEART IS STRONG. AS SHE LEARNS, SHE'LL UNDERSTAND, THE PURITY OF HER HEART CAN SAVE OUR LAND!

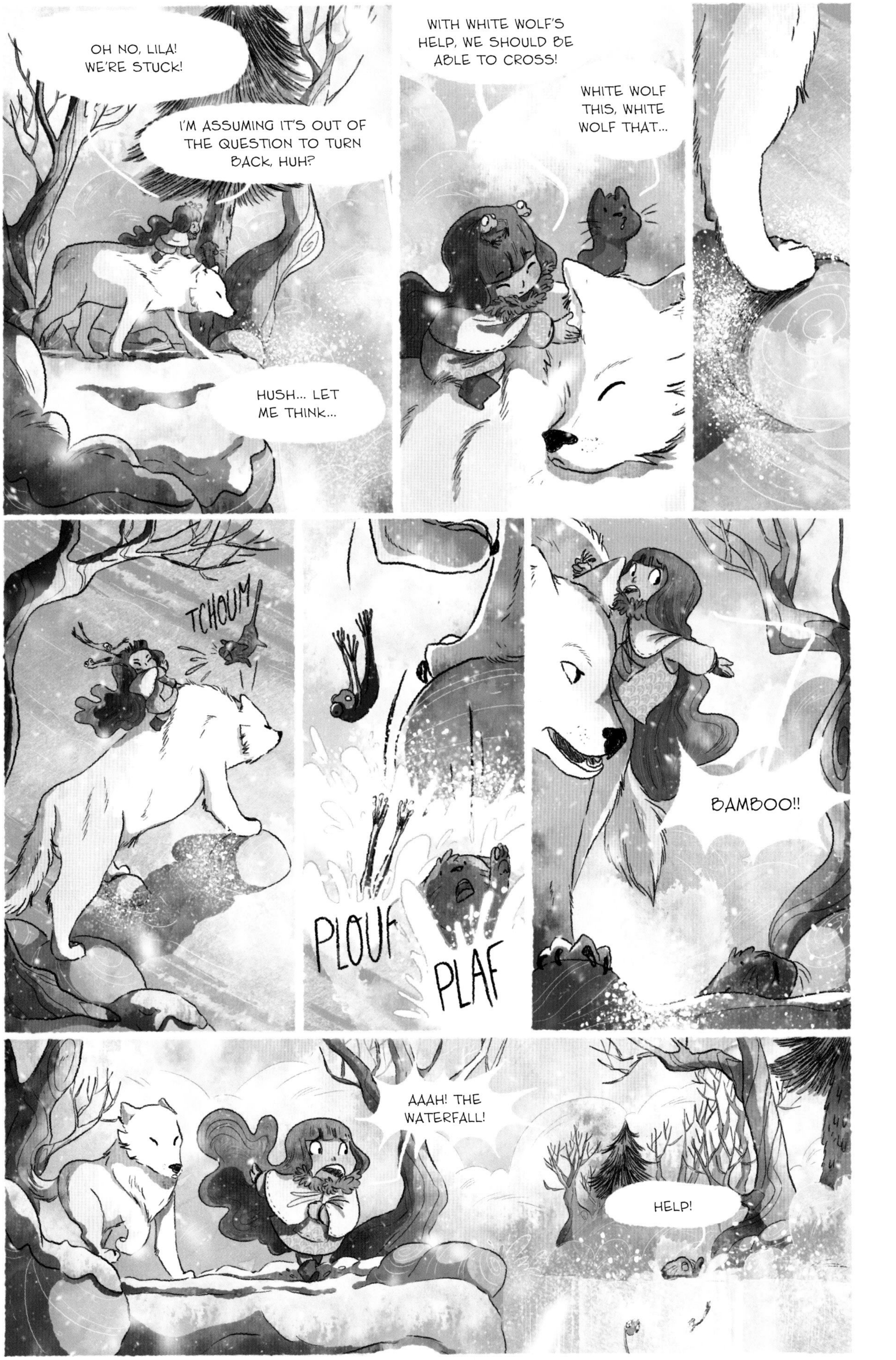
OH NO, LILA! WE'RE STUCK!
I'M ASSUMING IT'S OUT OF THE QUESTION TO TURN BACK, HUH?
HUSH... LET ME THINK...
WITH WHITE WOLF'S HELP, WE SHOULD BE ABLE TO CROSS!
WHITE WOLF THIS, WHITE WOLF THAT...
TCHOUM
PLOUF
PLAF
BAMBOO!!
AAAH! THE WATERFALL!
HELP!

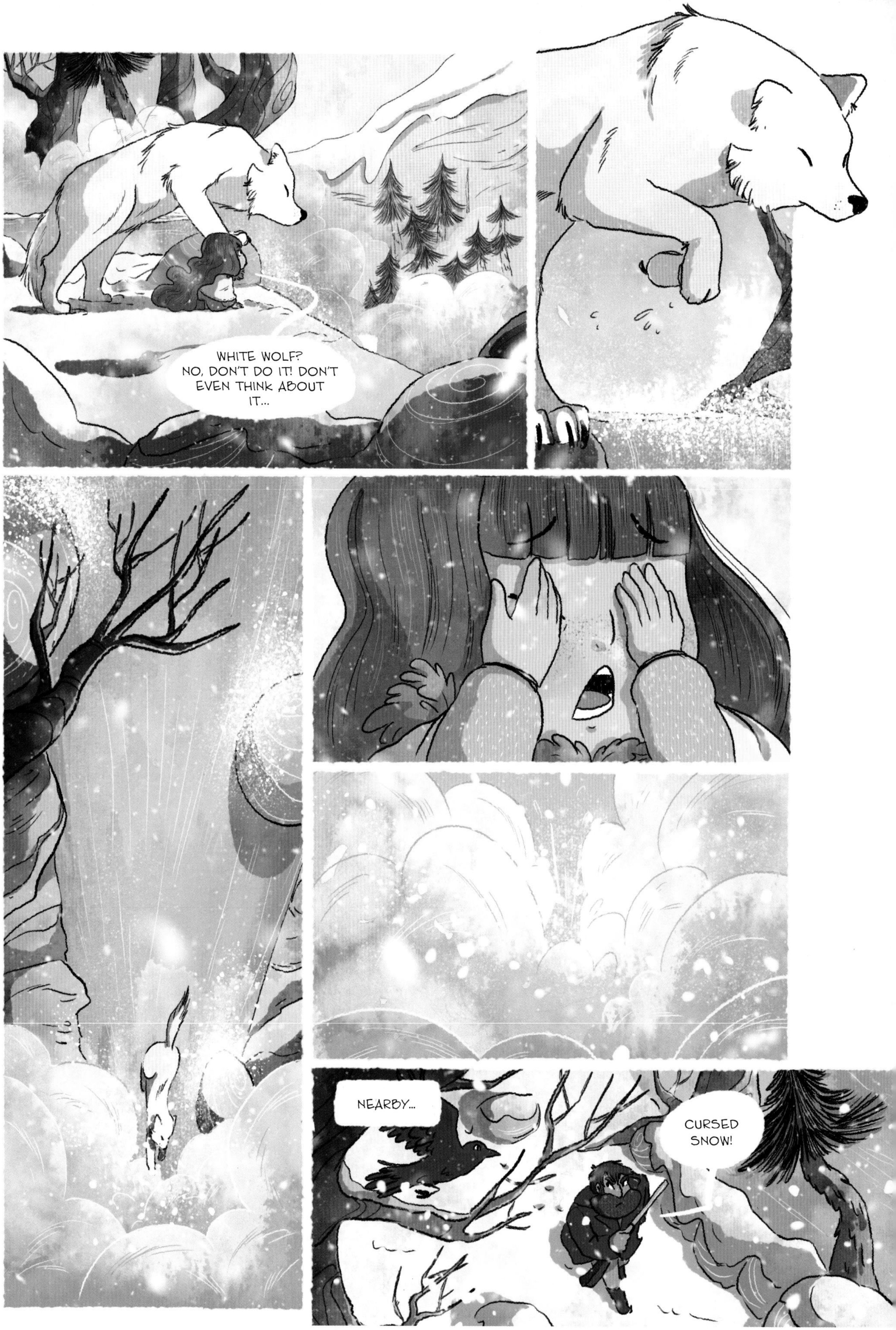
WHITE WOLF?
NO, DON'T DO IT! DON'T EVEN THINK ABOUT IT...
NEARBY...
CURSED SNOW!

The Lonely Cliff

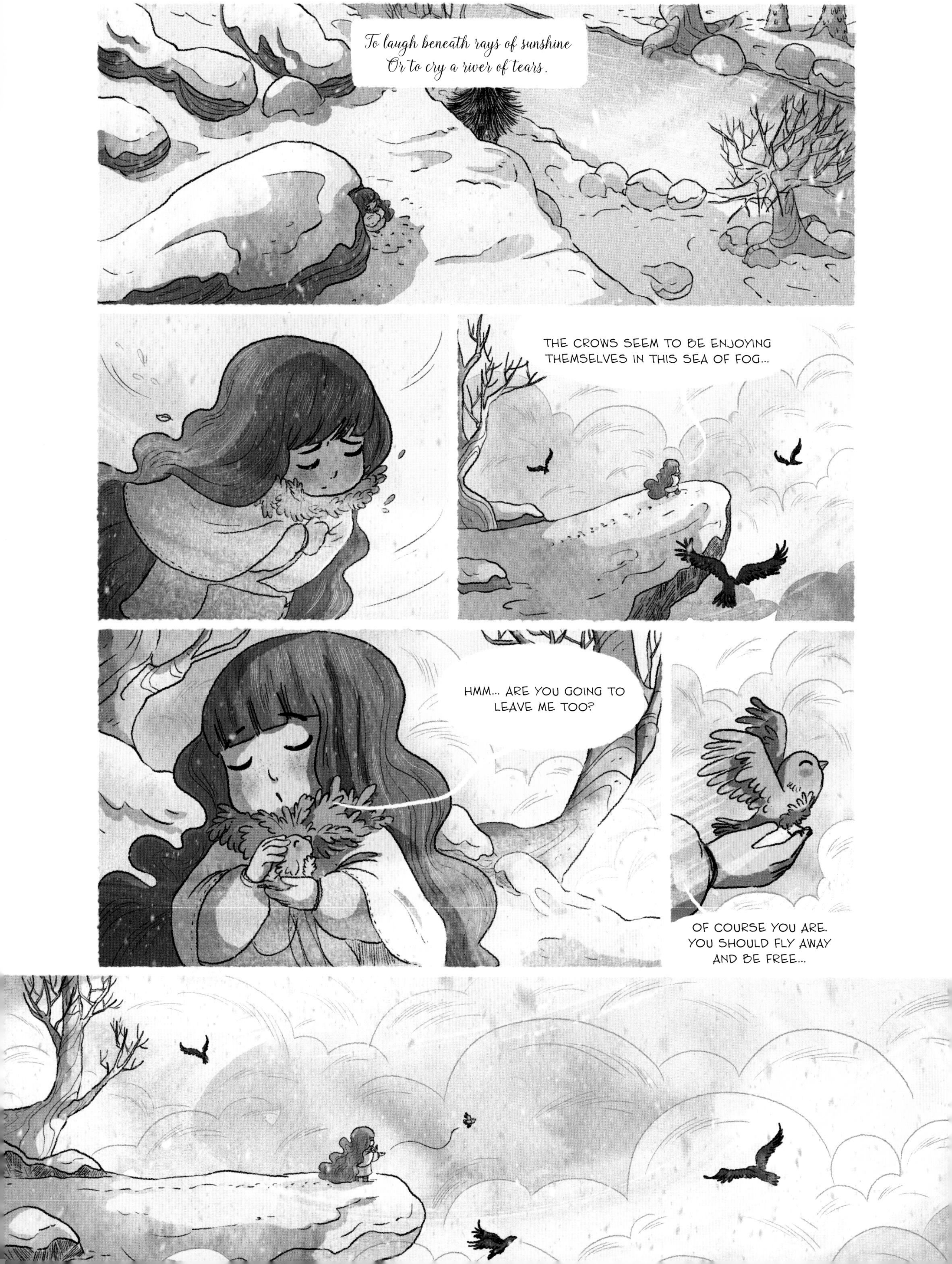
To laugh beneath rays of sunshine
Or to cry a river of tears.
THE CROWS SEEM TO BE ENJOYING THEMSELVES IN THIS SEA OF FOG...
HMM... ARE YOU GOING TO LEAVE ME TOO?
OF COURSE YOU ARE. YOU SHOULD FLY AWAY AND BE FREE...

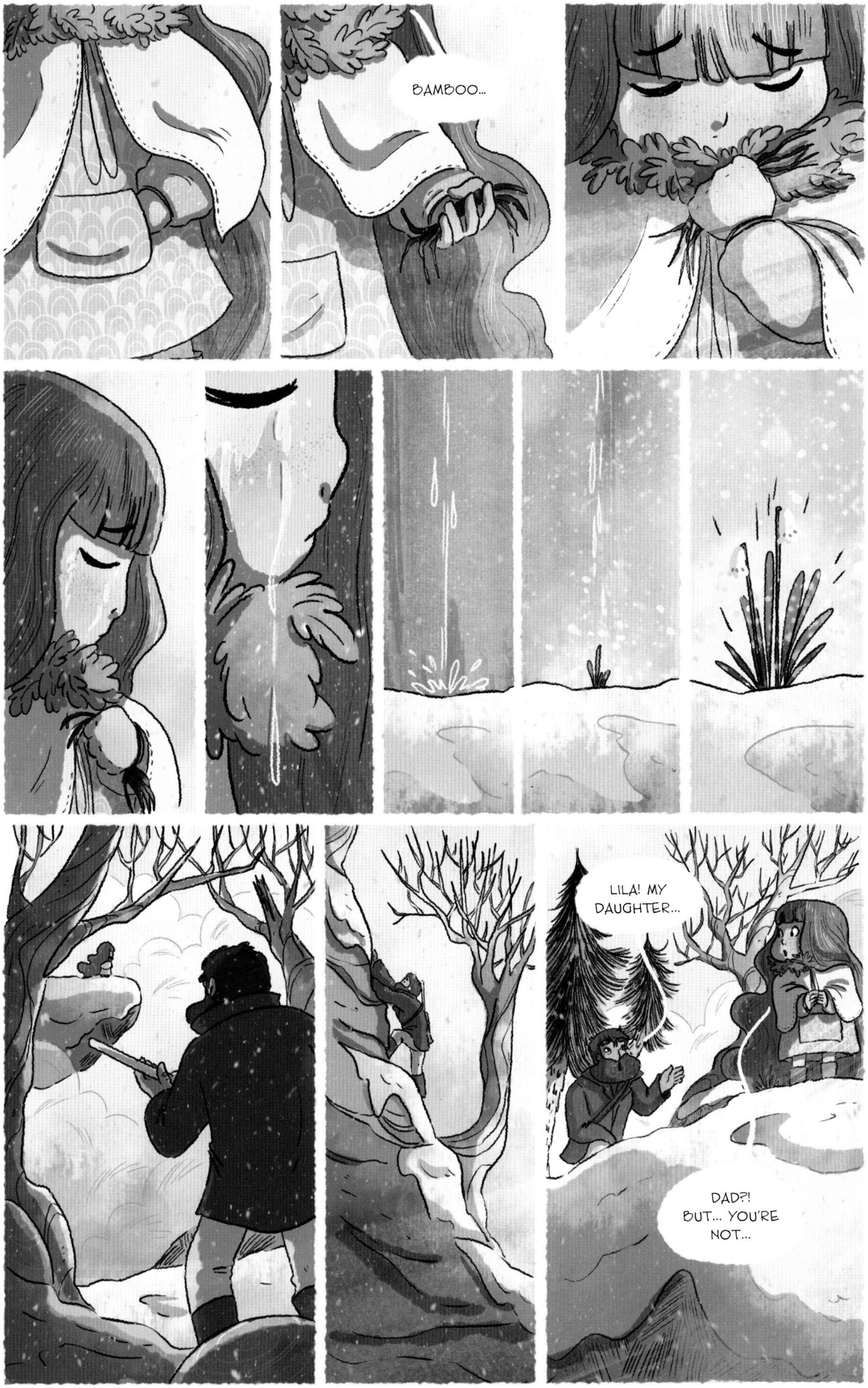
BAMBOO...
LILA! MY DAUGHTER...
DAD?! BUT... YOU'RE NOT...

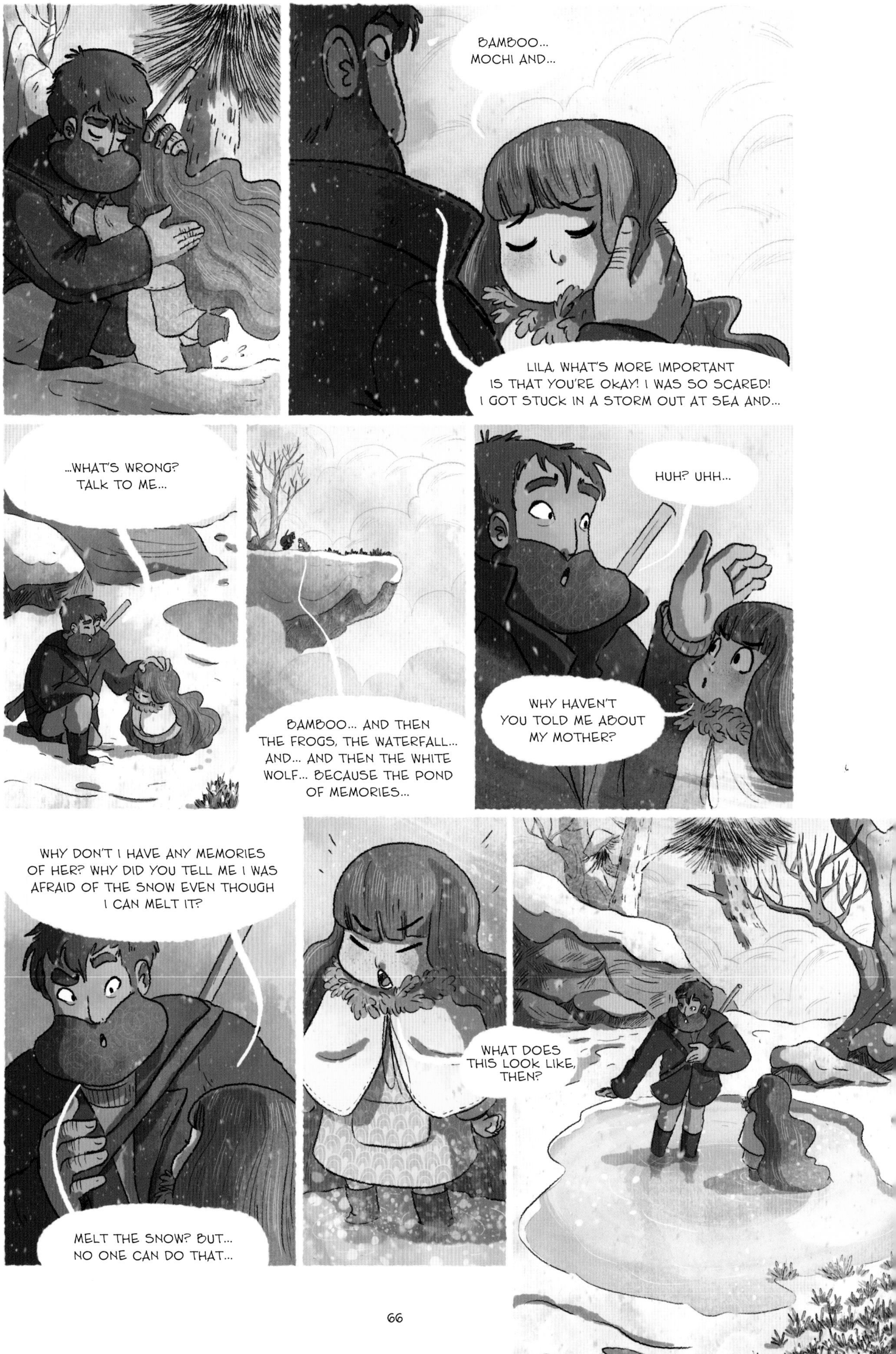

BAMBOO... MOCHI AND...
LILA, WHAT'S MORE IMPORTANT IS THAT YOU'RE OKAY! I WAS SO SCARED! I GOT STUCK IN A STORM OUT AT SEA AND...
...WHAT'S WRONG? TALK TO ME...
BAMBOO... AND THEN THE FROGS, THE WATERFALL... AND... AND THEN THE WHITE WOLF... BECAUSE THE POND OF MEMORIES...
HUH? UHH...
WHY HAVEN'T YOU TOLD ME ABOUT MY MOTHER?
WHY DON'T I HAVE ANY MEMORIES OF HER? WHY DID YOU TELL ME I WAS AFRAID OF THE SNOW EVEN THOUGH I CAN MELT IT?
MELT THE SNOW? BUT... NO ONE CAN DO THAT...
WHAT DOES THIS LOOK LIKE, THEN?

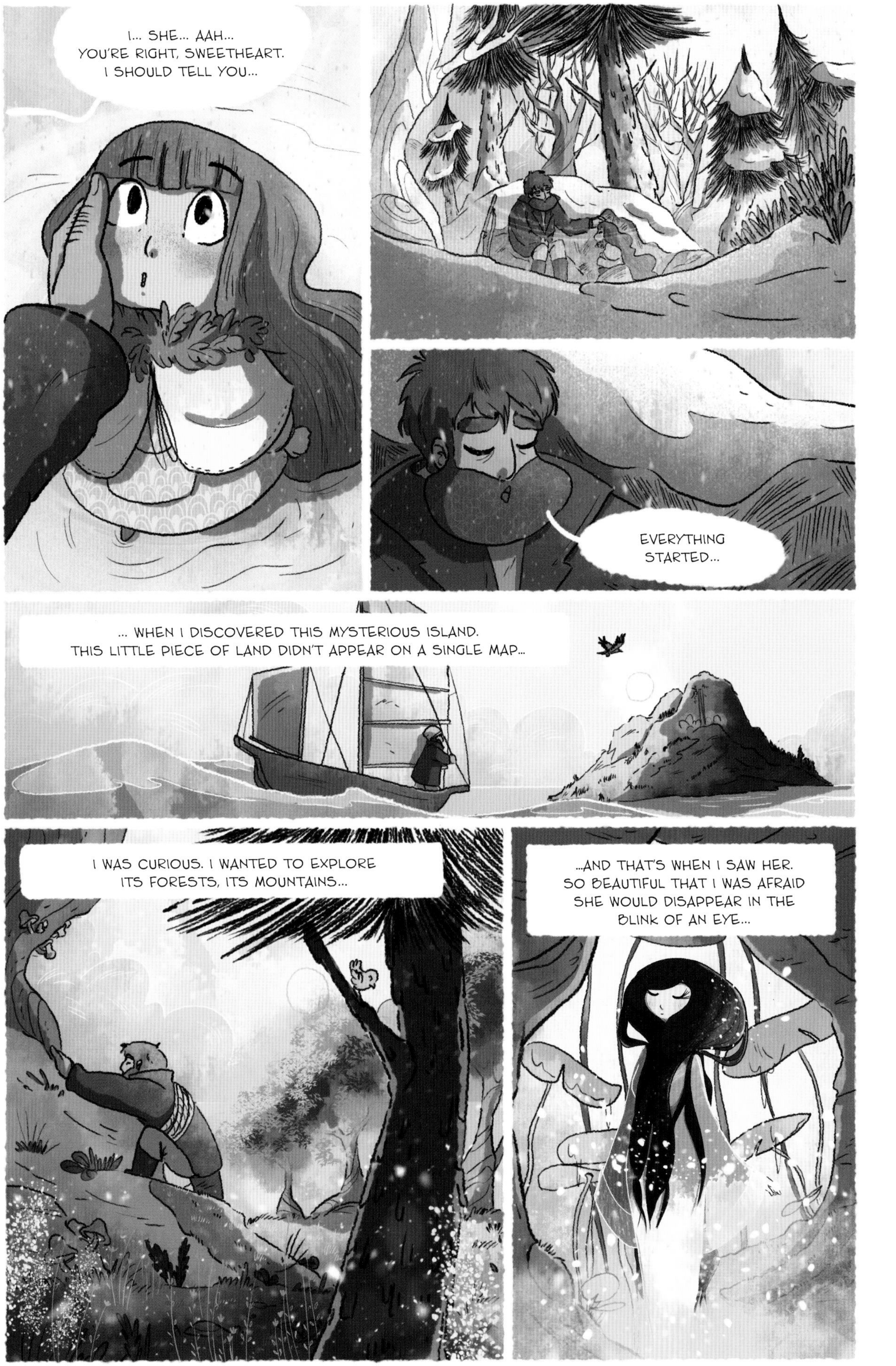
I... SHE... AAH...
YOU'RE RIGHT, SWEETHEART.
I SHOULD TELL YOU...
EVERYTHING
STARTED...
... WHEN I DISCOVERED THIS MYSTERIOUS ISLAND.
THIS LITTLE PIECE OF LAND DIDN'T APPEAR ON A SINGLE MAP...
I WAS CURIOUS. I WANTED TO EXPLORE
ITS FORESTS, ITS MOUNTAINS...
...AND THAT'S WHEN I SAW HER.
SO BEAUTIFUL THAT I WAS AFRAID
SHE WOULD DISAPPEAR IN THE
BLINK OF AN EYE...

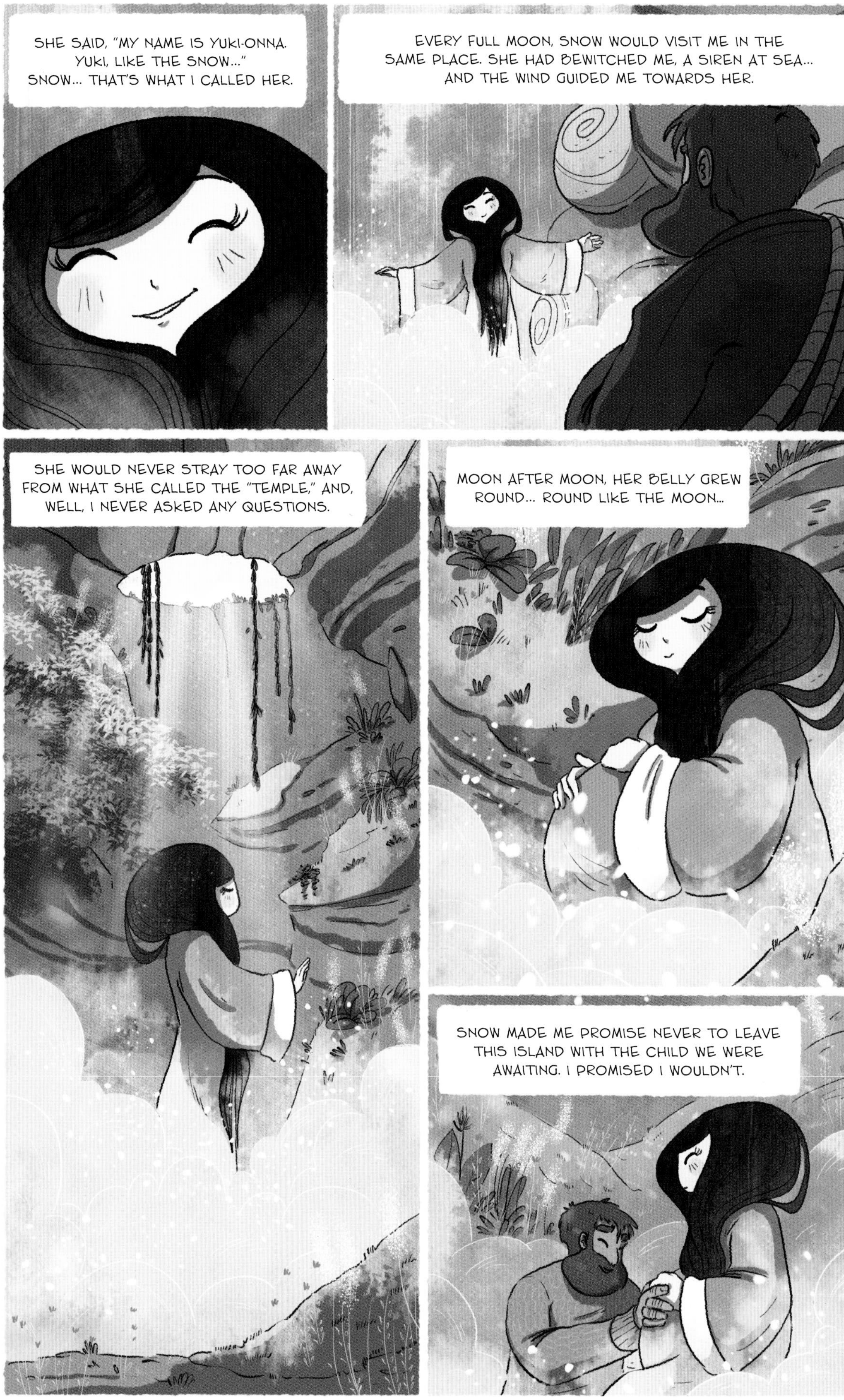
SHE SAID, "MY NAME IS YUKI-ONNA. YUKI, LIKE THE SNOW..." SNOW... THAT'S WHAT I CALLED HER.
EVERY FULL MOON, SNOW WOULD VISIT ME IN THE SAME PLACE. SHE HAD BEWITCHED ME, A SIREN AT SEA... AND THE WIND GUIDED ME TOWARDS HER.
SHE WOULD NEVER STRAY TOO FAR AWAY FROM WHAT SHE CALLED THE "TEMPLE," AND, WELL, I NEVER ASKED ANY QUESTIONS.
MOON AFTER MOON, HER BELLY GREW ROUND... ROUND LIKE THE MOON...
SNOW MADE ME PROMISE NEVER TO LEAVE THIS ISLAND WITH THE CHILD WE WERE AWAITING. I PROMISED I WOULDN'T.

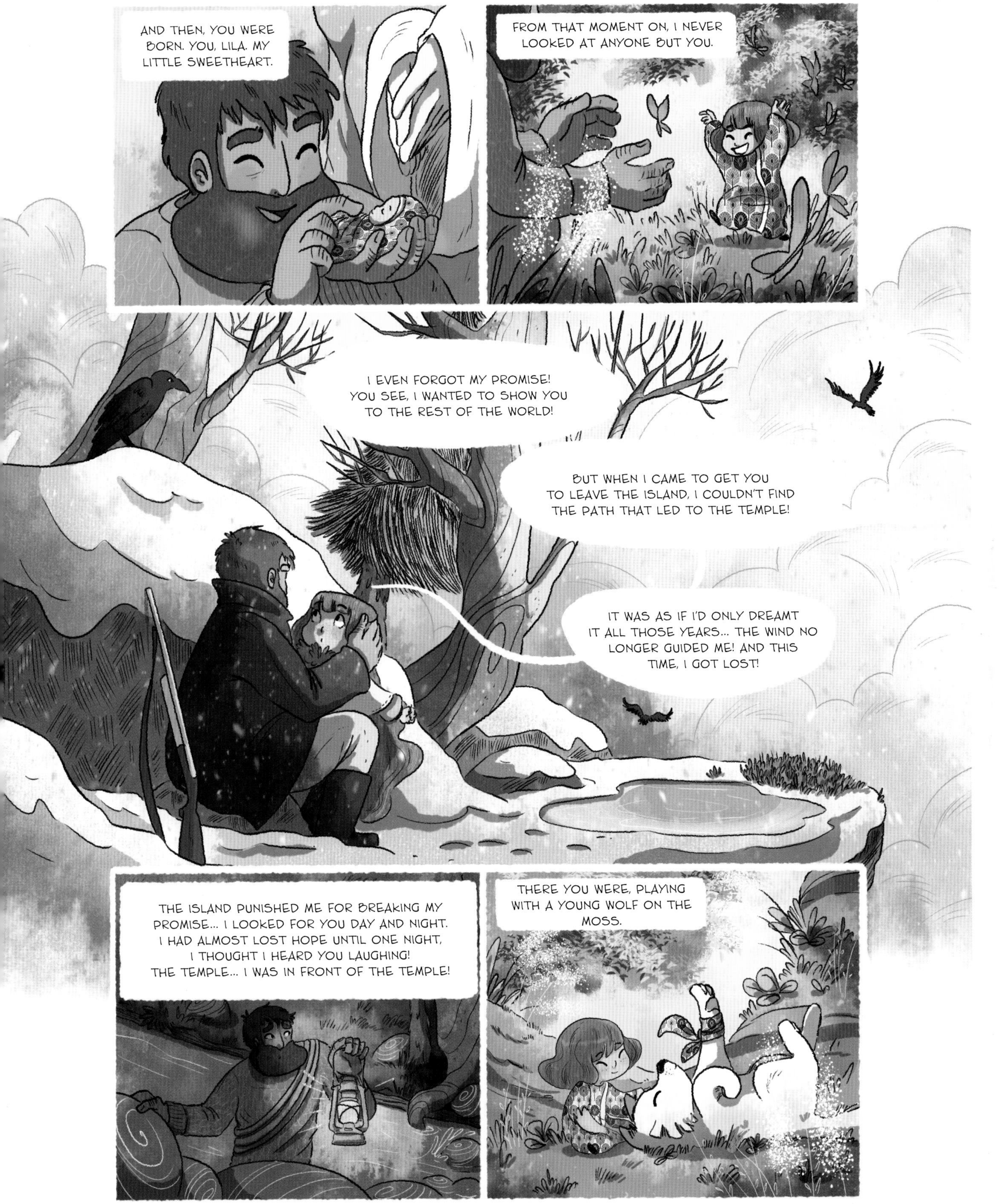
AND THEN, YOU WERE BORN. YOU, LILA. MY LITTLE SWEETHEART.
FROM THAT MOMENT ON, I NEVER LOOKED AT ANYONE BUT YOU.
I EVEN FORGOT MY PROMISE! YOU SEE, I WANTED TO SHOW YOU TO THE REST OF THE WORLD!
BUT WHEN I CAME TO GET YOU TO LEAVE THE ISLAND, I COULDN'T FIND THE PATH THAT LED TO THE TEMPLE!
IT WAS AS IF I'D ONLY DREAMT IT ALL THOSE YEARS... THE WIND NO LONGER GUIDED ME! AND THIS TIME, I GOT LOST!
THE ISLAND PUNISHED ME FOR BREAKING MY PROMISE... I LOOKED FOR YOU DAY AND NIGHT. I HAD ALMOST LOST HOPE UNTIL ONE NIGHT, I THOUGHT I HEARD YOU LAUGHING! THE TEMPLE... I WAS IN FRONT OF THE TEMPLE!
THERE YOU WERE, PLAYING WITH A YOUNG WOLF ON THE MOSS.

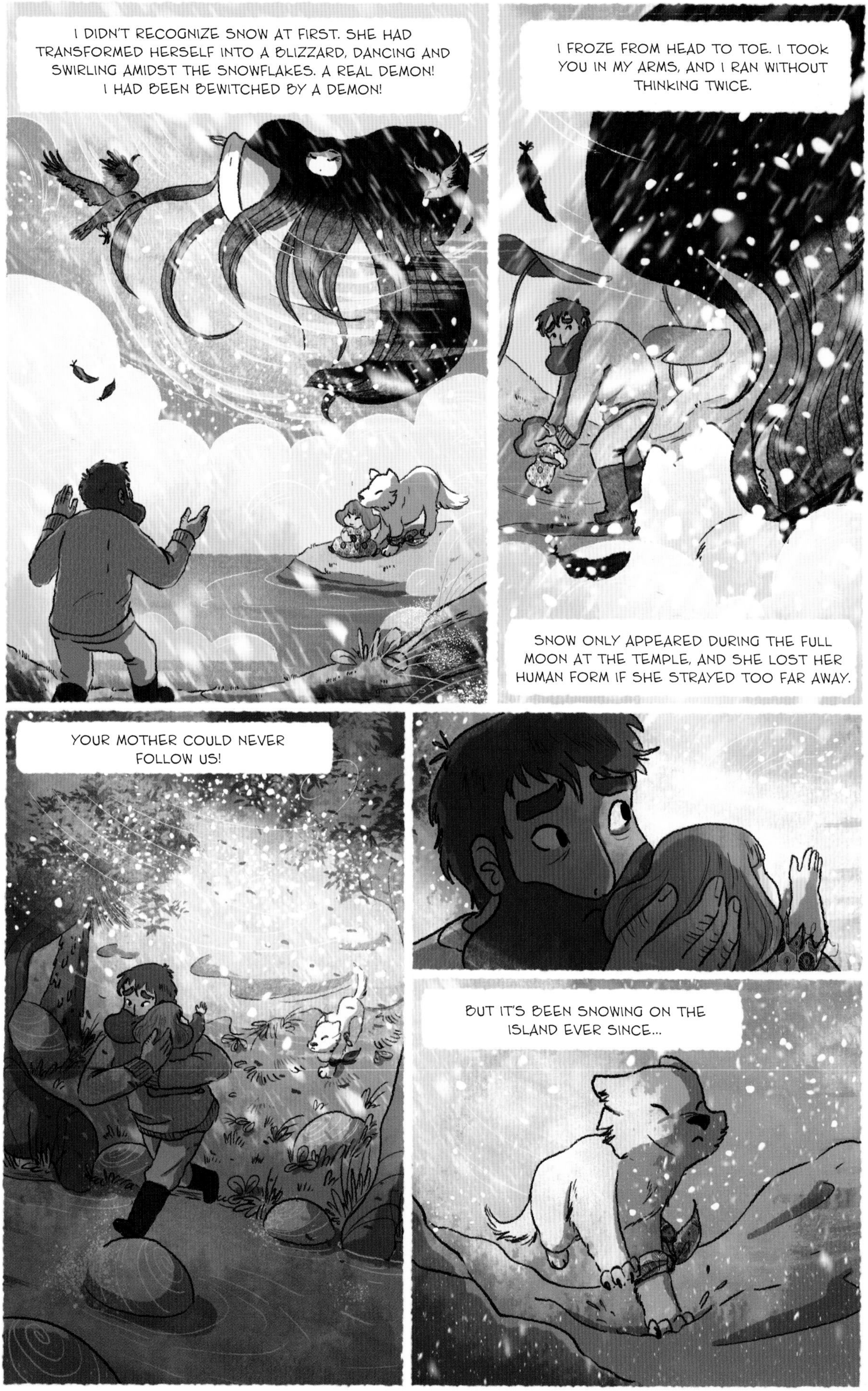
I DIDN'T RECOGNIZE SNOW AT FIRST. SHE HAD TRANSFORMED HERSELF INTO A BLIZZARD, DANCING AND SWIRLING AMIDST THE SNOWFLAKES. A REAL DEMON! I HAD BEEN BEWITCHED BY A DEMON!
I FROZE FROM HEAD TO TOE. I TOOK YOU IN MY ARMS, AND I RAN WITHOUT THINKING TWICE.
SNOW ONLY APPEARED DURING THE FULL MOON AT THE TEMPLE, AND SHE LOST HER HUMAN FORM IF SHE STRAYED TOO FAR AWAY.
YOUR MOTHER COULD NEVER FOLLOW US!
BUT IT'S BEEN SNOWING ON THE ISLAND EVER SINCE...

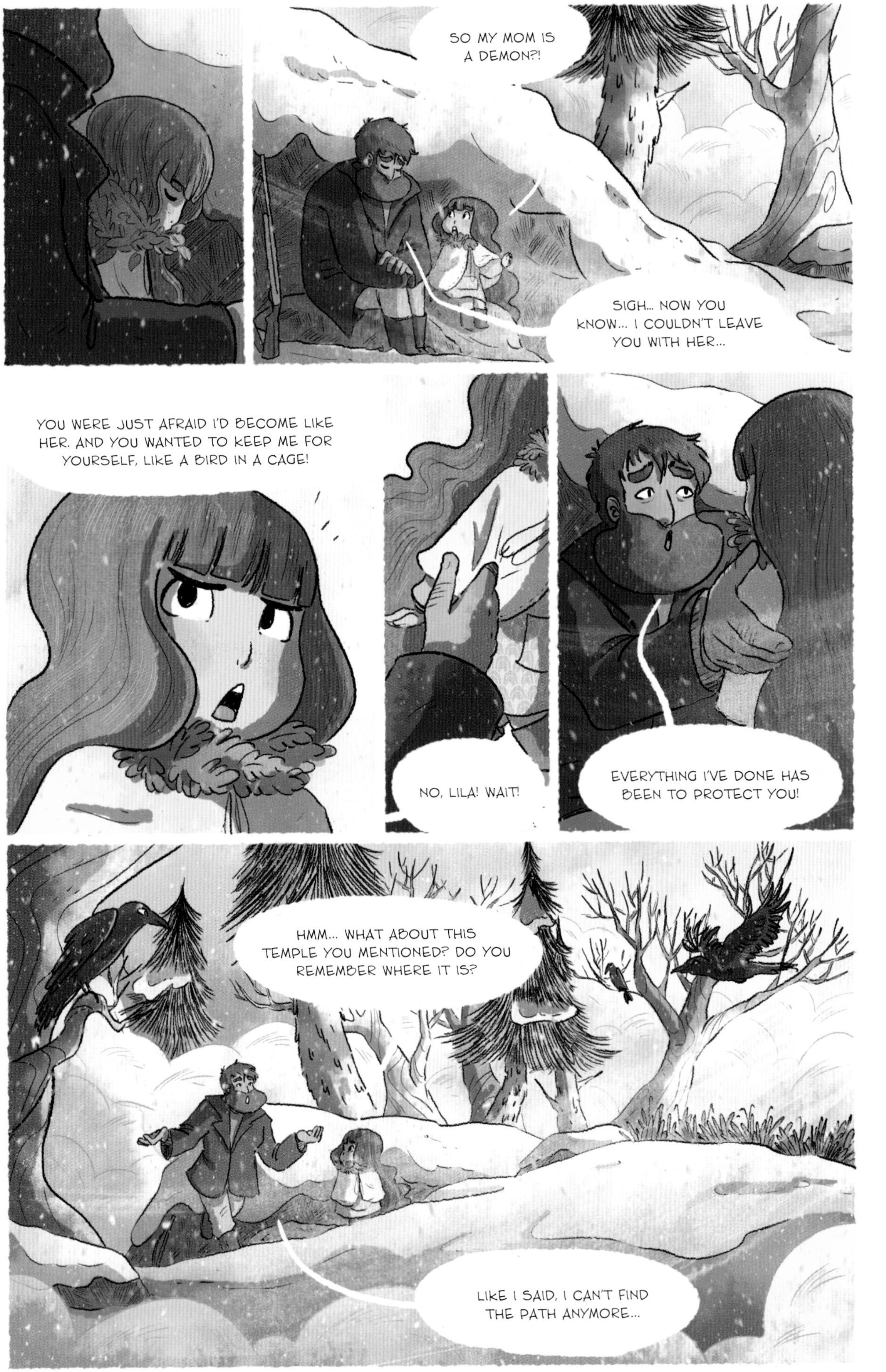
SO MY MOM IS A DEMON?!
SIGH... NOW YOU KNOW... I COULDN'T LEAVE YOU WITH HER...
YOU WERE JUST AFRAID I'D BECOME LIKE HER. AND YOU WANTED TO KEEP ME FOR YOURSELF, LIKE A BIRD IN A CAGE!
NO, LILA! WAIT!
EVERYTHING I'VE DONE HAS BEEN TO PROTECT YOU!
HMM... WHAT ABOUT THIS TEMPLE YOU MENTIONED? DO YOU REMEMBER WHERE IT IS?
LIKE I SAID, I CAN'T FIND THE PATH ANYMORE...

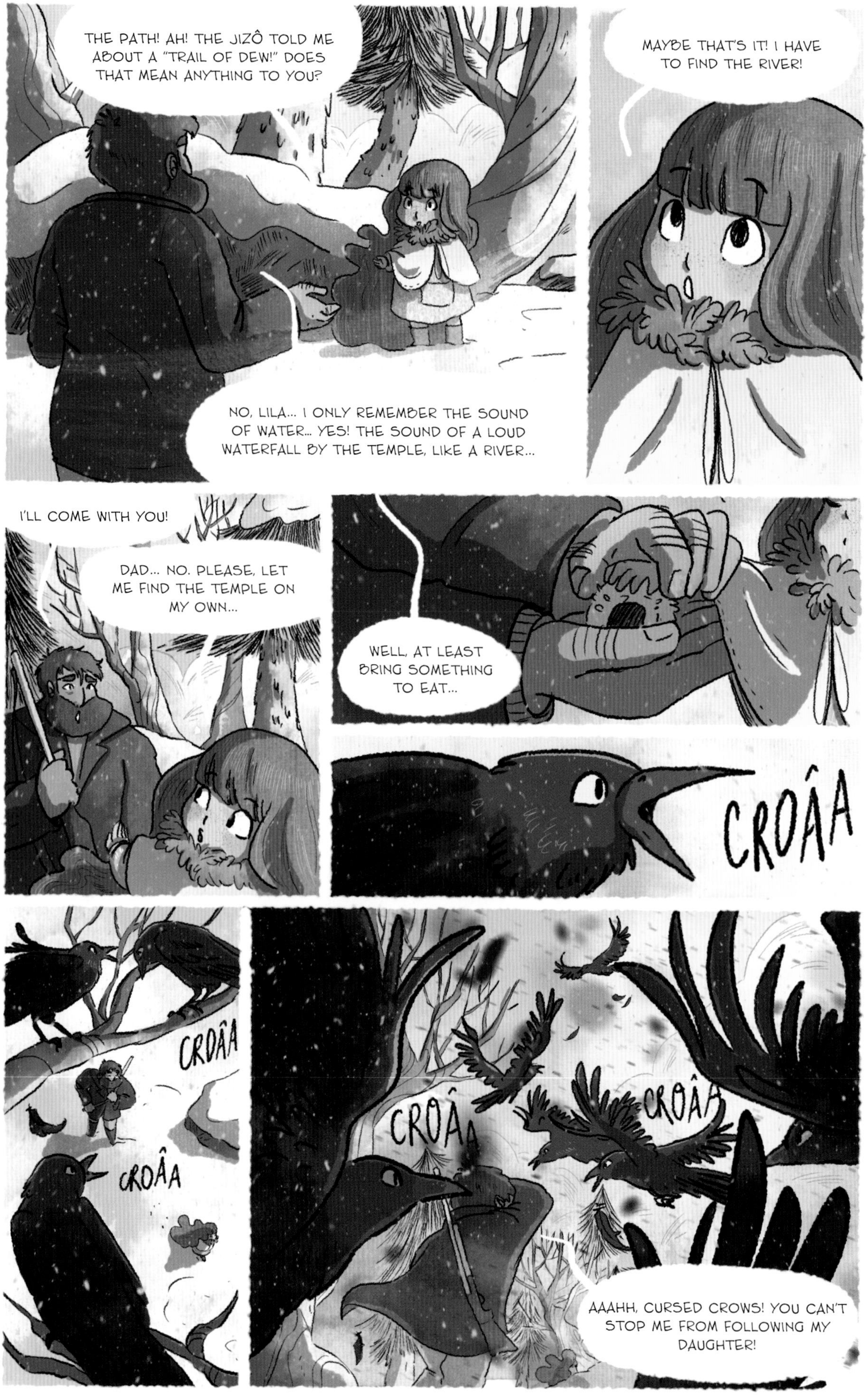

THE PATH! AH! THE JIZÔ TOLD ME ABOUT A "TRAIL OF DEW!" DOES THAT MEAN ANYTHING TO YOU?
NO, LILA... I ONLY REMEMBER THE SOUND OF WATER... YES! THE SOUND OF A LOUD WATERFALL BY THE TEMPLE, LIKE A RIVER...
MAYBE THAT'S IT! I HAVE TO FIND THE RIVER!
I'LL COME WITH YOU!
DAD... NO. PLEASE, LET ME FIND THE TEMPLE ON MY OWN...
WELL, AT LEAST BRING SOMETHING TO EAT...
CROÂA
CROÂA
CROÂA
CROÂA
CROÂA
AAAHH, CURSED CROWS! YOU CAN'T STOP ME FROM FOLLOWING MY DAUGHTER!

The Temple of Warmth

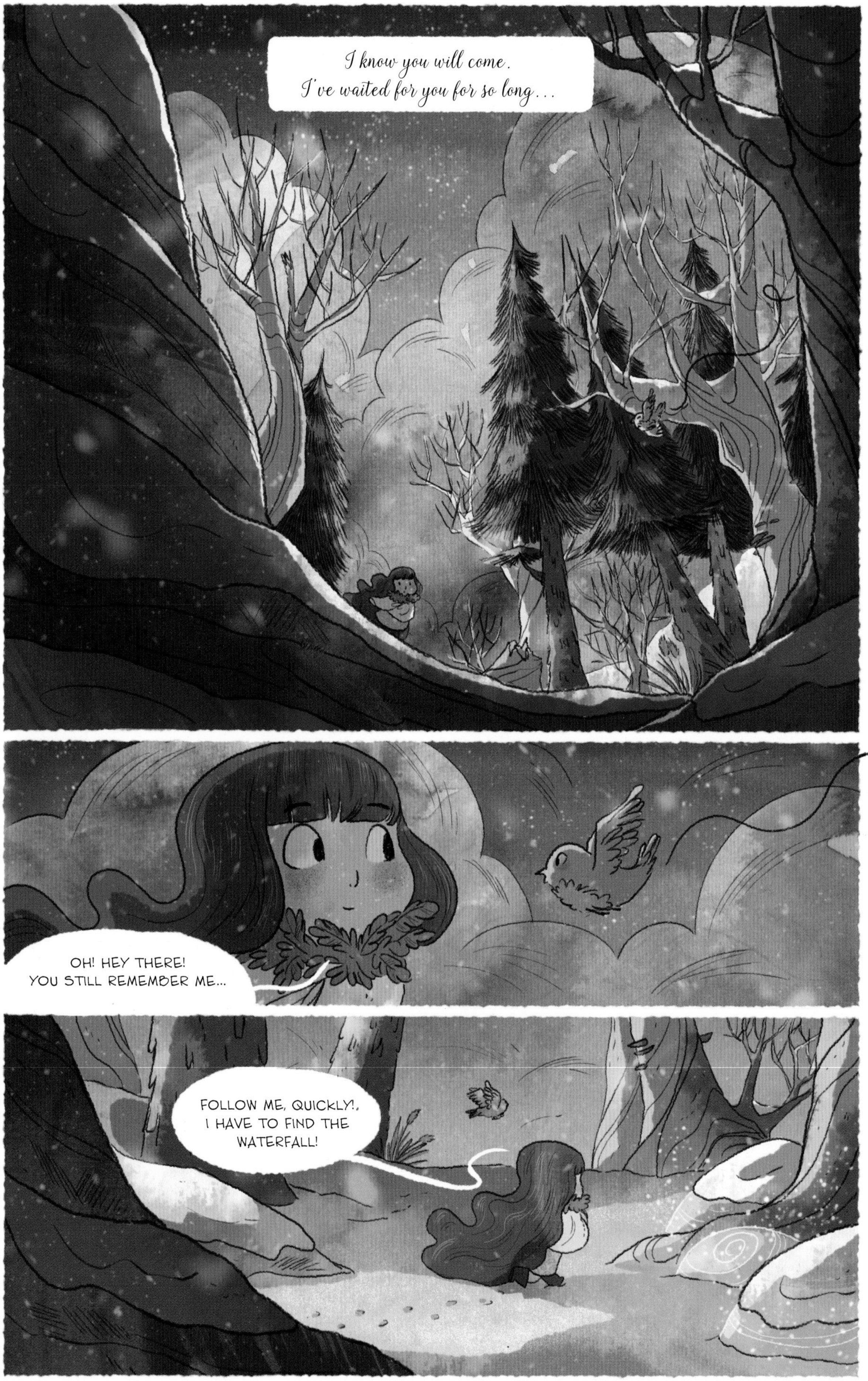
I know you will come.
I've waited for you for so long...
OH! HEY THERE! YOU STILL REMEMBER ME...
FOLLOW ME, QUICKLY!, I HAVE TO FIND THE WATERFALL!

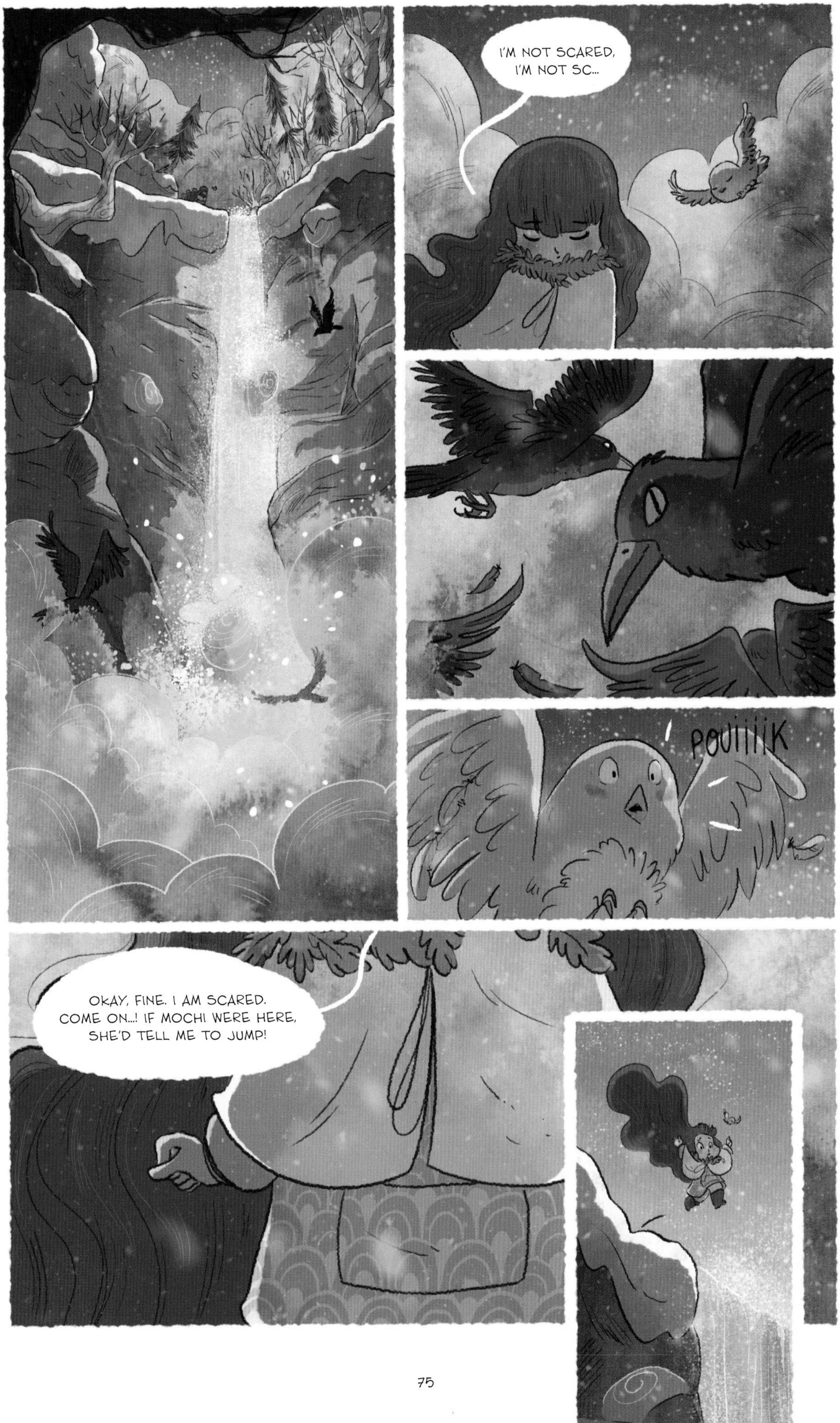
I'M NOT SCARED, I'M NOT SC...
POUIIIIK
OKAY, FINE. I AM SCARED. COME ON...! IF MOCHI WERE HERE, SHE'D TELL ME TO JUMP!

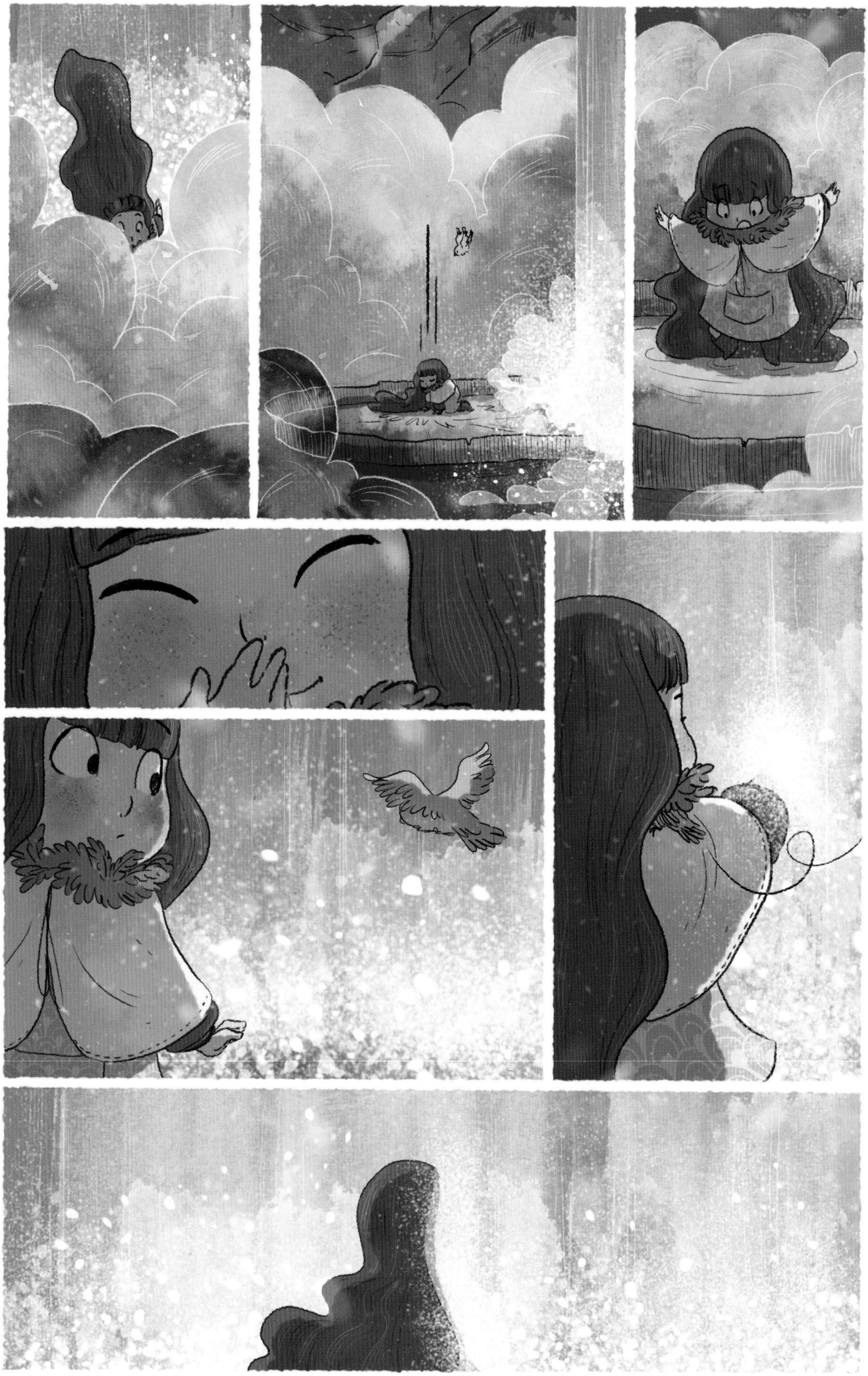

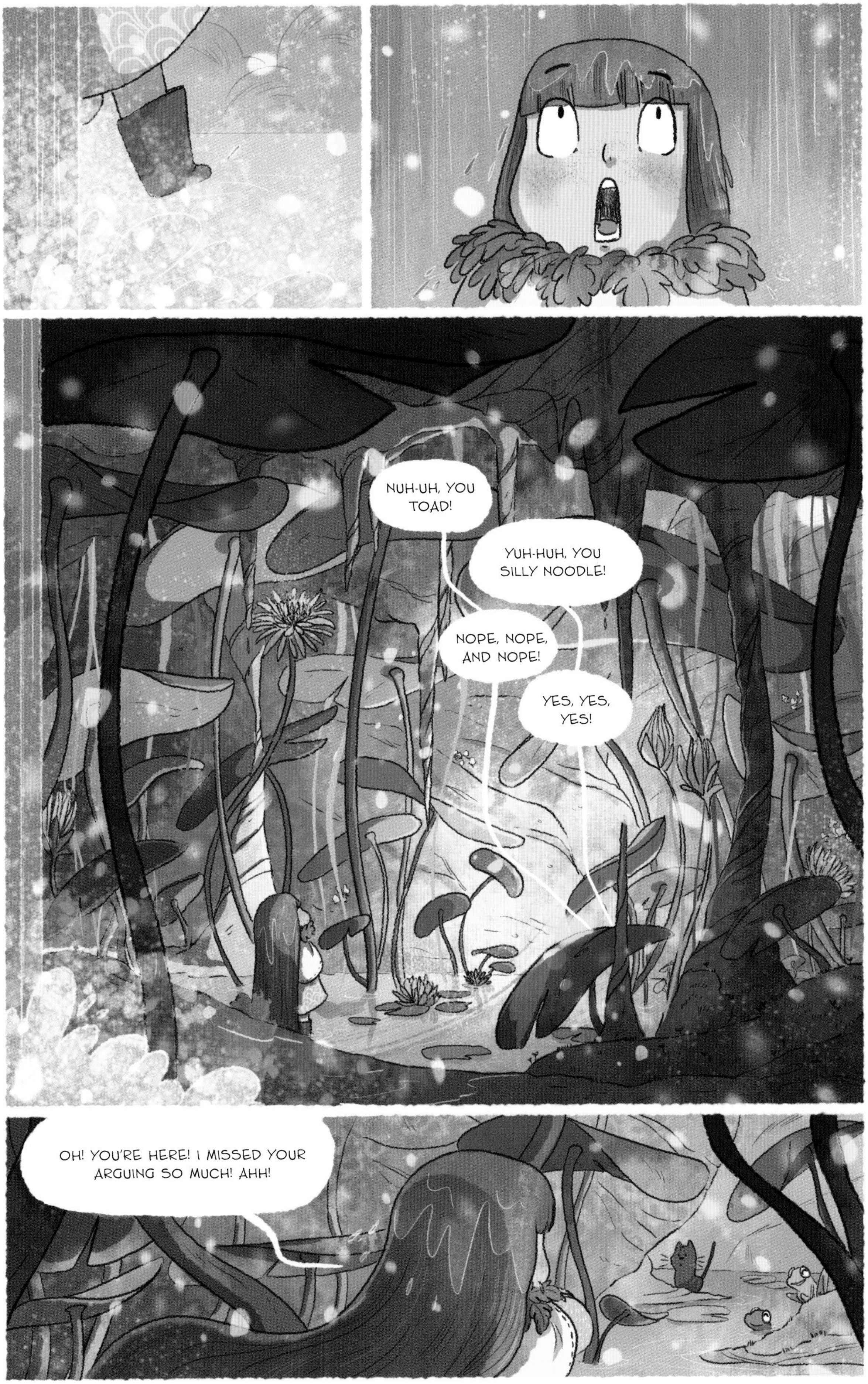

NUH-UH, YOU TOAD!
YUH-HUH, YOU SILLY NOODLE!
NOPE, NOPE, AND NOPE!
YES, YES, YES!
OH! YOU'RE HERE! I MISSED YOUR ARGUING SO MUCH! AHH!

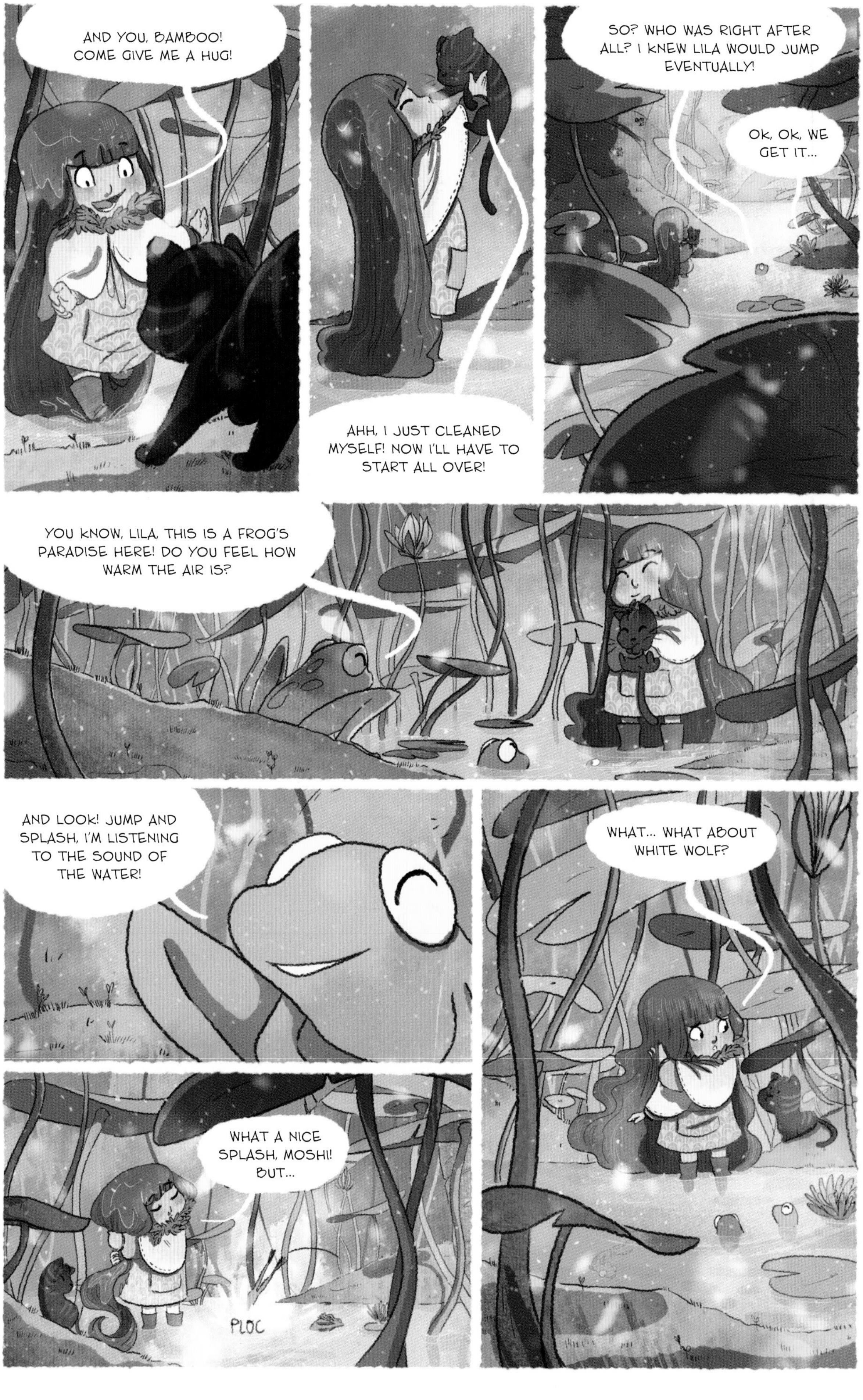
AND YOU, BAMBOO! COME GIVE ME A HUG!
AHH, I JUST CLEANED MYSELF! NOW I'LL HAVE TO START ALL OVER!
SO? WHO WAS RIGHT AFTER ALL? I KNEW LILA WOULD JUMP EVENTUALLY!
Ok, Ok, WE GET IT...
YOU KNOW, LILA, THIS IS A FROG'S PARADISE HERE! DO YOU FEEL HOW WARM THE AIR IS?
AND LOOK! JUMP AND SPLASH, I'M LISTENING TO THE SOUND OF THE WATER!
WHAT A NICE SPLASH, MOSHI! BUT...
PLOC
WHAT... WHAT ABOUT WHITE WOLF?

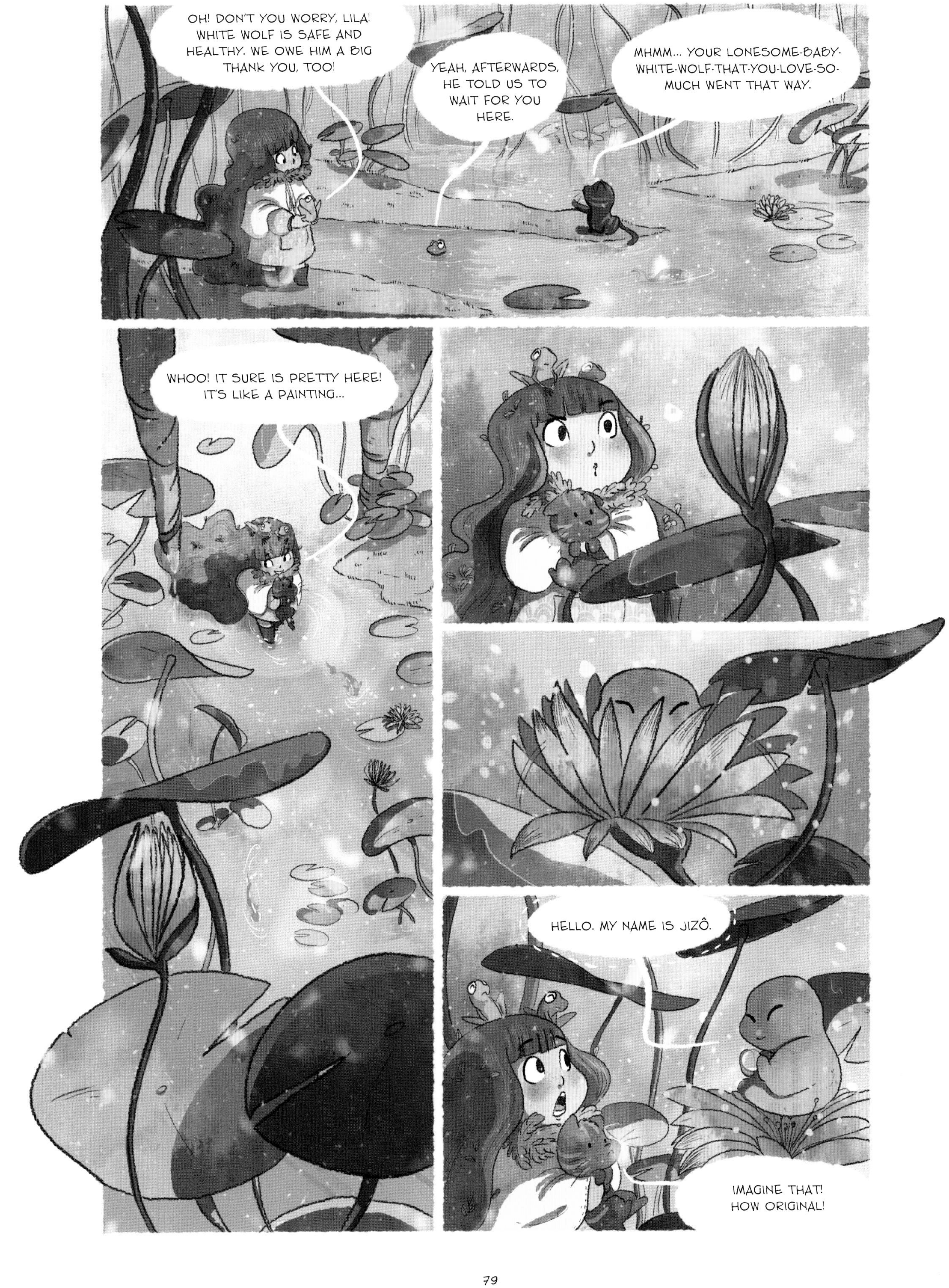
OH! DON'T YOU WORRY, LILA! WHITE WOLF IS SAFE AND HEALTHY. WE OWE HIM A BIG THANK YOU, TOO!
YEAH, AFTERWARDS, HE TOLD US TO WAIT FOR YOU HERE.
MHMM... YOUR LONESOME-BABY-WHITE-WOLF-THAT-YOU-LOVE-SO-MUCH WENT THAT WAY.
WHOO! IT SURE IS PRETTY HERE! IT'S LIKE A PAINTING...
HELLO. MY NAME IS JIZÔ.
IMAGINE THAT! HOW ORIGINAL!

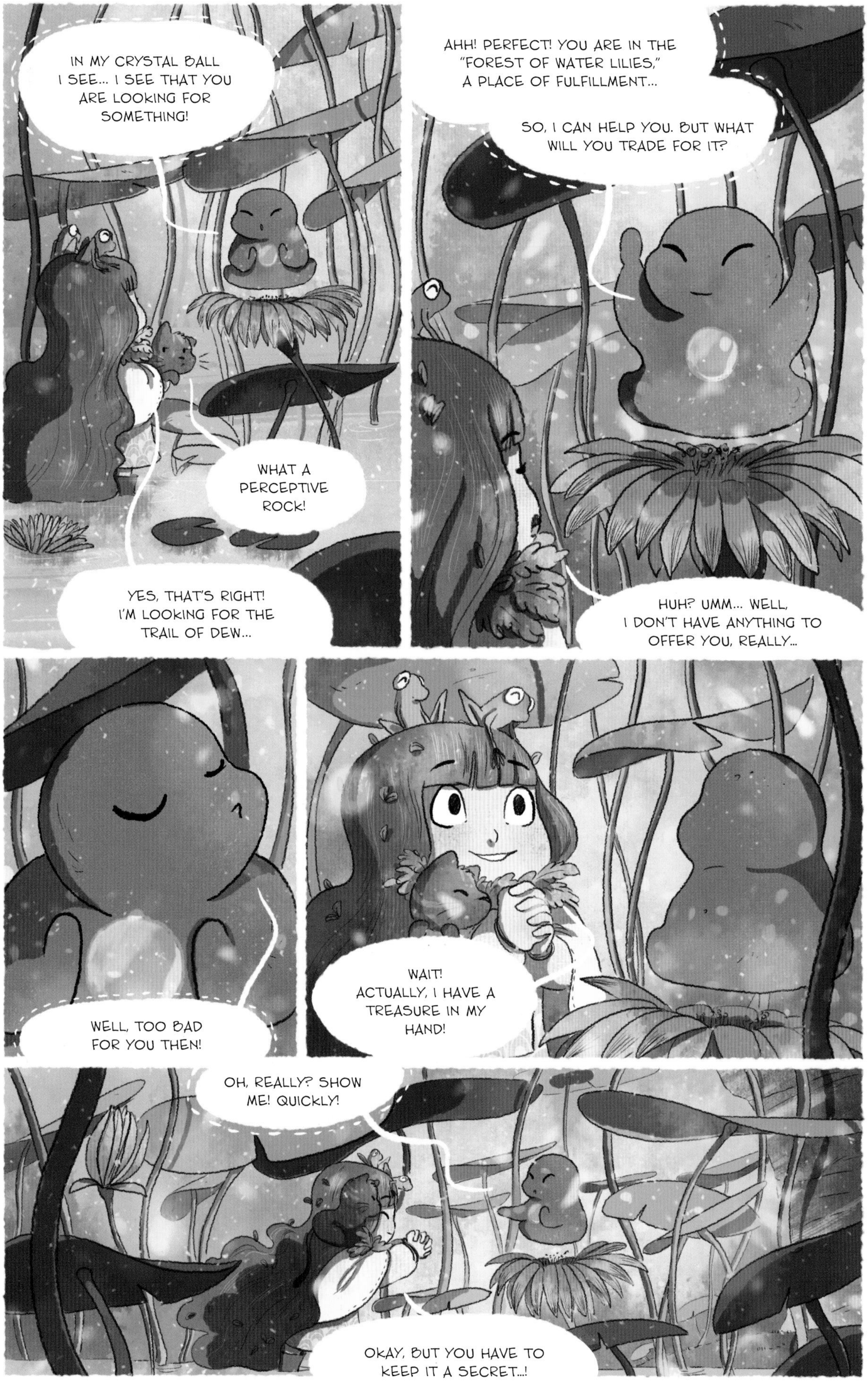
IN MY CRYSTAL BALL I SEE... I SEE THAT YOU ARE LOOKING FOR SOMETHING!
WHAT A PERCEPTIVE ROCK!
YES, THAT'S RIGHT! I'M LOOKING FOR THE TRAIL OF DEW...
AHH! PERFECT! YOU ARE IN THE "FOREST OF WATER LILIES," A PLACE OF FULFILLMENT...
SO, I CAN HELP YOU. BUT WHAT WILL YOU TRADE FOR IT?
HUH? UMM... WELL, I DON'T HAVE ANYTHING TO OFFER YOU, REALLY...
WELL, TOO BAD FOR YOU THEN!
WAIT! ACTUALLY, I HAVE A TREASURE IN MY HAND!
OH, REALLY? SHOW ME! QUICKLY!
OKAY, BUT YOU HAVE TO KEEP IT A SECRET...!

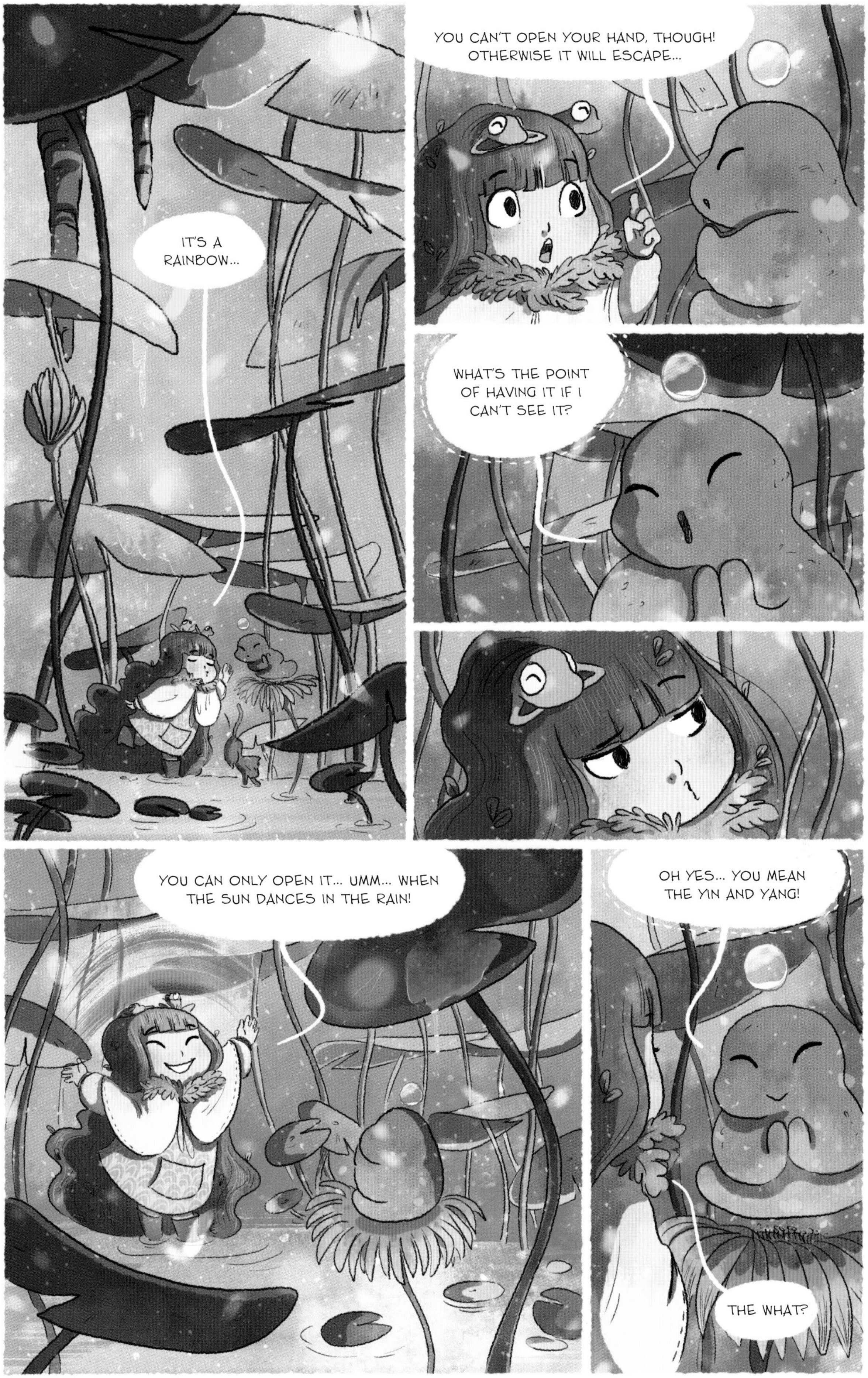
IT'S A RAINBOW...
YOU CAN'T OPEN YOUR HAND, THOUGH! OTHERWISE IT WILL ESCAPE...
WHAT'S THE POINT OF HAVING IT IF I CAN'T SEE IT?
YOU CAN ONLY OPEN IT... UMM... WHEN THE SUN DANCES IN THE RAIN!
OH YES... YOU MEAN THE YIN AND YANG!
THE WHAT?

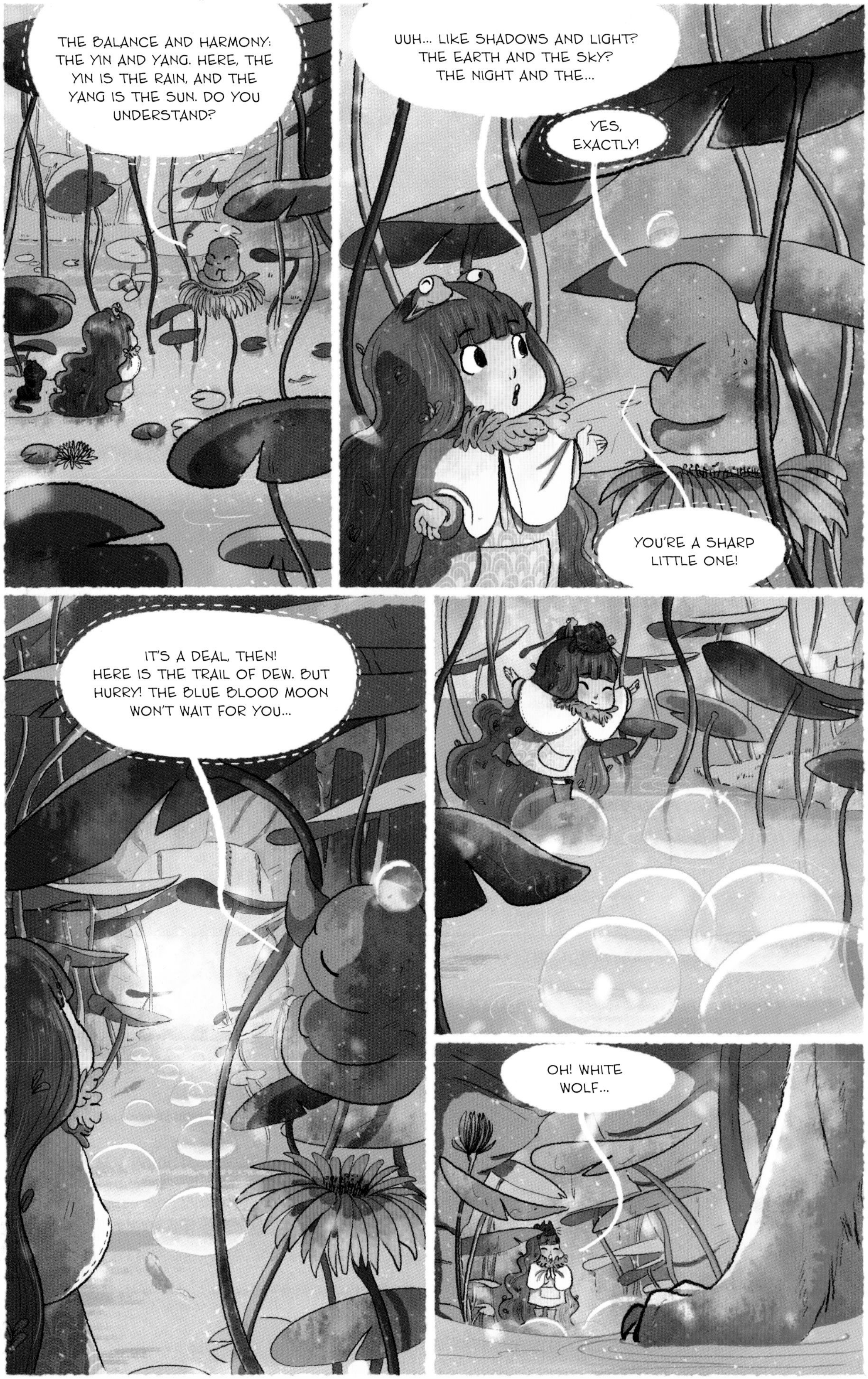
THE BALANCE AND HARMONY: THE YIN AND YANG. HERE, THE YIN IS THE RAIN, AND THE YANG IS THE SUN. DO YOU UNDERSTAND?
UUH... LIKE SHADOWS AND LIGHT? THE EARTH AND THE SKY? THE NIGHT AND THE...
YES, EXACTLY!
YOU'RE A SHARP LITTLE ONE!
IT'S A DEAL, THEN! HERE IS THE TRAIL OF DEW. BUT HURRY! THE BLUE BLOOD MOON WON'T WAIT FOR YOU...
OH! WHITE WOLF...

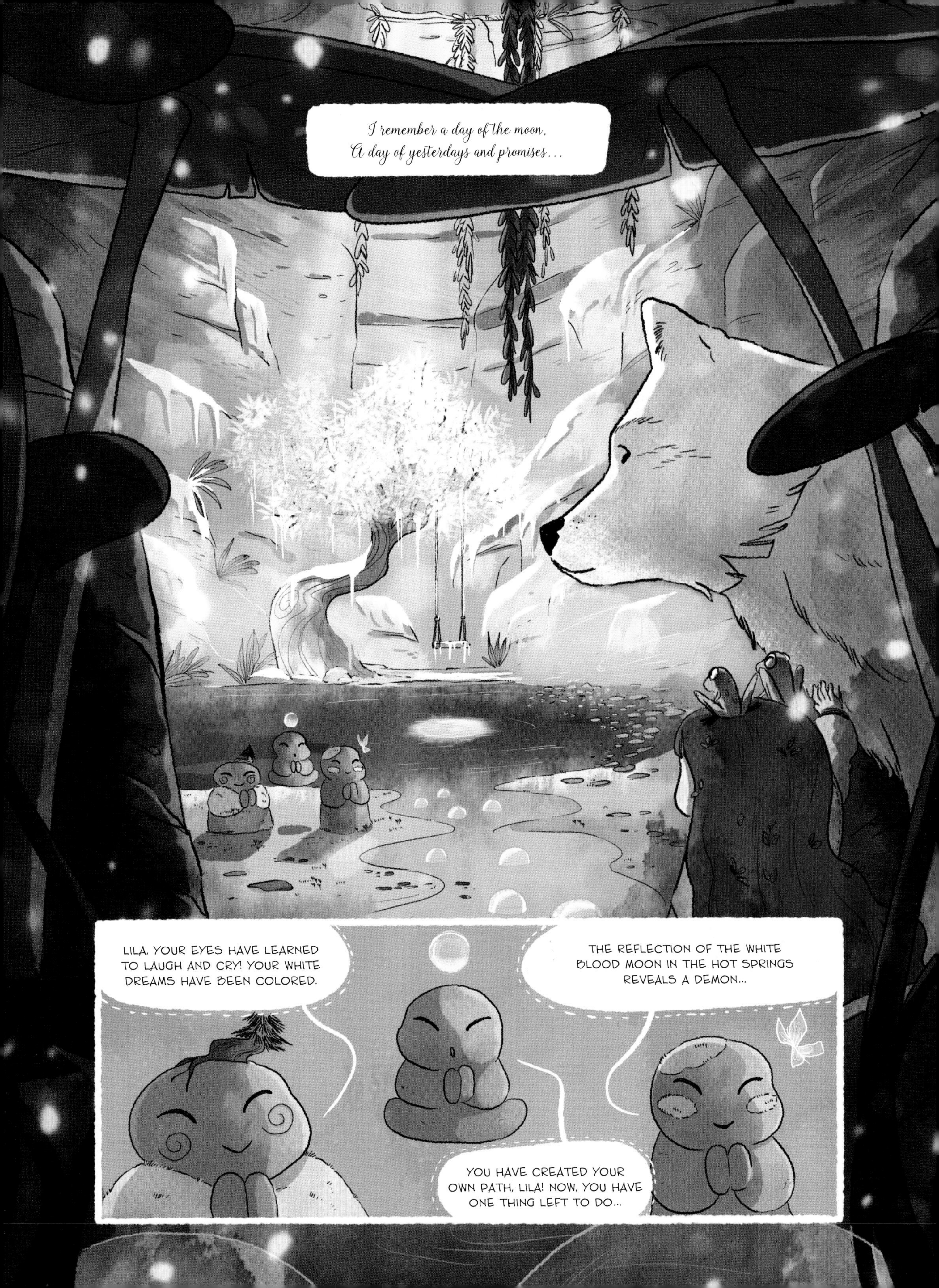
I remember a day of the moon,
A day of yesterdays and promises...
LILA, YOUR EYES HAVE LEARNED TO LAUGH AND CRY! YOUR WHITE DREAMS HAVE BEEN COLORED.
THE REFLECTION OF THE WHITE BLOOD MOON IN THE HOT SPRINGS REVEALS A DEMON...
YOU HAVE CREATED YOUR OWN PATH, LILA! NOW, YOU HAVE ONE THING LEFT TO DO...

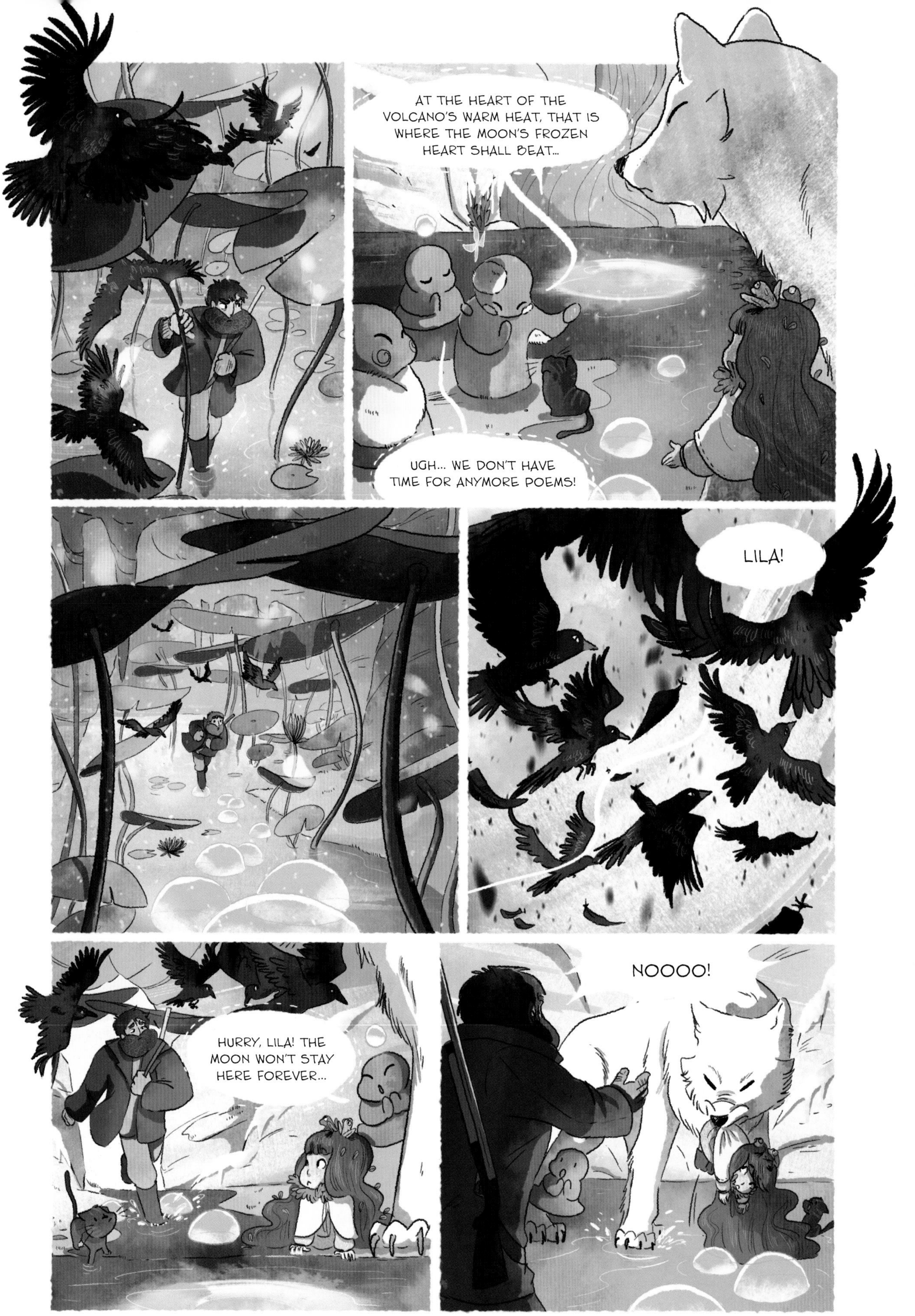
AT THE HEART OF THE VOLCANO'S WARM HEAT, THAT IS WHERE THE MOON'S FROZEN HEART SHALL BEAT...
UGH... WE DON'T HAVE TIME FOR ANYMORE POEMS!
LILA!
HURRY, LILA! THE MOON WON'T STAY HERE FOREVER...
NOOOO!

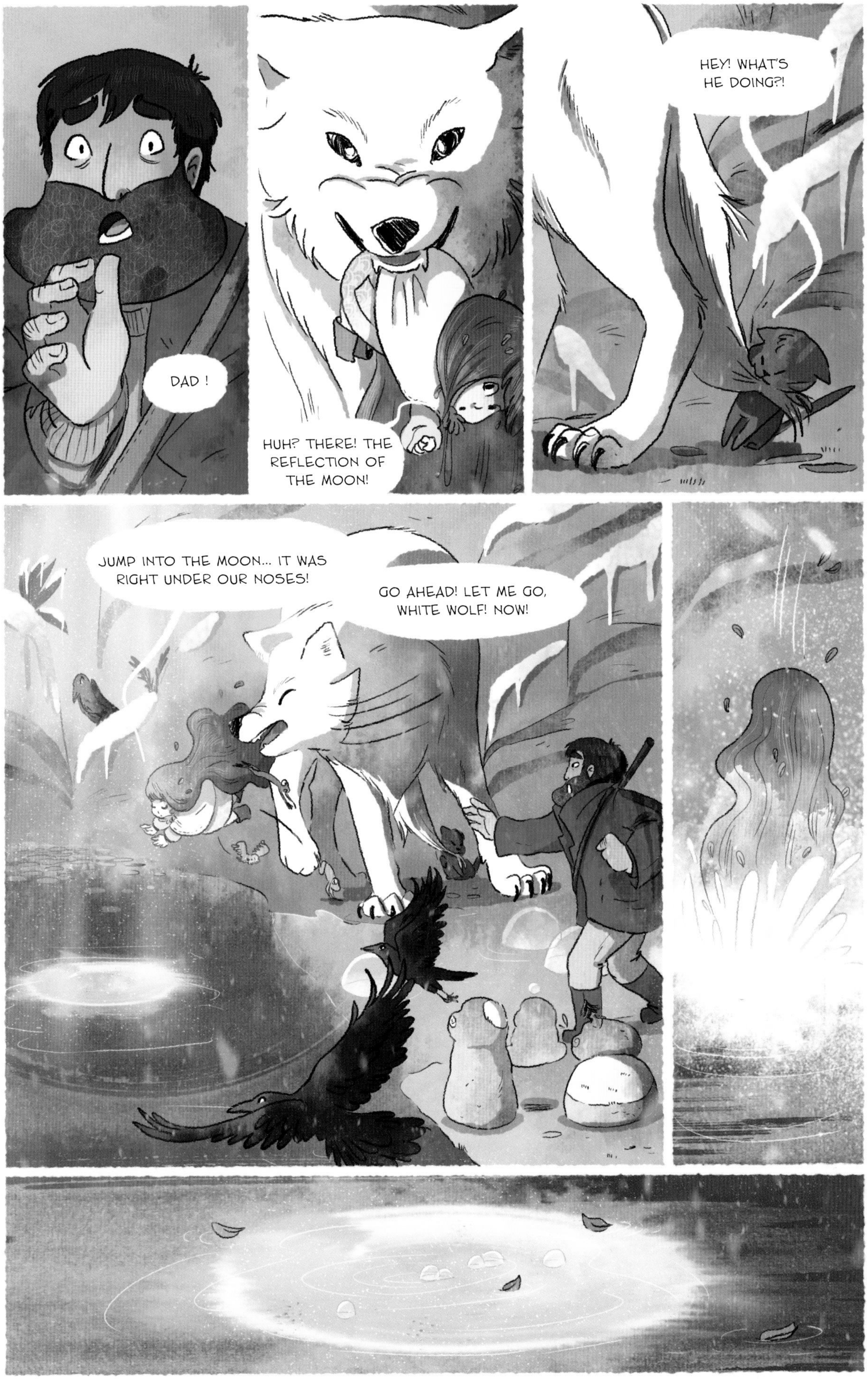
DAD !
HUH? THERE! THE REFLECTION OF THE MOON!
HEY! WHAT'S HE DOING?!
JUMP INTO THE MOON... IT WAS RIGHT UNDER OUR NOSES!
GO AHEAD! LET ME GO, WHITE WOLF! NOW!

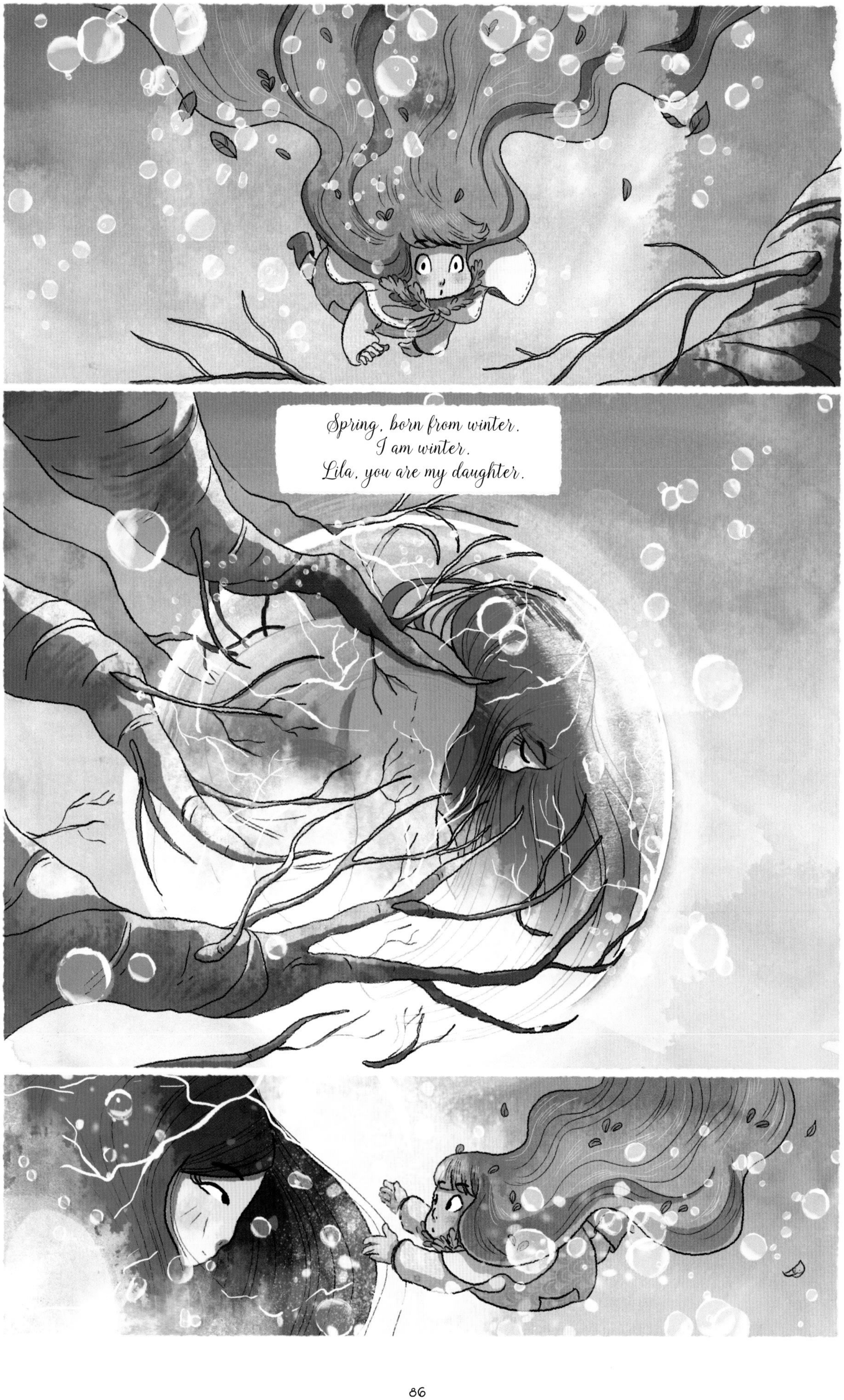
Spring, born from winter.
I am winter.
Lila, you are my daughter.

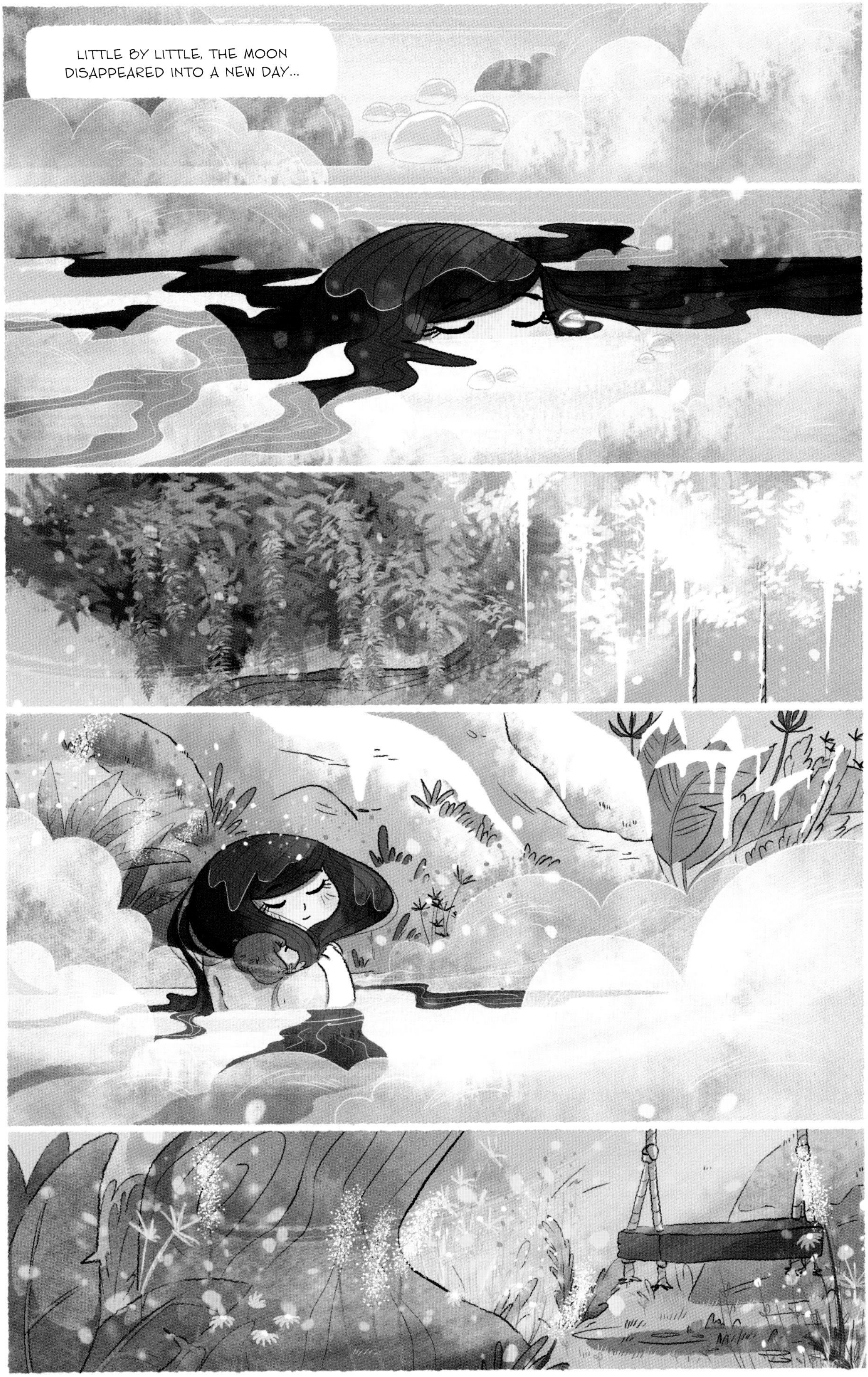
LITTLE BY LITTLE, THE MOON DISAPPEARED INTO A NEW DAY...

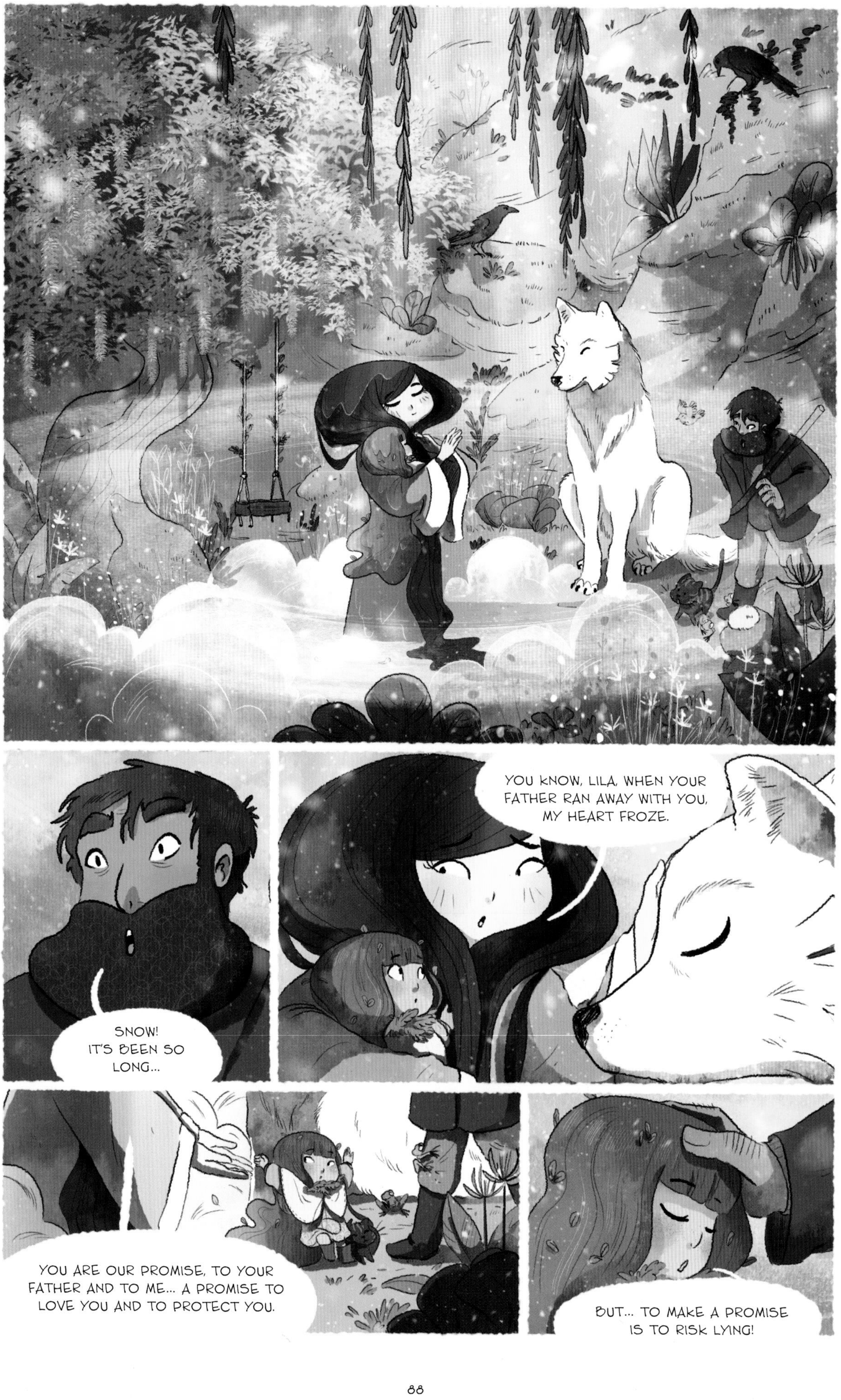
SNOW!
IT'S BEEN SO LONG...
YOU KNOW, LILA, WHEN YOUR FATHER RAN AWAY WITH YOU, MY HEART FROZE.
YOU ARE OUR PROMISE, TO YOUR FATHER AND TO ME... A PROMISE TO LOVE YOU AND TO PROTECT YOU.
BUT... TO MAKE A PROMISE IS TO RISK LYING!

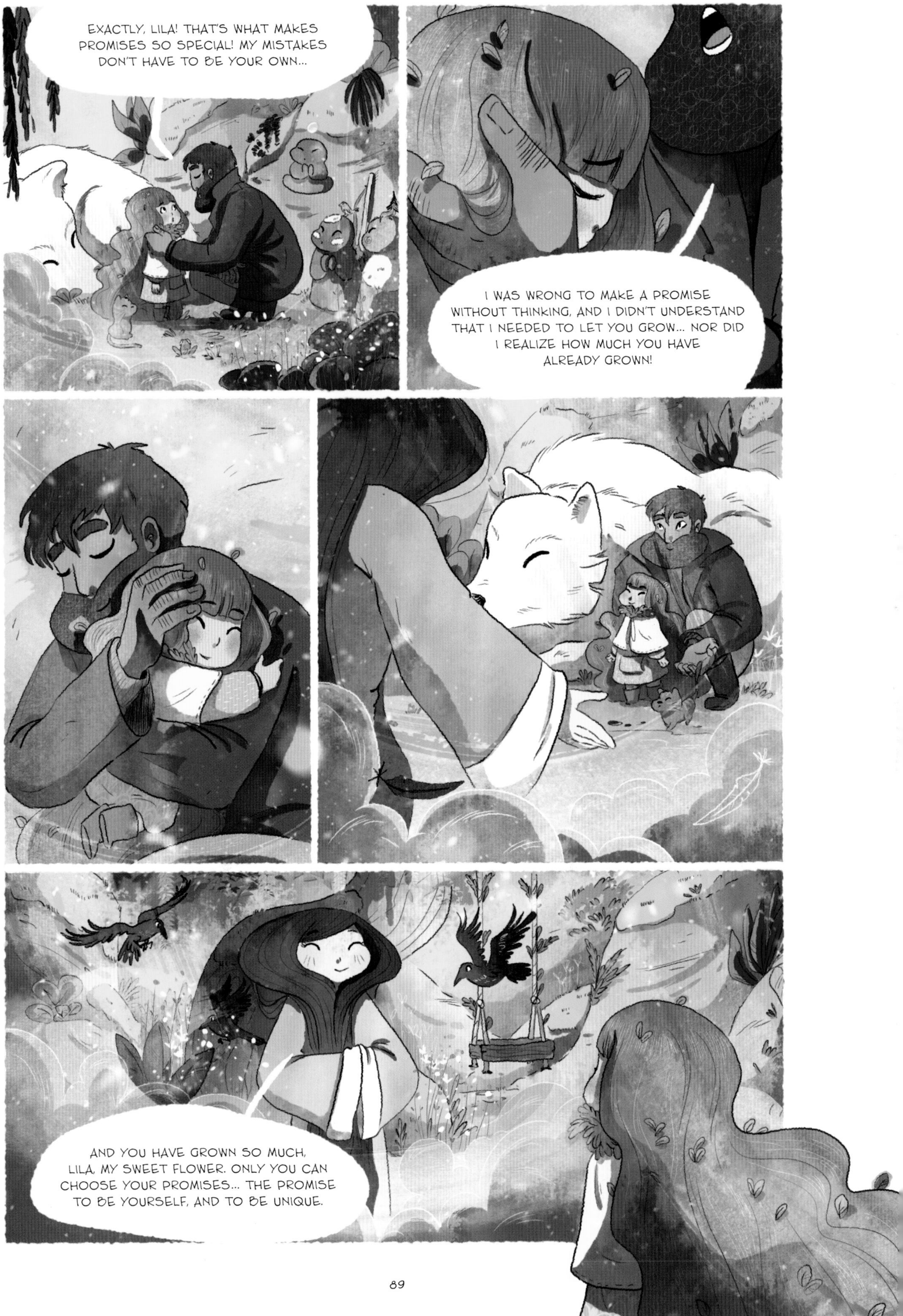
EXACTLY, LILA! THAT'S WHAT MAKES PROMISES SO SPECIAL! MY MISTAKES DON'T HAVE TO BE YOUR OWN...
I WAS WRONG TO MAKE A PROMISE WITHOUT THINKING, AND I DIDN'T UNDERSTAND THAT I NEEDED TO LET YOU GROW... NOR DID I REALIZE HOW MUCH YOU HAVE ALREADY GROWN!
AND YOU HAVE GROWN SO MUCH, LILA, MY SWEET FLOWER. ONLY YOU CAN CHOOSE YOUR PROMISES... THE PROMISE TO BE YOURSELF, AND TO BE UNIQUE.

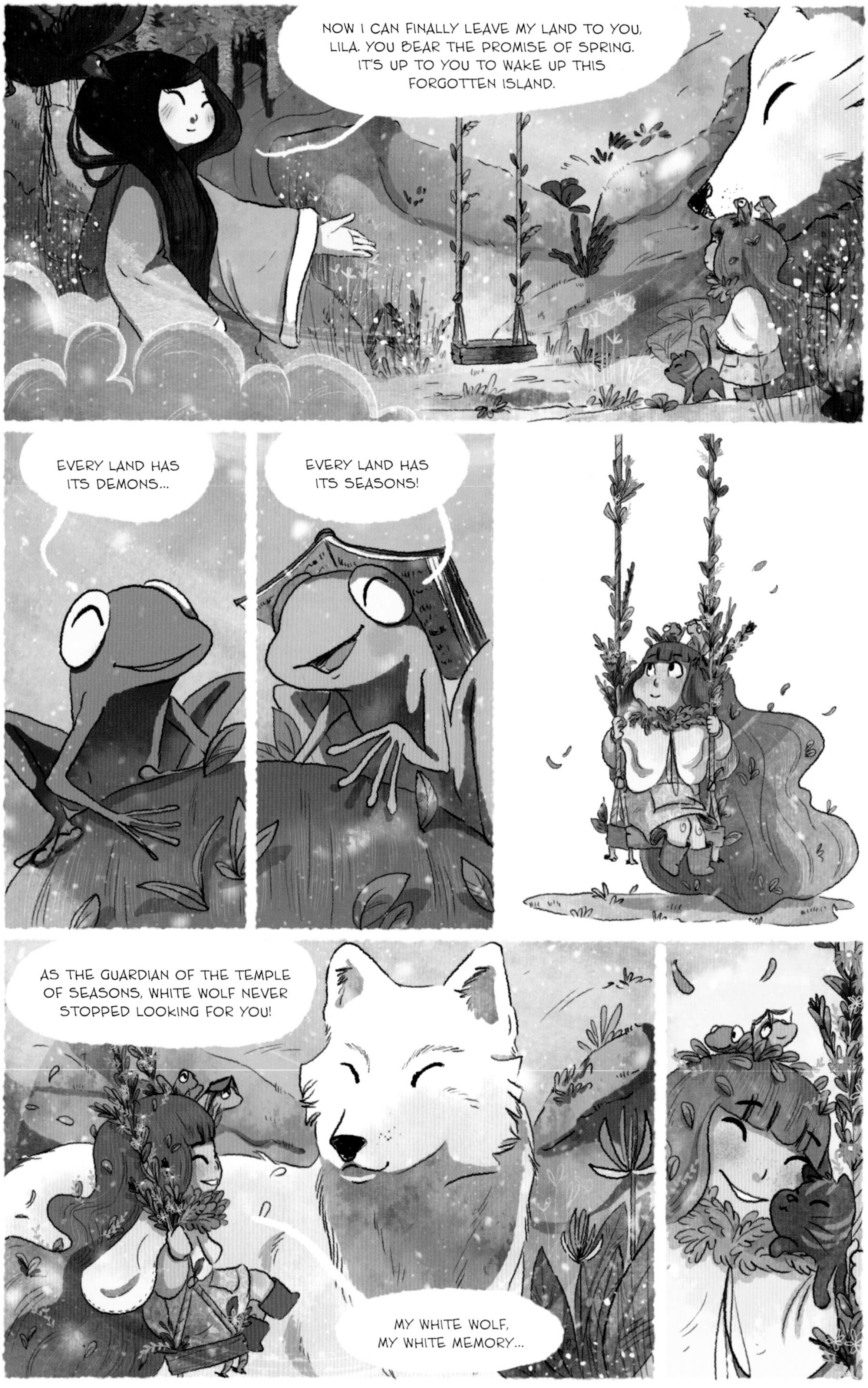
NOW I CAN FINALLY LEAVE MY LAND TO YOU, LILA. YOU BEAR THE PROMISE OF SPRING. IT'S UP TO YOU TO WAKE UP THIS FORGOTTEN ISLAND.
EVERY LAND HAS ITS DEMONS...
EVERY LAND HAS ITS SEASONS!
AS THE GUARDIAN OF THE TEMPLE OF SEASONS, WHITE WOLF NEVER STOPPED LOOKING FOR YOU!
MY WHITE WOLF, MY WHITE MEMORY...

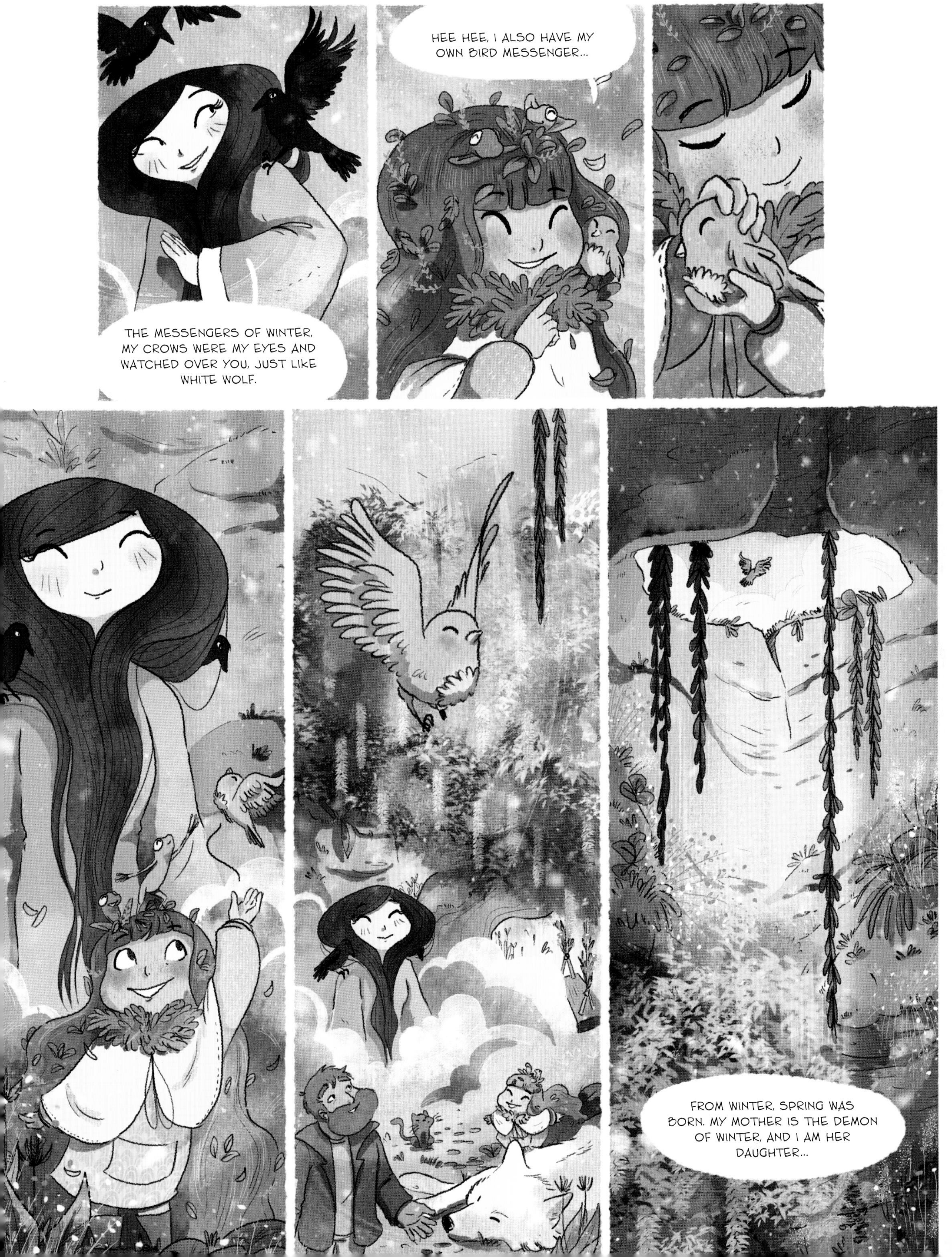
THE MESSENGERS OF WINTER, MY CROWS WERE MY EYES AND WATCHED OVER YOU, JUST LIKE WHITE WOLF.
HEE HEE, I ALSO HAVE MY OWN BIRD MESSENGER...
FROM WINTER, SPRING WAS BORN. MY MOTHER IS THE DEMON OF WINTER, AND I AM HER DAUGHTER...

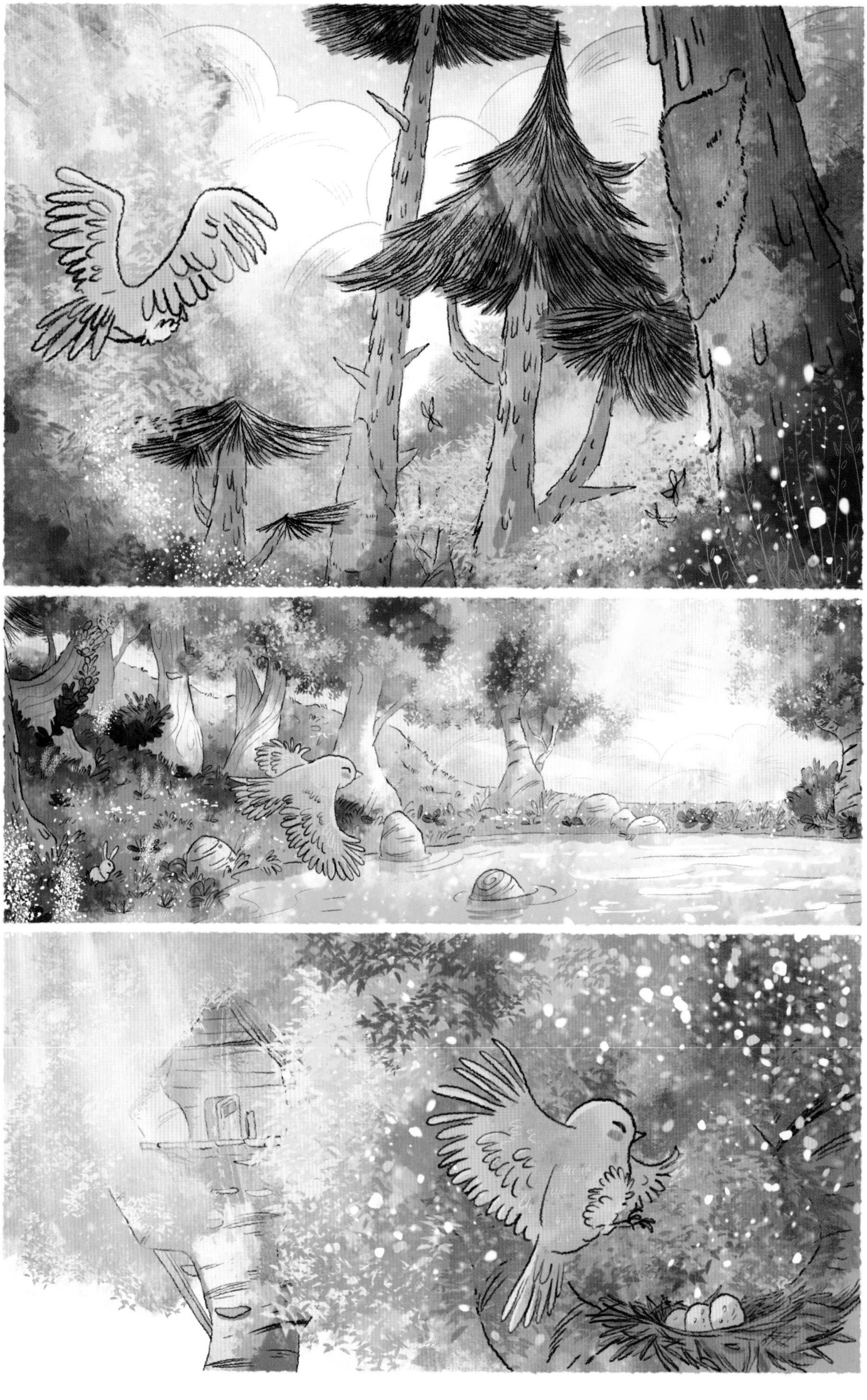

Poem of Snow

At the heart of a forgotten island,
Lila, you were born on a day of the moon
A day of yesterdays and promises.

You were born to run
Until you are out of breath
To fall but to always pick yourself back up.

Light and cheerful
You'll rock the earth
And charm the sun.

Lila, you are my poem
Murmured by the pebbles
And the smile of the wind.

You will remember
At the dawn of colors
That hesitate and stay silent

Lila, you are my most beautiful melody
Enchanted by birds
And the infinity of the sky.

To laugh beneath rays of sunshine
Or to cry a river of tears.

I know you will come.
I've waited for you for so long…

Spring, born from winter.
I am winter.
Lila, you are my daughter.